ALL THAT MATTERS

Pressing her lips against his, Honey kissed Stephen with all her might. There was little doubt from the warmth of the embrace and the strength of her arms that she meant to remove the thought of his family from his mind.

Stephen willingly succumbed to Honey's persuasive, bold caresses. He eased his arms around her lithe body and pulled her tightly against him. He could feel her heart pounding through her clothing with the excitement of their bold move. He knew that she never would have initiated a kiss of such a sensual nature if she had not desperately wanted to make him understand her feelings toward him. For his part, he was very willing to allow her to exert her womanly talents in any way she chose. For the moment at least, thoughts of his family were far away as his body responded to the fragrance of her shampoo and the closeness of her softness.

"Now," Honey said suddenly as she violently pushed him away, "I'm going to Jim Anderson's office. That's the last kiss you'll have from me until you decide who has the top spot in your life, me or your family's money. I won't play second fiddle to a purse full of money and neither will I sneak around like a common whore. When you make up your mind exactly which one of us you want, your precious inheritance or me, you'll know where to find me."

With that Honey stomped away to her car, stirring up a cloud of dust in her wake. She left Stephen standing with an expression on his face that vacillated between puzzlement and agony. She did not look back as she climbed into the seat and slammed the door.

BOOK YOUR PLACE ON OUR WEBSITE AND MAKE THE ARABESQUE ROMANCE CONNECTION!

We've created a customized website just for our very special Arabesque readers, where you can get the inside scoop on everything that's going on with Arabesque romance novels.

When you come online, you'll have the exciting opportunity to:

- View covers of upcoming books

- Learn about our future publishing schedule (listed by publication month and author)

- Find out when your favorite authors will be visiting a city near you

- Search for and order backlist books

- Check out author bios and background information

- Send e-mail to your favorite authors

- Join us in weekly chats with authors, readers and other guests

- Get writing guidelines

- AND MUCH MORE!

Visit our website at
http://www.arabesquebooks.com

ALL THAT MATTERS

Courtni Wright

ARABESQUE
BET BOOKS

BET Publications, LLC
www.msbet.com
www.arabesquebooks.com

ARABESQUE BOOKS are published by

BET Publications, LLC
c/o BET BOOKS
One BET Plaza
1900 W Place NE
Washington, D.C. 20018-1211

BET Books is a trademark of Black Entertainment Television,
Inc. ARABESQUE, the ARABESQUE logo and the BET
BOOKS logo are trademarks and registered trademarks.

First Printing: April, 2000
10 9 8 7 6 5 4 3 2 1

Printed in the United States of America

One

New Orleans, the Paris of the Americas, teemed with activity. Gleaming black sedans glided through the streets. Women in business suits mingled with those in shorts as they pressed against the windowpanes and stared at the latest fashions from Europe and their own top designers. Handsome gentlemen smiled as they walked past. Little girls tugged at little brothers in an effort to hurry them along. They wanted to stare into the windows, too. Downtown bustled as people moved through their busy days.

It was not only the fashions from Europe that fascinated the women and children, but also what they glimpsed through the puffy white curtain that parted slightly in the center and provided a peek at the sights within the shop. Inside the most famous of New Orleans's many prestigious shops, they caught a glimpse of an extraordinarily beautiful mannequin. However, she was no ordinary anatomically correct figure dressed in fabulous, eye-catching apparel. She was a live woman, a model, who posed in elegant attire for hours without moving more than to flutter her long brown lashes as rapidly as the beating of the wings of a hummingbird or to change from one provocative pose to another.

Everyone in town had heard about her although few had seen her closer than through the parted curtain. Only those women wealthy enough to afford a dress from Saint Philippe's shop would ever get to know her. Only those who had visited the world famous couturier since the recent arrival of his new model would have been honored with more than a glimpse of her. Of those who did experience her, they might not have realized that they had indeed gazed upon a living person until her subtle movements startled them from their shopping pleasure. She controlled her breathing so that her chest rose and fell ever so slightly. Her body remained frozen in its pose as if someone had cast a spell on her.

She wore the flawless soft beige skin of her face carefully masked in rosy powder and her cheeks skillfully tinted a subtle peach. She applied lipstick to her luscious lips with equal care so as not to distort the perfection of the line. With a hand that never trembled, she outlined her eyes in the deepest charcoal black she could buy to bring out the green color and size. When she stepped back from the mirror to survey her artistry, she was always pleased by what she saw. She should be, since she had spent hours learning the craft of transforming her naturally beautiful face into one that was stunning and arresting in its perfection.

She had only come to town three days ago and had been so busy that she had little time to associate with the New Orleanians who peered at her so curiously through the small opening in the curtain. She had arrived on the last flight long after most of the people had gone to bed. Only the town's prostitutes, drunkards, and voodoo practitioners saw the taxi driver unload her trunks in front of the most lavish and respected hotel in town.

She'd moved into a suite of rooms consisting of a living room with thick ornamental carpets, plush brocade upholstery, and heavy velvet drapes all done in shades of gold. The bedroom reflected the same elegance and sense of style as well as color in the counterpane and in the drapes around the four-poster bed and the one large shuttered window. On the table beside the bed lay a copy of the Bible and a rosary. She did not know who put either of them there, but she thought they were probably from the manager. They simply arrived while she was in the shop during her first day in town. She had not put either of them away, thinking that both might come in handy one day.

When the hotel receptionist asked how long she intended to stay, she had answered quietly, "Indefinitely." She noted on the card that she was from New York, but her speech was tinged with a trace of a Southern drawl that belied her origins. Her manner, too, reflected a Southern upbringing. She nodded politely to the elderly and gave up her seat on the Charles Street trolley to them.

When she passed people on the busy sidewalks, she hurried along with only a quick smile. Until she felt more comfortable with her new job, she had little time for casual associations. Her work was the source of her pleasure.

Her name, although few in the New Orleans dress shop had heard it, was as sweet and intoxicating as the magnolias that bloomed in her hometown. Her parents had named her Elizabeth Katherine, but they quickly gave her a nickname that reflected her disposition and personality. From the time she was a little girl barely able to toddle around the house and garden, everyone called her Honey because she was the kind of child who would do anything for anyone and who obeyed immediately when anyone spoke to her. Actually, no one ever disciplined Honey. Her instinctive goal in life had been to please others. From the time she was a young girl, she had always considered the feelings of others before her own. She was naturally good and sweet.

Honey had enlivened the household from the day she was born. Her father had doted on her, and her mother had lavished attention and praise on the little girl with the flowing auburn hair, sparkling green eyes, and gay laughter. She had possessed all of the most desirable Creole traits. Sitting beside her mother in the family room on long winter evenings, she quickly learned to read before any of her friends. She played quietly by herself and needed very little entertainment from others. She was very devoted to her family and lavished little gifts of flowers and chocolate on her friends when they came to visit. In the summer, Honey would run faster and climb higher than any of her male or female friends. She was equally at home running through the meadow as she was learning the finer touches of preparing fabulous dishes.

As she grew older and her beauty began to show, Honey started attracting the attention of boys. They would stop by the house in an effort to entice her to join them in a game of baseball. What they really wanted was to look into the face that was no longer smudged with dirt, but had changed into that of a pretty young girl. Honey's father watched protectively from the porch as she sat on the steps with one of the boys from the neighboring house. He only had to whistle to send the young man running from the yard and Honey into uncontrollable laughter. He knew that she was too young to fall in love with anyone. He was still her hero.

Then one day, her father died of a heart attack, throwing her world into chaos. Honey and her mother could not maintain the house, so they sold it to the first person with enough money to set them free of the collapse of their world. They packed up their things and said farewell to New Orleans, their dreams, and their past.

They moved to New York where Honey almost immediately found work in the fashion industry. Even as a teenager, her beauty and charm won the hearts of an industry that employed graceful young women who floated down the gangways in stunning fashions. At fifteen, she quickly became a favorite of everyone in town.

They lived comfortably but not lavishly in a small apartment as her mother wisely invested Honey's income and planned for her future. She enrolled Honey in the best schools that happily made accommodations for her hectic schedule. Despite the demands of modeling, Honey managed to graduate from college a year early.

Although Honey adjusted to the climate and pace of New York, her mother could never feel comfortable. Her mother made few friends because most of the women in the building thought she gave herself airs of superiority. They misunderstood her soft, gentle voice as haughtiness. Her mother's health failed from the unaccustomed cold and the heartbreak of living far from home. She slowly withered, unable to take comfort even in the success and company of her beautiful daughter. When her mother died some six years later, Honey returned to New Orleans and her memories of a better life. Her reputation as one of the top young models gave her the freedom she needed to strike out on her own.

Honey arrived at the shop for her first day at work long before the usual opening hours. She did not want a customer to see her before she was properly made up and in position. She had tired of life on the runway and wanted to try something different, so she trained herself to become a mannequin. Her job was to model the fabulous clothing as inconspicuously as possible. She had to showcase the clothing rather than herself. Every move she made and every step she took had to be for the purpose of displaying the dress. She was the figurine on which the wonderfully wrought creations rested. She was simply a clothes hanger that the couturier would dress with the intent of impressing customers with the beauty of his creation. She did not matter.

The fact that Honey was a human mannequin set her apart from other models who glided around fashion salons of New Orleans to display the fluidity of the fabrics. She had made a wonderful living in that occupation and now wanted to try her hand at another. She had established herself as a living but motionless tool for displaying the drape of a dress and for highlighting the flow of the fabric on the female form. She was unique in the fashion industry that had relied on stiff forms to display finished clothing in shop windows. Her flawless figure with ample but not heavy bust, small but not skeletal waist, and generous but not overdone hips exhibited the gowns to perfection. Her six years of experience in New York had added to her natural poise and grace and given her a wealth of knowledge not shared by the other New Orleans models.

For three days Honey had stood practically motionless in the center of the room as the wealthiest of New Orleans women examined the dresses that concealed the beauty of her body. They hoped that their less-than-ideal figures would magically be transformed as soon as the seamstresses in Saint Philippe's shop fashioned the creations to their measurements. They convinced themselves that their too-ample bosoms would be reduced, their thick waists would be whittled, and their wide hips would be constrained to look as voluptuous as those of the model who stood before them. The pale pastels would make their dull, lifeless eyes glow with the same luminescent green and their sallow skin shimmer with the same healthy rosiness. They were confident that their listless hair would suddenly reflect the rays of the sun if they put on the gossamer shawls that accentuated Honey's long thin neck as the halo of red shimmered around her head and made her look radiant.

They wanted to emulate her, and yet they never spoke to her or asked her name. Honey was as transparent in her borrowed finery as the formless, soulless seamstress's dress form had been before she arrived. They saw what they wanted to become, but never asked who she was or where she had been.

As the days passed, Honey began to recognize some of the faces that regularly pressed against the shop window to stare at the human model. She saw the same little boy of about ten who walked by with his heavy backpack slung across his shoulders. He wore his baseball cap low on his forehead. His hair was tightly curled and lay close to his round head. He always stopped on his way home from school. He wore too-large pants that he repeatedly had to pull up. His too-big, floppy tennis shoes seemed to slide around his feet and created the impression that he was walking through mud or sand that threatened to suck them from his feet. He would stand looking at her for a short while before the weight of the homework in his bag would send him off again. He would wave good-bye to her before continuing his trip home.

As Honey stared straight ahead, she could not respond, but she hoped the rapid fluttering of her lashes would serve as her sign of recognition. She did not want him to think his attention toward her went unnoticed. It was important to her to connect with someone, and he was the only one who had reached out to her.

Honey saw some of the same little girls, too. They stood in giggling clusters, wearing jeans and T-shirts or shorts and scraped knees as they pointed and stared. They talked about her behind their hands so she could not make out what they said, but she could tell from the way they poked each other and collapsed into gales of laughter that what they said was not complimentary. Often they would thrust out their flat chests in an attempt to form a bosom that would suggest the figure they might one day possess. They tossed their golden, red, and chestnut curls and patted their short tight afros until they, too, continued their walk home. Older girls with after-school jobs looked with envy at the outfits that did not fit into their budgets.

If Honey had allowed herself an occasional laugh, she would have shown that she found the mothers as comical as their daughters. They patted their stomachs as if the action would flatten out years of overindulging in the foods of which she deprived herself. They tried to lift their sagging, matronly bosoms as they imagined themselves in the slim slacks and close-fitting sweaters. Usually they shrugged their shoulders and walked away without entering the shop, telling themselves that they really did not want yet another outfit anyway. Some left with wistful expressions on their faces, knowing they would never be able to afford the expensive clothes even though they could fit into them.

The lucky ones who could wear and afford the creations entered the shop with a sense of pride and entitlement. They knew they were above the others who could not purchase the luxurious trappings of wealth at Saint Philippe's shop on the corner of Canal and Royal Streets. As they sauntered past the motionless model on their way out of the shop, they did not give her a second look. Honey had served her purpose. They would purchase the outfit she wore in their size, and Honey was of little interest to them beyond that.

When the last customer left in the evening, Saint Philippe himself would turn out the lights that illuminated the massive chandeliers and turn on the alarm before closing and locking the door. He took pride in doing the little things that set his shop apart from the others in town, like brewing the tea or coffee. He waited patiently as Honey changed out of the somber colors, skin-tight slacks, and tailored blouses that she modeled. She preferred linen slacks and blouses in the spring and summer and lightweight wool during the winter. Her choice of colors was more vivid than what was reflected in the clothing she modeled. She liked reds and strong, vibrant blues and hardly ever wore black or brown. When she really wanted to get comfortable, Honey would pull on a pair of faded old jeans with torn knees. She would ease her toes into worn, cloth slippers that caressed her tired feet.

Whenever she had a short break from the shop, she liked to walk about the city to see the sights and mingle with the people as they went about their daily activities. She had learned while in New York that she could not blend into the crowd while wearing her high-fashion dresses or her makeup. She would change into shorts and a T-shirt or jeans and a blouse tied at the waist after washing the powder and carefully applied blush from her cheeks and the crimson from her lips. Dressed as herself, no one recognized her as the model from Saint Philippe's shop. If they looked as if they might suspect, she would quickly look away and hide her face before they could be certain.

One day, Honey did not turn away fast enough and a handsome young man caught her eye. As he smiled and said hello, she could feel the warm blush come to her freshly scrubbed cheeks. Smiling, she hurried away, leaving him to appreciate the perfection of her figure, the radiant glow of her hair, and the sweet scent of roses that flowed from her body.

Honey had seen him on her first day in the shop as she stared motionlessly through the separation in the curtains. She had spied him across the street in conversation with another man of about his age but not as handsome. The afternoon sun had glistened off his deep brown hair. His thin mustache accentuated the strong, chiseled features and the mischievous, sparkling, light brown eyes. His tall straight back spoke of military training. The sweeping manner in which he gesticulated with his thin, tapered hands indicated a rapidity of speech that would be useful in the courtroom. The way he threw back his head and laughed with abandon spoke of his strong sense of humor.

As she quickly changed into her dress for the next few hours of modeling, Honey secretly hoped he would stop by the window and look at her. From her position in Saint Philippe's shop, she felt her heart pound at the memory of him. She hoped she would see him again.

Yet, when she did encounter him one afternoon a week later as she left the salon for her usual lunchtime break, Honey assumed the body language and posture of a woman trying to convey the message that she did not wish to encourage his attentions. She hid the fact that she desperately wanted to meet him. As he walked toward her, she pulled herself into a small private package that spoke of her hesitation to reach out to others. After so many years in New York, Honey was surprised to find that she was still basically shy about meeting new people.

"Excuse me, Miss, I don't mean to intrude, but . . ." he began in a softly accented voice that immediately reminded Honey of her father's deep baritone.

"No, I'm sorry . . ." Honey replied curtly as she turned away with a quick wave of her hand.

In her heart, she had hoped he would follow her. Instead,

seeing her contained expression and tightly closed body, he turned away from her with a shrug. He had permitted her to pass, leaving her to gaze longingly at the tips of the black boots that vanished behind her.

Now she stood at her position watching out the window and waiting for him to appear. Her carefully applied makeup only partially concealed the flush of color that tinged her cheeks. The purse hanging from its strap over her shoulder jiggled from the rapid rise and fall of her chest as she eagerly scanned the faces of everyone who passed by the window.

Honey was so excited at the prospect of seeing him again that she almost called out a greeting to the little boy with the backpack as he stopped by on his way home. He looked at her and slightly frowned as if realizing that something was not quite as it had been in the past when he looked in the window at her. He sensed that she had changed and appeared more animated even in her stillness. Even the way she fluttered her lashes at him seemed more alive than usual, almost as if she were shouting at him in her desire to attract his attention. Shrugging his shoulders, he put her out of his mind as he trudged home with his too-large tennis shoes, kicking up a cloud of dust along the way.

When the familiar group of beautiful tan- and brown-skinned girls stopped to stare and laugh behind their hands on their way home from school, Honey had to suppress the urge to stick out her tongue at them. They also sensed that she was in some way different although she stood in her usual spot and remained perfectly still despite their efforts to engage her and force her to move. Something in the slight tilt of her head told them she had changed. Honey was not fun anymore. She looked as if she might try to speak to them and perhaps scold them for their behavior. No longer finding her interesting, they left the sidewalk in front of the store and disappeared out of view.

Honey watched and waited. Through two changes of outfits, she looked for him. When the sun shifted direction and late afternoon approached, she searched the crowd of people on their way home for a sign of him. As she followed Saint Philippe into the evening air, she scanned the almost empty streets for him. When she stepped into her hotel for a lonely dinner in her suite, she turned one last time and surveyed the street on both sides. Seeing no one following her, she went inside and entered the empty elevator for the solitary ride to the third floor and her rooms.

That night as Honey slipped into her long nightgown, she noticed that the anonymous person had left something new beside the Bible and rosary on the table next to her bed. Fingering the small bottle, she saw a carefully inscribed label that read "Get-Together Drops" in bold black ink. Gently lifting the top, she sniffed the liquid. The scent was strong but not overpowering. It reminded her of the wisteria that used to grow along the trellis of the south porch and intertwined among the tree branches of the live oak trees in front of her old house.

Honey found it a little unsettling to know that someone had watched her activities and knew that she would be away from the hotel the entire day. This person knew when to enter her room without either interfering with her toilet or being seen by her. Yet, she felt strangely connected to the person. Whoever it was, he or she had taken the time to procure the objects for her. That person had shown interest in her life while everyone else had only stared at her but never made contact.

Settling under the covers, Honey realized that she had been back in New Orleans for more than a month. She had neither spoken casually with anyone nor shared a meal with anyone. She had not even visited the famous Café du Monde for beignets and coffee with chicory. No one had asked her name or inquired about her health except for Saint Philippe and the hotel manager whose interests were self-serving; they both wanted to assure her continued money-making ability.

On her list of things she had not done, Honey mentally

added that she had not attended the theater, a party, a barbe-cue, or a church service. She had not taken a walk in the park or enjoyed a paddleboat ride on the mighty Mississippi River that thundered past the Crescent City. She also had not visited her old home.

Turning out the light, Honey decided that tomorrow she would have to stop hiding from the pain of her past and begin making her future. She thought it was time to wash off the makeup that separated her from the rest of the town. It was time for her to put aside the fancy clothes that separated her from the rest of the citizens of the Crescent City. She needed to pull on her jeans, roll up her sleeves, and venture into the life of New Orleans. She had to stop being a voyeur from Saint Philippe's window and start living if New Orleans was to be her home again.

Two

New Orleans, the City that Care Forgot, was alive and vibrant even on Sunday morning as Honey blended with the foot traffic and made her way to church. She had been raised a Catholic although she had practiced her faith very little while living in New York.

Although the church bells rang loudly and accusingly every Sunday morning, Honey and her mother had kept to themselves and never visited St. Patrick's Cathedral in New York. Honey had spent the past six years of her life working six days each week and resting on Sunday. Since her mother did not encourage her to attend church, Honey would spend her free time reading or going to a movie or the theater. Sometimes, she would slip away with a few friends who were also caught up in the hectic modeling life. They would go bowling or ice skating in Rockefeller Center. Their favorite treat was a reduced-price ticket to a Broadway play. They would purchase them after standing in line among residents who did not recognize them as the famous models that they were.

Occasionally, when the flowers in the park were especially beautiful or the sky had turned a remarkable shade of blue, Honey would repeat a prayer that her father had taught her, not because of its religious significance but because it reinforced the connection with him. She did not want to forget the sound of his voice and the gentleness of his touch. When she said his prayer, she could hear his voice in her ears and feel his fingers helping her through the decades of her rosary. Now at twenty-one, Honey felt that she needed to visit her family's old church and the old religion.

Walking up the wide marble stairs, Honey felt all the old memories flooding back. She could envision her father on one side of her and her mother on the other as they sat in St. Louis Cathedral together. As she joined in the singing of the psalms and the canticles, she could almost hear their voices leading her through the difficult passages. Fingering the Bible and the rosary from her hotel suite, she read the gospel passage and wondered at the way it paralleled her life. She, too, had returned home after a long time in exile. She wondered if the city would be as generous and welcoming as the father in the story of the prodigal son had been. The busy streets had silenced and the rush of workaday life had been put aside for a while.

When she was a child growing up in their huge home on the outskirts of town, Honey and her parents would climb into the car every Sunday for the short trip to the cathedral. When they arrived, Honey's family would occupy the same pews that had been their seats in the church since before she was born. When the service ended, Honey's family would go to the Café du Monde for coffee and beignets.

Her mother would begin the preparations for the Sunday church service on Saturday night by washing, ironing, and arranging the clothing that she and her family would wear the next day. She also tended to the task of washing and drying Honey's thick auburn hair. She did not really consider grooming her only child a chore since the obedient youngster would sit perfectly still as the water dripped into her eyes, ran down her face, and soaked the towel that lay across her shoulders to protect her pajamas from dampness. In the summertime, Honey would sit outside watching fireflies dart across the lawn. On rainy nights, she would play games or watch television with her father while her hair dried. In the winter, she would endure the blasts of hot air as her mother blow-dried her sometimes stubborn curls into submission.

Her mother would carefully roll her hair around spongy, pink rollers. The curlers would keep it from becoming tangled as Honey slept and force her naturally curly locks into submission. The next morning, a few passes with a brush would tame any stray hairs. Honey would be dressed and ready for church with very little effort.

Sometimes as she shivered in the winter breezes off the Mississippi, she wondered what had attracted her parents to that house. Eventually, when she grew older, they had explained the irony of their ownership to her. Armed with this knowledge, Honey spent long hours in the town's library and courthouse researching the previous ownership and the connection to slavery.

This time, as she entered the cathedral, Honey was alone. Taking her seat in the pew that had been occupied by her family during her childhood, Honey knelt on the little flower-embroidered pillow. She recited prayers she remembered from her youth when her life had been blissfully happy. The pillow felt familiar beneath her knees as her fingers gently counted the decades of her rosary. When she finished, she sat back on the pew and drank in the feeling of home that permeated the church.

Looking at the sun streaming through the stained-glass windows, Honey felt a sense of comfort and peace settle over her inner spirit. When she stood as a model dressed in elaborate couturier fashions, she had to will herself to remain still. She breathed deeply and set her mind on a distant vision or recited a fairy story from her childhood or her favorite poetry. Here in the church with the smell of incense in the air and the whispers of the other worshipers floating around her, she did not have to force the quiet to take possession of her. It simply settled around her shoulders like an often-worn shawl or the loving arms of her mother. It brought with it a feeling of total belonging and tranquility.

Watching her fellow worshipers recite their rosaries, Honey wondered at the reasons that brought them to church. In this city that never slept, she marveled at the number of people who sought comfort, peace, release, or forgiveness within the walls of the grand cathedral. Lines of people waited at the confessionals with their prayer books, Bibles, and rosaries clutched in their fists and their faces set in poses of devotion. Many more knelt to receive Communion at the altar with expressions of wonder transforming their tired faces. The wealthy and the poor joined together in reciting the "Our Father" and in singing the hymns. White and black, Northerners and Southerners, men and women gathered together to take their troubles to God, believing that He would absolve them and lead them on the path of righteousness that led to the promised land of the Scriptures.

Occasionally while she lived in New York, Honey had peeked into St. Patrick's Cathedral to see the same rapt expressions on the faces of the worshipers. Not wanting to upset her mother's delicate health further, she never stayed more than a few minutes. However, in that short time, she felt the same sense of release of care and community among the congregation. She wondered why her mother did not seek the same comfort rather than live with the constant pain of grief and disillusionment. Honey knew that Josephine would have been a much happier woman if she could have accepted the changes in her lifestyle rather than railing against the injustice of losing her livelihood, her home, and her husband.

Sometimes Honey tried to share her thoughts about the church with her mother in the hopes that she might change her mother's mind. However, whenever she began the conversation, her mother would raise her hand and signal for silence. Quietly, she would repeat to the listening child her litany of opposition and once again ask her daughter to refrain from visiting the cathedral up the street. She never asked Honey to promise that she would not attend the services; she must have realized that the pull to the church was as strong in her daughter as it had been in her husband. Instead, she requested that Honey not mention the church or God in her presence. Since her mother was one of the very few people with whom Honey shared her life, her mother's request had the effect of silencing her on that topic.

Now, sitting in the midst of bowed heads, Honey found herself wondering again at her mother's reluctance to return to the church. At the very least, the hour spent in the cool of the marble building would have provided her with relief from the heat and humidity of a summer day in New York. Although their apartment was air-conditioned, any outside physical activity produced discomfort when the temperature rose in July and August.

Honey knew that her mother had not really died of the cancer that racked her delicate frame and made it almost impossible for her to walk the three flights from the subway to their apartment. She died from a sense of disillusionment and hopelessness too large to shoulder without help and from complete abandonment of herself to grief. Although she could not return to the church in life, Josephine turned to it in death and requested that her daughter give her a proper Catholic funeral.

St. Louis Cathedral was very much like the one from which Honey had buried her mother. Although it was not quite as large as the one in New York, it had many of the same smaller side altars and statues of Mary along the walls. The same hush pervaded the atmosphere of the building as people communicated their hopes and aspirations to God in that public place.

Leaving the cathedral, Honey squinted into the sun and quickly put on her sunglasses. Picking her way through the crowd, she walked toward her hotel. Honey had not eaten since dinner last night and was very hungry. She decided to stop in one of the many restaurants that served beignets and strong Creole coffee flavored with chicory. Since none of the families that filled the café at that hour of the day asked her to join their table, she sat alone and waited for the waiter to serve her light meal.

Honey had not eaten one of the New Orleans specialties since she was a little girl and had forgotten the rich taste of its sugary sweetness. Immediately, memories of years long gone flashed through her mind as the beignet melted in her mouth. Although she was hungry, Honey knew after the first bite that she would not be able to eat more than one of the delicious square pastries. The crusty sugar stuck to her fingers and flaked on her lips. She had to resist the temptation to lick its sweetness from her fingertips as she had when she was a child. Wiping them instead, she looked around the café to see children doing exactly what she wished she could have done.

Smiling slightly as she sipped her hot, steaming coffee, Honey remembered a time when her family had visited the café after Sunday mass. They had occupied the table in the center of the room where the family of the redheaded children now sat. They had feasted on beignets and café au lait. She and her father had licked their fingers clean despite her mother's gentle scolding.

Slipping the strap of her purse over her shoulder, Honey once again joined the throng of people on the sidewalk. She allowed the current of their movement to propel her along. She had no definite plans and felt no obligation to be any-where. The day was hers to spend as she liked, and the weather was perfect. The shop was closed on Sunday, so she had the day to herself. She did not feel the need to return to the hotel at any particular time because no one had noticed when she left and no one awaited her return.

As she walked along, Honey thought about the hot, hazy summer in New Orleans. She remembered days that were so sticky with humidity that it almost dripped from the branches of the leaf-heavy trees. This Sunday the sun shone hot and bright but a gentle breeze stirred the air enough to keep the city from lying in a blanket of moisture. As she walked along,

Honey saw that the owners of the houses along the way had thrown open their shutters to allow the fresh air to push out the stale smells from the past few days of rain. All the flowers looked healthy and vibrant as they trailed from boxes and grew in splendid gardens. The bougainvillea and banana trees looked especially lush in their blooms and wide leaves.

The rain, however, had cast its magic over the city. The white and gentle pastel paints of the houses shone clean as if newly applied, and the ironwork colonnades glistened a shimmering black. Peeking around the corner, Honey saw that the flagstone driveway led the way to elegant secluded court-yards that overflowed with thriving, lush flowers and carefully placed benches for reflection. Fresh, neat gingerbread trim decorated the rooflines of many houses and black shutters accented others.

Music drifted from the gabled Creole cottages as women and children whose skin glistened in beautiful shades of brown and café au lait drifted in and out with the breeze. Some of them carried packages in their arms. Others entered wearing Sunday-best clothes. Still others looked as if they had not retired from their Saturday night revelry. They softly hummed the music that had kept their toes tapping and their fingers snapping all night. This was the New Orleans that Honey remembered from her childhood.

When Honey was young, her father loved to drive through the Creole section of town. He would point out the different flowers and identify the aromas of foods foreign to Honey's tastes but well-known to him. He introduced her to the world of music with an African or French beat and melody and people who walked with a proud spring in their step. Some-times he would stop in front of the houses so that she could see the people who made this section so colorful. They dressed in all the smartest and most fashionable clothing.

There was yet another section of town that Honey's father particularly enjoyed. In that neighborhood, the large, stately houses had elaborate ironwork and lush gardens. Her mother always tried to stop him from pulling up in front of one particularly spectacular white house with black shutters, cast iron balconies, and bougainvillea growing all over it. Despite her objections, he would linger for a moment before driving away. Honey always felt as if he hoped to see someone he knew come from the house, but he never did. He would sigh and lean back against the seat with a sad expression on his face. Seeing him, her mother would dab at the corners of her eyes with her thin fingers. Honey never asked her parents about the house or why it made them sad to see it.

As the current of pedestrians flowed along, taking her with it, Honey decided that she would try to find that house again. She did not remember the name of the street and doubted that she would have any luck. It had been over ten years since she had seen it. Time had probably changed its appearance by now.

Wandering along the side streets, Honey discovered that she should not have worried about not remembering the location of the house. With every step she took, she felt as if she were being drawn closer and closer to the large white brick structure. It was almost as if the house wanted her to find it.

As Honey rounded still another corner, she stopped short. There in front of her, just as she remembered it, stood the house. Its white brick was just as clean and sparkling in its starkness as it had been when she last saw it, and its black shutters looked equally as dark. The bougainvillea still grew in wild profusion along the balcony and down the side of the house. The soft strains of piano and violin wafted from the open windows just as they had when she sat beside her father on Sunday afternoon.

Gazing at the house, Honey could not understand what had troubled her mother about its exterior or the inhabitants. The tall, elegant structure was impressive in its size and style but no more so than what she remembered of their own house. The flower gardens that surrounded it were immaculately maintained, but they did not contain more varieties than those that grew around their home. The house, although stunningly appointed with its wide porches and sweeping weeping willow trees and stately magnolias, was no more enchanting than any other on the same street.

As she was preparing to turn away, Honey noticed that the front door had opened and a woman dressed in faded jeans and a red T-shirt had emerged. She wore dangling hoop earrings that sparkled beneath her dark short hair. Her rich brown complexion tinged with subtle peach appeared flawless, although Honey thought the woman had applied a touch of blush to her cheeks. Honey gazed curiously as the young woman appeared to float down the steps toward the sidewalk where she stood.

"Oh, hello. Are you looking for someone?" the elegant young woman of about Honey's age asked. Her voice was lightly touched by the same gentle brand of southern accent that marked all New Orleanians.

"No, actually, I'm just out for a walk," Honey answered as she studied the face of one of the most beautiful women she had ever seen. "I've only recently moved back to New Orleans and I'm trying to relearn the city."

"This is certainly a lovely day for it. The rain of the last few days has made everything come to life again. I don't think I've ever seen my flowers looking more beautiful. I'm going for a walk myself. Do you mind if I walk along with you?" the young woman asked as she joined Honey on the sidewalk.

"No, not at all. Perhaps you could point out some of the local landmarks as we walk," Honey replied as the other woman linked arms with her.

"I suppose I should introduce myself now that I've intruded on your solitude. I'm Jacqueline du Prix. My family has lived in this house for as long as I can remember. There isn't much that I can't tell you about this neighborhood or the people who live in it," Jacqueline said with enthusiasm.

"Wonderful! I could use a guide. My name is Honey Tate. Actually, it's Elizabeth Katherine, but everyone calls me Honey. My family used to own a large house just outside the city limits until our finances took a turn for the worse and we were forced to move. I've been living in New York and only just returned home," Honey said as they slowly walked through the winding streets and under the overhanging lush branches. Passing the house on the corner, she felt as if someone were watching them from an upstairs window. Seeing no one, she quickly pushed the thought from her mind.

"You must be the model everyone's talking about," Jacqueline chattered as they rounded another corner. "I drove past Saint Philippe's shop only yesterday, but I didn't stop. I could see that you were causing quite a stir. I watched masses of people stand in front of the store and stare at you. The funniest sight was the children who made faces at the window. I suppose they were trying to make you laugh."

The houses on this block alternated between the large, stately type in which Jacqueline lived and the smaller ones that Honey remembered her father refer to as shotgun houses. He said that a man could fire a shotgun through the front door and out the back without hitting anything because the rooms flanked the long narrow center hall.

"Some of them try," Honey answered. "A little girl and her brother regularly stop by the window to make faces at me. She's really quite funny. I look forward to seeing her although I never let on that I recognize her. I do try to make eye contact with a little boy. He's always weighed down by a heavy backpack, but he looks so happy to be out of school that I enjoy seeing him. He waves and smiles every day. I hope to meet him one day."

Honey could listen to Jacqueline's soft, accented drawl for hours. It was so like her father's that she wanted her new friend never to stop talking. She had missed the gentle cadence of southern speech while she lived in busy New York.

"Sometimes I think I'd like to take a job. I often discussed it with my mother in the years before her death, but she would not allow it," Jacqueline said as she picked a magnolia blossom for her hair and one for Honey. "She said that our family was not meant to work the way other people were. It is not that we're so very wealthy because we were not. We simply lived a different kind of lifestyle. But then, I suppose we all do when we're children."

Inhaling the heady fragrance of the flower, Honey responded, "Things were very different while my father was alive. We lived well. He was a very successful Creole attorney. After his death, everything changed. My mother and I moved to New York. To our dismay, we found that my father had not invested well or planned for the future. His death left us with only a small life insurance policy and little else."

Jacqueline commented, pointing to another stately house covered in bougainvillea, "Except for some time I spent in Richmond, I haven't lived anyplace other than New Orleans. I have thought about moving, but I really love it here. I'd miss the sound of the boats on the Mississippi, the smell of magnolias, and the taste of the wonderful foods we enjoy here. I doubt that I would find any other city in the world with the variety of cuisine that we have. Some of my female friends have traveled to Europe, but they say that New Orleans is the only place to live. I ask you, where else would you find houses like this?"

"Certainly not in New York," Honey laughed as she watched a woman in a small sporty convertible speed down the street.

"Have you met any men since you returned to New Orleans?" Jacqueline asked in the whisper of two old friends confiding in each other.

"No, but I've seen one I'd like to meet," Honey said with a tinge of sadness in her soft voice and green eyes. "He spoke to me, but I froze. I'm still a little nervous about being here alone. I certainly hope he will try again. He is incredibly handsome and tall."

Jacqueline replied with confidence in their Southern way of life and manners, "Even though it's old-fashioned these days, I don't think a little game of cat and mouse will hurt anything. In fact, it might make him more anxious to meet you. From your perspective, he still looks interesting and even exciting. You know nothing about him, and, therefore, he retains his mystery. I like finding out about people very slowly. I don't want to learn too quickly that I do not like them."

"Well, we certainly are playing a game of cat and mouse. All I know with any certainty is that he wears suits that fit him perfectly and has the most fabulous piercing eyes and gorgeous dark brown hair," Honey gushed to the amusement of her friend.

"My dear Honey, so do many of the men in New Orleans," Jacqueline responded with a manner that appeared older than her years. "Your description fits any number of gentlemen whom I see. We'll have to find your mystery man so that you can learn more about him and share the information with me. In the meantime, I would like some ice cream. Let's stop in this little café."

As they nibbled at their chocolate ice cream, Honey felt as if the other diners were carefully watching them. She could not imagine why they would draw so much attention. Even if someone had recognized her from the shop window, she did not think anyone would be rude enough to stare and listen to her conversation. However, whenever she looked up from her snack or away from Jacqueline's face, she saw that they were indeed the center of attention. Clusters of women whispered behind their hands about them and cast sidelong glances in their direction. Men raised their eyebrows and smiled knowingly as they boldly studied their faces and figures. If their voices had been just a little louder, she would have heard everything they said.

Unable to ignore the feeling of discomfort that prevented

her from enjoying her ice cream any longer, Honey asked, "Why do you suppose that everyone is watching us?"

"I've found that people often stare when they have nothing else to do. Ignore them and they'll stop," Jacqueline responded without turning her attention from her food. She did not seem the least bit affected by the unwanted attention. It was almost as if she were accustomed to being the center of loudly whispered criticism.

"That is certainly easier said than done. Besides, I don't think those gentlemen at the table by the window are exactly admiring us. I've seen expressions on faces of men like that when they see prostitutes pass on the street. If they don't stop, I'll have to set them straight," Honey replied. The men were all but drooling as they looked at them.

"I wouldn't call any more attention to our situation than already exists. Ignore them. Finish your ice cream so we can leave," Jacqueline suggested without seeming the least bit annoyed or irritated by the men.

"I've lost my appetite. We can leave whenever you're ready. I really can't take this staring and whispering any longer. If you'd rather that I not say anything, we're out of here. If we stay another minute, I'll have to report them to the owner at least," Honey replied, pushing her half-empty bowl away and tossing her napkin onto the table in disgust.

"Let's go then. Put your money away. This is my treat. Next time, I'll allow you to pick up the tab," Jacqueline said as she deposited the necessary bills on the table and rose. Linking her arm once again in Honey's, the two young women left the café amid twitters of laughter.

Honey struggled with her turbulent emotions all the way back to Jacqueline's house. Never had she been treated so rudely. She had modeled bathing suits and caused less of a stir than she did today. She could not imagine that being new to New Orleans would cause this much attention. She had spent the first month of her return in total anonymity. Now, suddenly she and Jacqueline had become the center of attention.

"If you have time next week, I would like to take you to the city of the dead. Our cemeteries are quite famous," Jacqueline said. Her face and demeanor showed no sign that anything had affected her enjoyment of the afternoon.

"I would love a guided tour. I'll give you a call on Friday and stop by again after mass next Sunday if the weather's good. Will I see you at Saint Philippe's shop any time soon?" Honey asked as she stood on the sidewalk in front of Jacqueline's quiet house.

"No, don't expect to see me there. I only shop after hours and by appointment. I stay pretty much to myself during the day," Jacqueline replied sadly. "I only go out to run errands. Stopping in the café was a true treat for me. No, I will meet you at the cathedral on Sunday. By the way, don't give further thought to the rudeness of the people today. It wasn't you they were sneering at, it was me. I have lived with their attitudes all my life. Their behavior doesn't bother me anymore. If you're too busy to call, don't worry. I'll be here. See you next Sunday."

Waving good-bye, Jacqueline climbed the steps and disappeared through the front door. As she closed it, the sad melody of a lone violin floated out to Honey. She wondered who might be playing such a lonely tune. Almost immediately, it was joined by an equally forlorn piano.

Quickly returning to her hotel, Honey wondered what secrets lay behind the carefully controlled façade of her new friend. She wanted to know why Jacqueline had not been as upset by the unwanted attention as she had been. She marveled at the young woman's ability to maintain her composure as her own slipped under the prying eyes and rude whispers. The reason for the careful observation of the other diners must have been directly related to Jacqueline and her stunning beauty.

As Honey entered the lobby with the assistance of the attentive doorman, Saint Philippe waved happily in greeting. He had dined in the restaurant and enjoyed a round of cards in the drawing room. He was now on his way home for the evening. Over cigars he had heard about the stir Honey and Jacqueline had caused in the little café. As her employer, he wanted to bring up the subject, but he found it too delicate to broach. He waited, hoping she would share her afternoon with him.

"And how was your Sunday, Honey?" Saint Philippe asked as they walked across the lobby to the stairs that led up to the suites.

"Lovely, thank you. I explored several beautiful neighborhoods, made a new friend, and ate ice cream in a cute little café. We have planned to visit the cemeteries together next week," Honey replied as she turned to face him. "I am a little concerned, however, about something that happened in the ice cream shop today. I was really shocked at the rudeness of several men."

"Let me assure you, my dear, that the attention was not directed at you," Saint Philippe responded with the color rising to his cheeks. "I have heard about the incident in the café and feel that it is my duty to explain something about your companion to you. You see, Honey, your new friend is rumored to be a courtesan, as we call them down here— wealthy man's mistress, as her mother was before her and her grandmother and great grandmother before that. You, of course, did not know about her social standing. People, rude as they were, felt that she had stepped outside of her circle and was intruding in theirs."

Although Saint Philippe had himself been the subject of much gossip, he continued to defend the behavior of many of the residents. Blushing, his sexual leanings made it very difficult for him to discuss the various romantic arrangements that existed in New Orleans. He wished that someone else could discuss these matters with Honey, but her lack of friends placed the responsibility on his shoulders.

"Gossip certainly travels quickly in this town," Honey replied in disbelief. "I can't imagine that she would do something like that. I don't believe it. I think it's just gossip because people are jealous of her beauty. I have seen plenty of prostitutes and call girls in New York, but they seldom had Jacqueline's look of innocence."

"I'm sure that it is difficult for someone of your moral values and sensibilities to believe that a new friend could be engaged in that profession, but I assure you that she is from one of the oldest families of courtesans in the city. Her mother was famous for her relationship with two very prominent men. Her grandmother before her was even more notorious because of her political activism and romantic ties. And then there was her great-great grandmother, who hosted some of the wildest Mardi Gras parties in town. Her great-great grandmother was legendary as the mistress of one of the most prominent Yankee generals to occupy New Orleans during the Civil War. You must quickly give up this new relationship in order to preserve your reputation. You don't want anyone to think that you practice the same . . . make your living the same . . . well, you understand," Saint Philippe stuttered under Honey's direct gaze.

"I understand completely, Saint Philippe. I appreciate your efforts on my behalf. I will certainly take your suggestion under consideration. I am sure that you only have my welfare at heart. However, I will ask Jacqueline myself about her profession before I act on unsubstantiated hearsay. If what you have told me compares with her story, I will certainly need to reconsider my friendship with her. Thank you, sir, and good night," Honey said with considerable effort.

Although Honey was surprised to find that the young woman with whom she had just become acquainted was a well-known courtesan, she still did not want to believe Saint Philippe. However, she wondered how many of the men who watched her with knowing eyes might actually have been her customers. With that in mind, Honey could understand the hostile manner in which the men acted. They were frightened that Jacqueline would reveal their acquaintanceship to their wives. Jacqueline said she had many appointments to keep during the week. Honey almost giggled when she thought about their possible nature.

"I am sure that you will do what is best in this circumstance, dear Honey. I'll see you at the shop in the morning," Saint Philippe replied, easing toward the door. He felt comfortable that Honey would not continue her friendship with this Jacqueline woman after receiving his advice and verifying the truth of its content.

Leaving Saint Philippe in the lobby, Honey returned to her room. Carefully removing the Bible and the rosary from her bag, she laid them on the bedside table next to the bottle of elixir. As she slipped out of her clothes and into her jeans and T-shirt, Honey realized that she was very tired. The tension of the afternoon had been more than she had originally thought. She could feel it weighing down her shoulders and causing her feet to feel heavy and leaden. She was happy to be back in the privacy of her own room.

As she lay on the chaise and struggled to read the book open at her side, Honey wondered if her mother had known about a relationship with the woman who lived in that house. Had her mother suspected her father of having a relationship with this woman or did she simply dislike the idea of stopping there for fear someone would recognize their car and make assumptions? Remembering her father's longing stares as they sat in front of the white house, she realized that her mother must have known and suffered the humiliation in silence. She wondered if his infidelity had contributed to her mother's death as a tormented, lonely woman more than the grief over losing her beloved husband, station in life, and home. For the first time in her life, Honey saw her father in a totally different light.

Before she could make New Orleans her home again, Honey would have to discover the truth buried in this town of strictly followed rules of southern etiquette and carefully constructed canals. With sadness, Honey admitted that the truth probably resided among the back streets and bars and in houses like Jacqueline's.

Three

The next week passed quickly, with Honey modeling clothing that the wealthy women of New Orleans rushed into Saint Philippe's shop to purchase. As word of her elegant demeanor and fabulous figure continued to spread, the cash register never stopped tinkling. Saint Philippe fluttered with happiness each time he heard its sweet little song.

Many women Honey had not seen in her first days in town came to peer at her. From their barely hushed whispers, she knew they had heard the rumor about her keeping company with a reputed courtesan. Although none of them would admit to knowing any personally, they were very curious.

They had seen news reports of madams being jailed and thought that all of them wore too much makeup, hot pants, halter tops, and spike heels. At the very least, they operated out of lavish apartments and drove fancy cars while wearing expensive suits and furs. Although the women in the shop dared not ask her, they hoped Honey would describe the woman to them if they loitered around the shop long enough. They wondered if Honey looked different now that she had shared an afternoon with a woman of questionable family.

When Honey did not mention her meeting to them and did not appear changed by the experience, they left the shop disappointed that she had not grown a scarlet letter on her chest purely by association. They consoled themselves smugly with the thought that their husbands had not visited such a woman, or at least had maintained the proper decorum and not made the association public knowledge.

Before the matrons departed, they counseled Saint Philippe that, as Honey's employer and benefactor, he had the responsibility to guide her in the expected behavior for a young woman. They understood that Honey had been the sole means of support of her ailing mother while living in New York, but she needed direction to prevent her from going astray now that she had returned to her hometown.

Honey accepted their words of advice with gentle grace and genuine appreciation. She had not intended to visit a courtesan and had not known that her new friend was one until Saint Philippe broke the news to her. She was even more distressed than the ladies to discover that Jacqueline and her mother were members of the oldest profession known to man. She had assumed that Jacqueline was a woman of independent means.

As she listened to the motherly advice of the town's well-meaning matrons who gathered around Saint Philippe's desk, Honey wondered what conditions led a young woman to selecting that lifestyle. Jacqueline had mentioned that the women of her family had not been raised to work, but Honey had thought nothing of the remark. Her father's prominence in his field had made her life comfortable, too, but she had not sold her body to make ends meet. As a child, she had enjoyed playing with all the latest toys, traveling the country, and studying at the best schools. If he had not died and left them with a mortgage they could not afford, she would have been buying expensive dresses rather than modeling them for women who should not consider wedging their bodies into them.

As Honey listened, she reflected that she had never been a person to make friends quickly, but when she met Jacqueline, she warmed to her immediately. Although she found the news of her profession unsettling, Honey continued to feel affection toward her new friend. She disliked the tone and content of the women's discussion and wished that they would leave her in peace. She needed time to digest all they had said and to seek out Jacqueline for verification.

Despite her aching feet from standing all day, Honey could not imagine choosing the life that Jacqueline appeared to have. With women serving in the military, the House, and the Senate, as well as holding upper-level management positions in Fortune 500 companies, a woman could rise to levels of importance in government and commerce. She certainly did not need to serve as the mistress to a wealthy man in order to support herself.

Returning to her position in front of the window, Honey allowed the antics of the passersby to distract her mind from thoughts of Jacqueline. As always, the children gathered in front of the window to watch the model. Honey would have thought that by now they would have tired of waiting for her to move or speak, but the same little faces pressed against the shop window. She recognized them immediately and suppressed the urge to smile and wave. She also noticed that a few of the older girls had started wearing their hair in a style that closely resembled her own. If she wore a braid of hair over her right shoulder on Monday, on Tuesday they would appear with theirs in the same style. When she wore hers tucked under a baseball cap while wearing a shorts set, the next day they did the same.

After Saint Philippe noticed the impact Honey had on the girls, he began to stock the accessories that she wore so well. Gradually, the teenagers stopped staring longingly into the window and began coming into the shop to purchase the items Honey had used to accentuate her outfits. Their mothers did not seem to mind that their daughters copied the model's fashions. They could not criticize their daughters when they themselves flocked to the shop to purchase the same styles that Honey had modeled.

Despite the gossip about Jacqueline, Saint Philippe had never been happier or more content with a business decision. As his

bank account balance increased, he patted himself on the back
for having the wisdom to bring the first human model into a
New Orleans house of fine fashion. He had always prided himself on being a trendsetter. After all, his shop was the first to
employ saleswomen to model the fashions while they waited
on their customers, in the manner of the French salons. His
reputation as a designer had soared with that simple change;
this one had caused his fame to skyrocket. His clientele reached
far past the boundaries of New Orleans. As he counted his
growing assets, Saint Philippe imagined that shortly he would
be as famous as the New York fashion houses or maybe even
vie for a position among the French elite.

Yet Saint Philippe knew that as much as Honey could help
his success, a scandal could ruin both of them. He realized
that the advice of the matrons had been correct. He had to
counsel Honey on the expectations New Orleans society
placed on young women. She had to understand that associating with certain people could result in her destruction. It
was not enough that she lived in the best and most respected
hotel in town and worked for him. She had to maintain an
expected level of respectability as well. Her association with
a suspected courtesan had to stop immediately. He had
worked too hard to establish himself in town to allow an
employee to pull him down with her.

As Saint Philippe busied himself around his shop, he formulated a plan for introducing Honey to New Orleans society.
He was certain that the young woman was very lonely with
only his customers to keep her company. She worked six days
a week and had little time to associate with the other young
people in the town. He knew from the hotel manager that
she retired to her suite early after taking her dinner alone at
a side table in the dining room. She always read a book to
keep uninvited men from joining her at the table. He had
never seen her speak to a man and had actually witnessed
her scurry away when a very eligible young bachelor had
approached her.

Realizing that he had to do something, Saint Philippe decided to host a masked party. He had not given a party in ages and was well overdue. Everyone said that he threw the most enjoyable parties in New Orleans. He certainly worked hard to make them the most elaborate. He always employed jugglers and clowns as well as the usual musicians and the best chefs his money could buy. He decided that a masked party would not only be fun but would add to his coffers as the women would flock to his shop to purchase the dresses they would wear for the special evening. Saint Philippe set himself to the immediate task of writing the invitations.

Placing himself at his desk, from which he could watch the comings and goings of his customers and the activities of his models and seamstresses, Saint Philippe inscribed thick, cream-colored vellum in his easily recognizable swooping handwriting in bold black ink. He wanted the invitation to be as stunning as the affair itself. In his mind there was little point in holding anything in reserve. He believed in living life to its fullest every day. He had seen too many tomorrows snuffed out by illness, lost fortunes, and unhappiness and no longer believed that he needed to postpone anything for the future.

Leaning over his desk with an expression of concentration on his ageless, carefully powdered face, Saint Philippe wrote:

My dearest friends,
*   In honor of the arrival of my latest creations and my*
enchanting model, Honey Tate, I will be hosting a
masked party at my home on Saturday evening. You are
all invited to attend, revel, and dine. My shop will, of
course, be open to satisfy your costuming needs.

Posting each one, he never doubted that everyone he invited would attend. He could not imagine that anyone would not want to see his fashions and to meet his human model.

Stepping close to Honey, Saint Philippe whispered in her

ear, saying, "I am giving a masquerade party this weekend
to introduce you and my new fashions to New Orleans. You'll
come, of course. I will not take no for an answer. My humble
soiree would not be a success without you." Saint Philippe
did not wait for more than a slight nod of her head. Not
wanting to disturb her any further, he trotted away in a flurry
of enthusiasm to hire a messenger to hand deliver the invitations. It would be money well spent.

If Honey had been able to move, she would have smiled
at the joie de vivre of this eccentric little man who loved to
dress in ruffled tuxedo shirt and shades of violet. He had
already become as dear to her as an uncle. She would not
think of missing his party. Besides, Honey had already decided she had spent enough time alone and that she needed
to meet the people of New Orleans now that she was home
again. Honey wanted to see for herself if the parties were as
wild as she had heard they were.

As the afternoon progressed, Honey became aware of the
increased flow of customers past the window and into the
shop. Their excited chatter told her they had received Saint
Philippe's invitation and were coming to purchase the necessary clothing for the party. Stopping to stare at her as she
struck yet another provocative pose, they wondered what the
much-discussed model would wear for her gala introduction
to New Orleans society. They wondered if it would be the
divine creation she modeled that afternoon. It certainly was
sufficiently elaborate for a party. Saint Philippe had fitted
Honey with a mask and feathery headdress that reflected the
colors of the sequins on the wide-skirted ivory dress with the
tight bodice that would make an ideal Marie Antoinette costume. The elegant tapestry slippers barely showed beneath the
hem of the voluminous skirt as a strand of pearls glistened
on Honey's skin. The outfit was very Mardi Gras.

The discussion of Jacqueline's reputation and the constant
changing of clothes to lure customers into the shop had
Honey so busy that she enjoyed little opportunity to think

about her handsome mystery man whose face usually filled her daydreams. When she did, she could feel her cheeks grow warm with the blush that spread down her neck. She wondered if he had seen her in one of the many alluring costumes she had modeled that day. More importantly, she hoped that he would attend Saint Philippe's party. She wanted the pleasure of dancing with him.

After escorting the last of his customers out of the shop, Saint Philippe waited for Honey to change clothes. As was his habit, he lingered to walk her safely to her hotel. New Orleans at night could be dangerous, as any big, bustling city could be. Saint Philippe took it upon his shoulders to be Honey's protector.

Tonight as he waited, he paced the floor nervously. Saint Philippe, despite his handsome, mature looks, had never had much experience with women other than as their fashion designer or employer. He had never married or fathered children. Now, he found himself thrown into the role of father and guardian for a fetching young woman who had stumbled quite innocently into a potentially dangerous situation. Saint Philippe dreaded the conversation that he would have with her as soon as she reappeared from the dressing room.

Looking at his reflection in the mirror, Saint Philippe felt his customary sense of pride in his appearance. He admitted to being fifty although he was almost sixty, while in his mind he thought that he looked forty. His carefully combed black hair had lost some of its sheen with age and was lightly streaked with pure white, not the yellowish gray that tormented others. Most importantly, it had not lost its volume. When his friends complained of balding, he proudly ran his fingers through his thick mane.

His physique had also remained remarkably youthful despite the passage of time. His short body was still trim with only a little extra girth around the middle that signified his prosperity rather than age. His feet, however, suffered from the long hours of standing in his shop. Sometimes the pain was so severe that it forced Saint Philippe to abandon the orthopedic shoes with their two-inch lifts that he preferred for the comfort of the soft slipper leather shoes that pampered his tormented toes. He would sigh contentedly as he slid his throbbing feet into them and wiggle his toes merrily in their extra width.

Saint Philippe's unlined face helped him conceal the years. Since he still had all of his own teeth and had never smoked, his lips had not withered and puckered like those of some mature people. With just a touch of lipstick, he restored their youthful color and suppleness.

However, it was Saint Philippe's light gray eyes, although a little puffy in the lids, that were his best feature. They still twinkled mischievously and barely squinted when he tried to read. He occasionally wore thin tortoiseshell glasses that he felt made him look distinguished rather than old. He kept them on a gold chain attached to his vest and said that everyone should have a pair. He proclaimed them to be quite the fashion accessory for gentlemen.

Despite his confidence in his appearance and his success in business, Saint Philippe did not look forward to the discussion with Honey. He had purposefully avoided the intimate company of women. He found them too jumpy and nervous for his taste. They upset his sense of balance. Besides, he preferred the company of men. Now, he was thrown into a relationship he could not avoid when all he had wanted was someone to model his fashions. He had not planned on gaining a niece in the process. However, she had no one else to turn to, and he was dreadfully fond of the dear young woman.

Taking a deep breath, Saint Philippe called, "Honey, are you almost ready? I have a dinner engagement, dear, and there's something we really must discuss before I'm free to go. Will you be much longer?"

"I'm coming right now, Saint Philippe," Honey replied as she tied the laces of her tennis shoes. Surveying her appearance in the mirror, Honey saw that the soft emerald green pullover made her eyes glow brighter than usual. Smiling, she picked up her purse and joined him in the main salon.

"Honey, we really must talk about your relationship with a certain young woman of our community. Please take a seat for a moment. How should I phrase this? I must stress the importance of appearances in a closed little circle like ours. This is not an easy discussion for me, so please do not ask any questions until I have finished," Saint Philippe said as he offered Honey a chair.

Greatly touched by his concern for her and his embarrassment, Honey immediately perched upon the offered straight-backed chair. She knew her new friendship with Jacqueline had become the talk of the town, but she did not realize that it had affected Saint Philippe to this extent. She felt dreadful about the torment that wracked him and was genuinely sorry for her part in it. Although she was a grown woman and very capable of making her own decisions, Honey was always concerned about the feelings of others, just as she had been as a little girl.

Clearing his throat and adjusting his tie, Saint Philippe began what for him was a very painful discussion. "Honey, I am aware that you have lived a very unusual life. However, as your employer and friend, I find it my duty to speak with you about your new friendship with a certain young woman by the name of Jacqueline du Prix.

"Miss du Prix is not the kind of young woman with whom you should form a relationship. Although she is your age, I have heard that she is a call girl. She is part of the well-established society of courtesans. They do not mingle with families outside of their social circle except for business purposes. It is not that they are forbidden to do so, it is simply that over the years they have found it more comfortable not to do it. They are women who never marry. Again, they are not forbidden to take husbands, but they find it an arrangement that usually escapes their grasp.

"As you could undoubtedly tell from the appearance of the

house in which Miss du Prix resides, the women who select this way of life find that they live quite well if their companions are generous. I am sure, knowing the generosity of the men in New Orleans, that she wants for nothing. As a matter of fact, she and others of her profession are among my most frequent customers. They love the latest fashions and entertain often, making a large wardrobe a necessity, and they have the financial wherewithal to make the necessary purchases. I understand, although I've never personally attended one, that their parties are legendary.

"However, my dear, she is not an appropriate associate for you. Despite all of her charm and gentility, she is not of your circle. I must ask you not to see her again. Your reputation might suffer irreparable damage if the association continues. I realize that this information has just been thrust upon you and that I have given you little time to reflect upon all you have heard. However, as your friend, my dear, I must warn you that to be seen in Jacqueline du Prix's company, even for the purpose of hearing her disclose the truth of her livelihood, could be ruinous to your reputation."

"But, Saint Philippe, Jacqueline has offered to show me around the city of the dead on Sunday," Honey responded sincerely but with an equal amount of determination and sarcasm. "I do appreciate your concern for me, but I cannot understand the need for such caution. What possible harm could come of going for a stroll in the city's cemeteries with her? I promise that I will not enter her house, although I am quite curious about its interior."

Saint Philippe had failed to hear the teasing in Honey's voice, only hearing the determination. He wrung the handkerchief that lay a wrinkled mass of softest linen in his hand. "Be that as it may, I am sure that I can find someone more suitable to guide you. Perhaps you will meet someone at my party who would make a much more appropriate companion. If not, I will take you myself. I will do anything to preserve your reputation."

"I could not think of putting you to so much trouble when Jacqueline has already made the offer," Honey said. She did not want to upset Saint Philippe any further, but she also did not want to relinquish her plans. "Besides, my father used to drive us past that house almost every Sunday after mass. He would stop and look at it as if waiting to see someone. I would like to discover the identity of that person who held so much fascination for him if I can."

With a sniff, Saint Philippe replied, "I daresay that a great many men drove past that house in your father's day. As beautiful as Jacqueline is, her mother was even more so. I myself was tempted to visit the fair Madeline."

"Are you saying that my father visited a courtesan, that she was his mistress? My father never would have done anything like that," Honey bristled as she defended her father's memory. Yet, she remembered the expression of longing that took possession of his face every time he drove by the white house.

Saint Philippe sniffed again. "I am certainly not saying anything of the sort. However, many men fell under her spell by simply looking at her. Some said she practiced voodoo to attract men for her own financial gain. Perhaps she cast a spell on him, too, but he was strong enough to resist. Maybe he simply found her beauty something that he had to admire from the safe distance of his car and his wife's side. Whatever the reason for his fascination, you know the kind of woman who was the object of his attraction. Remember, Honey, that your father was only human. He had the same thoughts as other men or at least men of his persuasion."

Saint Philippe had suffered through enough of this conversation and was ready to escort Honey home. He had already decided that if she did not heed his advice, he would have to fire her rather than take the chance that her behavior would reflect on his shop. She had contributed to his most recent financial success, but he did not owe her either a livelihood or his protection if she was too stubborn to take his advice.

His affection for her and sense of responsibility toward her could only go so far.

"I'm sure you are more familiar with the ways of men than I am, Saint Philippe, but I do not want to believe that my father only visited that house for the reasons that you imply," Honey responded with wounded pride. "I intend to find out what other motives drove him to stop there every week, especially since his wife and child accompanied him. I assure you that I will act with the utmost discretion and not cause any stain to fall on my family name or your shop."

Honey's father, in her memory, was the closest she had ever come to a perfect person. She did not want anyone, not even Saint Philippe, to cast a shadow of doubt in her mind. She could not bring herself to admit that he had human flaws and weaknesses that might include frequenting and maintaining women of ill repute.

Deeply upset by what he envisioned as his slight to Honey's sensibilities, Saint Philippe pleaded, "Oh, no, my dear, I would never suggest that your father would do anything that might in any way disgrace his name. What I am merely saying is that whereas your father could stop his car in front of that house and not be ridiculed, you do not have that freedom or luxury. You must protect yourself at all costs.

"Now, let us speak of something more pleasant. I am, after all, giving the masquerade party to introduce you and my fashions to New Orleans. Did you see any particular one of my creations that especially caught your fancy, or should I whip up something special for you? I live only to please."

With a dry chuckle, Honey excused Saint Philippe's comment about her father. She could not remain angry with anyone for very long, and especially not with someone who had been so kind to her. Yet, she was aware that he had clearly given her a message that she must heed, or she would lose her job. Saint Philippe, despite all of his fluttering, was a businessman who did not intend to sacrifice his creative success, position in society, and bank account for anyone. She made a mental note to tread carefully on the topic of Jacqueline du Prix.

"I'm rather fond of the pale gold gown with the sparkling ruffles at the neckline and cuffs. If I could, I'd like to wear that one. Perhaps you might make a hat of some sort for me to wear with it. Lots of feathers would be heavenly. And, of course I'll need the appropriate slippers to complete the ensemble. Might I wear those lovely, tapestry ones I modeled today? I think I'll wear my hair in a cascade of curls to the right side. Could you design something that would complement that hair style?" Honey asked. She had deliberately selected clothing that would show off her hair and smiling eyes. Her taste had gravitated toward Saint Philippe's personal favorites, too. She meant the selection as the highest form of flattery and gratitude for his interest in her welfare. His Mardi Gras costumes, of which that ensemble was a favorite, were the toast of the town.

Saint Philippe responded, linking his arm in hers and directing her toward her hotel. *"Ma cheri,* you may wear anything you would like, as you know. However, with your sense of style, you could not have chosen more elegant fashions from among my treasures if you had tried. Your taste is exquisite. I will set my hands to making the perfect little hat tomorrow."

He could hardly wait to tell his dinner companion that his prized model had selected the most extravagant and expensive creation in his collection to wear to the party. He could already hear the singing of the cash register on Monday morning.

As they waved their good nights, Honey wondered when and how she would find the time and the opportunity to visit Jacqueline and the elegant white house again. She did not want to have these discussions on the phone, preferring personal contact for such delicate matters. She had to know why her father had been attracted to the women who lived there.

She needed to understand her quick bond to Jacqueline, too.
She had to have answers, and she knew that no one in New
Orleans would give them to her.

Four

The crowds of women in Saint Philippe's shop during the week kept Honey so busy that she had little time to think about Jacqueline, her mystery man, or the party. She modeled one elaborate creation after the other as shoppers made their selections and waited for fittings. Saint Philippe was so busy he did not have time to complain about anything. Not even the aching of his poor feet could spoil his days. His usually taciturn assistant giggled with glee at his employer's unaccustomed silence.

The preparations for the party extended beyond Saint Philippe's shop to his huge mansion in the highly fashionable Garden District. The ornate ironworks were dwarfed by the abundance of the colorful bunting he instructed the caterer to hang from the balconies and colonnades. He spared no expense in ordering massive pots of flowers and shrubs to augment the ones that bloomed in profusion in his carefully tended gardens.

Saint Philippe had purchased every candle in New Orleans that was not in use in a church or voodoo ceremony. His decorator had set up torches of every height and description throughout the grounds. When night came, his yard and gardens would sparkle like fireworks on Lake Pontchartrain on the Fourth of July.

The sky on the evening of the party was so clear that everyone thought Saint Philippe had paid someone to conjure the spectacular display of stars. With the sky and the gardens all aglow with twinkling lights, New Orleans looked as if heaven and earth had joined forces to make the night perfect.

Saint Philippe stood tall on high heels as he cut an elegant figure in the Louis XVI costume he had fashioned for himself. The silvery silk brocade knee-length trousers and matching vest reflected the many colors of the candles that flickered beside him. On his head he wore a massive white powdered wig. Hand-sewn tapestry slippers adorned his feet. He smiled happily into the masked but not unknown faces of all of his closest friends . . . all two hundred of them. Saint Philippe was in his element and enjoying every minute of reigning as king over his masquerade party.

All the dignitaries of New Orleans nibbled on shrimp, mango, paté, and other treats. Animated conversation flowed from one cluster of happy revelers to the other as old friends chatted contentedly. Huge diamonds in almost gaudy clusters and weighty solitaires sparkled around the necks of the women and on the fingers of both men and women. Shoe buckles with faux gems vied for equal attention as twinkling feet padded along the red carpet that led to the receiving line.

Honey was a vision as she stood at Saint Philippe's side. The two of them made the perfect Marie Antoinette and Louis. However, unlike Saint Philippe, she had not covered her own lustrous tresses with a wig but instead wore her hair over her right ear in ringlets that peered from under the huge headdress that he had created for the evening. Its many layers of feathers, gossamer fabric, and sparkling sequins glittered as brightly as did her mother's diamonds at her throat.

She, too, was in her element as his queen. Honey had loved playing dress-up as a child and had found that her fascination with clothing had not lessened with the passing of the years. She not only enjoyed modeling them for other women to buy, but she loved wearing beautiful outfits herself.

As a waiter dressed in burgundy velvet sounded a note from the lonely trumpet, Saint Philippe took Honey's arm and

led her into the mansion's huge living room from which he
had ordered the furniture removed to create a royal reception
room. Taking their places, they officially announced the formal portion of the evening by forming the receiving line.

Honey graciously inclined her head as Saint Philippe presented her to the invited ladies and offered her hand to the
men. She smiled sweetly as they bowed low and placed discreet kisses on her bejeweled fingers in the tradition of days
long forgotten. If any of the men lingered a bit too long,
their wives quickly tugged at their sleeves to force them to
move along. Saint Philippe beamed as each woman passed.
He recognized his creations on the backs of all of them. No
one had dared to wear a creation designed by one of his
competitors.

Saint Philippe had not neglected the interior of his mansion
in his decorating efforts. Arrangements of potted flowers and
ferns crowded every corner and tabletop. He had hired a pianist to play the rented concert grand piano in the library. A
small orchestra played in the ballroom that by day served as
the storage room for the fabric and fashions he sold in his
shop. He had transformed the dining room into an overflowing serving room in which he displayed every possible deli-
cacy that might possibly tempt the palate of the most
discerning diner. Delicate china platters heaped with candies,
chocolate-dipped strawberries, caviar, and cakes sat atop lacy
cloths surrounded by crystal bowls and heavily ornamented
silver serving pieces. If one of Saint Philippe's guests did not
see an especially desired treat, all he had to do was request
it and the chef would produce it immediately.

As the receiving line closed, Saint Philippe led Honey away
from the platform on which they had stood for the past two
hours and into the grand ballroom. Passing one elegantly
decorated room after the other, she peered through open doors
into candlelit parlors filled with oil paintings, gilt-framed mirrors, genuine French period furniture, and thick, hand-woven
carpets on gleaming wood floors. Honey felt as if she had

stepped back in time to an era of opulence and elegance. Few in New Orleans lived as Saint Philippe did. Honey guessed that only a select few in white America enjoyed his wealth. She felt pride at being in the company of a black man who had risen to this level of wealth and position.

Entering the ballroom, Honey studied the masked faces of the guests to see if her mystery man stood among them. She had not recognized him from the receiving line and was anxious to meet him. Saint Philippe had promised that she would meet suitable gentlemen escorts who would show her around New Orleans and remove her from the company of Jacqueline du Prix. Honey already had her eye on the perfect substitute if she could ever meet him.

As the first notes of the waltz filled the air, Saint Philippe bowed low in imitation of the grand style of bygone days and asked her to dance. Leading her to the center of the dance floor, he bowed elegantly and offered himself as a partner. Dropping a curtsy, Honey stepped forward and accepted his offer. Amidst appropriately appreciative applause from the assembled guests, he slipped his arm around her waist and guided her around the room.

As they twirled under the glittering chandelier, Honey spoke with true appreciation for his skills, saying, "You certainly are a man of many talents, Saint Philippe. You dance divinely, create fabulously elegant gowns, and give the most elaborate parties in town. I don't know how you have the energy to do it all."

Beaming like a schoolboy, Saint Philippe responded with his customary flutter and flourish, "My dear, as I have told you before, I live to please and to serve. I love to see my friends have a good time. I do my part to enliven our poor little lives here in New Orleans."

"Well, I cannot imagine anyone not having a perfectly delightful time tonight. Any other party would pale by comparison to yours," Honey replied as she continued to search the faces of the guests who watched them navigate the ballroom floor.

Noticing that although Honey followed his masterful lead with ease, she was not really paying attention to him, Saint Philippe asked, "Honey, dear, for whom are you searching? If I were a less understanding man, I would be insulted that you are not giving me your undivided attention."

"Oh, I am sorry, Saint Philippe, but I was hoping to find the young man I happened to see the other day. Unfortunately, I have not seen him. Perhaps he was not on your list," Honey replied. She was genuinely sorry she had not been more attentive, but she had to take whatever opportunities presented themselves to search for her mystery man.

"I assure you, my dear Miss Tate, that I have invited everyone of note in New Orleans. If the young man in whom you are interested is not here, he is not worth meeting," Saint Philippe sniffed with genuine disdain for the people he did not consider worthy of an invitation to his soiree. He was quite wounded in his own way that she would think that someone important had not been invited to his party.

As the music slowed, Saint Philippe led Honey to their chairs at the top of the room. He had ordered the best carpenters in New Orleans to construct a stage on which sat genuine period thrones that he kept in storage for such occasions as these extravagant parties. He had purchased them on one of his many trips to Europe in search of fashion trends. From their vantage point, they could see everyone who entered the ballroom.

Not since she was a young girl at her father's expansive home during one of his frequent barbecues had Honey seen so many people gathered in one place to enjoy an evening. They danced the waltzes, tangos, and more modern steps with gay abandon in cutaway jackets, flowing gowns, and masks that disguised the top portion of their faces but left their lips exposed for easy conversation and stolen kisses. The people she knew in New York seemed to enjoy smaller, more intimate gatherings. While she lived there, Honey had learned to appreciate their taste. However, now that she was home again, she realized that she had missed the impact of the crush of people making merry.

Honey had always enjoyed her father's parties and the sense of togetherness that they produced. She had especially enjoyed seeing so many black people in high positions who possessed power and the wealth that accompanied it. For too long, wealth had belonged only to whites. Seeing black people in elaborate gowns, driven by chauffeurs, and coifed by leading stylists told Honey that powerful African-Americans had attained the same status as their white counterparts.

Now, Honey found herself totally overwhelmed by a feeling of closeness with these people. Although she knew that many of them attended for the purpose of gaining material for future gossip, she liked being among the soft Southern voices and laughter that had filled her childhood. She loved to watch the way these assembled members of New Orleans black aristocracy kissed the air to show affection as they lightly touched cheeks or shook hands. She chuckled each time she saw two women put their heads together. Behind their elaborate fans, which were part of their equally elaborate costumes, they shared secrets they had saved just for tonight, criticism of their good friends, and hopes that certain available young men would ask them to dance. Most of the men, however, clustered together as if they preferred the safety of their number, and perhaps they were right. From the expressions on the faces of several of the women, Honey decided that the men were no safer than a turkey at Thanksgiving. Losing interest in their plight, she shrugged and looked away.

Turning her gaze to a group of people standing to the right, Honey watched the expressions of the men and women as they exchanged pleasantries. The carefully composed faces hid the envy, jealousy, and deception that were always part of a gathering of social equals. She tried to guess the topic of discussion by watching the darting glances that directed the listener to look in the indicated direction. They were obviously chatting about missing group members because their discussion stopped as soon as a newcomer entered their circle. A few moments later, it resumed with the same level of comfort and animation until someone else new appeared. She wondered how many of Saint Philippe's friends had already dissected him, and her, too, for that matter.

Changing the direction of her gaze once more, Honey became so engaged in observing the conversation of two young women in the far right corner that she did not see the young man approach her from the left. "Good evening," he said, startling Honey out of her reverie. "I hope you've saved at least one waltz for me."

Before she could answer, Saint Philippe turned at the sound of the young man's voice. "Stephen Turner, I thought you had forgotten all about my little party. Have you met Honey Tate? She's the most beautiful and talented model in the country and probably the world," he gushed with a flutter of his hand.

Stephen inclined his body in a deliberately formal, low bow and kissed her hand. Then he replied, "I have never had the pleasure of being introduced to Miss Tate although I have seen her through your shop window on many occasions of late. Once in the marketplace, I almost had the good fortune of meeting her, but something came between us. If I remember correctly, I think it was an oversized purse. I am delighted, Honey."

Honey controlled the wild pounding of her heart and inclined her head graciously. The role of a great lady suited her perfectly. "Good evening, Stephen. I too remember seeing you at the market," she responded formally, not wanting to appear too eager to make his acquaintance. Honey did not want him to know that she had scoured the faces of all in attendance at the party in a futile effort to search for him since the evening began.

"I am sorry, Saint Philippe, for arriving late. My car had

a flat and I had a terrible time finding anyone to fix it. It seems that everyone in this town is partying tonight. I hope I haven't missed anything scandalous or exciting," Stephen said as he dragged his attention from Honey's beautiful face. She was even more stunning than he had originally thought from the quick glimpse he had enjoyed of her before she placed her purse between them.

"Nothing extraordinary has happened yet, but just give it time!" Saint Philippe gushed. Turning to Honey, he said, "Stephen and his father are partners in the same law firm. As long as there have been Turners in New Orleans, they have been attorneys. It's a wonderful tradition that I hope will continue forever."

Waving off the compliment, Stephen replied with a proud smile, "It's nothing. We're a family that likes to talk. We could think of no better way to do it than by becoming lawyers. But, Honey, I'm sure you find my family tree rather boring."

"Not at all," Honey responded. "I find it quite interesting. I might need your services one day. Besides, my father was an attorney here. I'm used to shop talk."

Pretending interest in the dancers, Honey took quick glances at Stephen as he continued to chat with Saint Philippe. Even with the mask over the upper portion of his face, he was far more handsome than she had originally thought. In her first assessment, she had missed the twinkle in his light brown eyes and the playful dimple in his chin. She had not heard the laughter that started deep in his chest and rumbled upward until it ended with a head-back roar that shook his entire body. She had not felt the soft tickle of his mustache on her hand or the light caress of his lips. Honey had misjudged his height and now realized that at six feet two inches, Stephen was one of the tallest men in the room. His deep brown hair against the healthy warm skin tones certainly made him one of the most handsome. From the overt stares of the other women, Honey could tell that she was not the only one who found Stephen Turner handsome.

Yet, standing there in his Sir Walter Raleigh costume that revealed the muscular shape of his calves, Stephen did not appear at all aware of the admiring gazes sent in his direction by the unattached women at Saint Philippe's party. He continued to chat amiably with the host, seemingly without noticing that many of the women had ceased their conversation as soon as he appeared and that many more were giggling because of him. Honey decided that his nonchalant manner was the result of good breeding and proper upbringing, which had instilled in him the perfect Southern manners. It was either that or the fact that he was quite accustomed to being the center of attention and took it all in stride.

Having spent the required time in casual conversation with Saint Philippe, Stephen turned his attention to Honey, who felt her powdered cheeks blush brightly. She was so taken by his steady, unflinching gaze that she did not hear him ask her to dance until he repeated his question, saying with Old-World formality, "Miss Tate, I would indeed be beholden to you if you would honor me with this dance. I promise I will not tread too heavily on your feet." Deep, playful dimples appeared on either side of his well-shaped mouth as he spoke.

"Mr. Turner, it is I who would be honored," Honey replied as she lifted the train of her skirt and looped it over her arm.

Walking her to the middle of the dance floor, Stephen again bowed with great elegance and took Honey into his arms. She inhaled the heady maleness of him as he pulled her against his chest and swung her around the floor. She felt so small in his arms that Honey wondered if her feet touched the ground or if she floated on the strength of his muscles.

"You certainly do waltz divinely, Stephen," Honey commented. She quickly discovered that the compliment sprang easily to her lips as Stephen directed her skillfully through the steps of her favorite dance. He was such a masterful dancer that Honey experienced no difficulty at all in following his lead.

"Honey, I have discovered that a gentleman's skill at dancing is directly related to that of his partner. In this instance, you make me look like a dancing instructor," Stephen replied, giving Honey an extra little flourish.

"And exactly how did you make this discovery? Have you danced with many women?" Honey asked, finding that the relaxed small talk came easily with Stephen.

"Oh, I've danced with my fair share of lovely young women, Honey, but none so lovely as you. New Orleans is a city that offers many opportunities for dancing, as I'm sure you've noticed. We seem to have at least one party every week, and I'm usually invited to all as one of the town's most eligible bachelors. I try to attend as many as I can," Stephen replied with a chuckle.

Just then, the waltz ended and a lovely tango began. Honey could feel the electricity flow between their bodies as Stephen pressed her close and steered her around the floor. She wondered if Stephen felt the same way. From the way his eyes never left her face even as they danced with other partners in the intricate steps, she thought that the fascination was mutual.

As the music ended, waiters wearing French attire from the time of Louis and Marie Antoinette appeared carrying tables covered in damask cloths, baskets of elegantly detailed china, sparkling crystal, and heavy silver candlesticks and flatware. An army of servers followed them with their arms overflowing with trays of steaming food. Maids in highly starched hats brought in elaborate floral arrangements for each table and a spectacular spray of roses, magnolias, and bougainvillea for the head table. To Honey, it looked as if Saint Philippe had ordered enough food to feed all of New Orleans, not just his invited friends. There were certainly sufficient flowers to deck every altar in town.

With Honey by his side and all the guests comfortably

seated at their tables, Saint Philippe did indeed look every bit the part of a king. His elaborate wig covered in glittery powder sparkled almost as brightly as the gems on his fingers as he stood behind his chair.

Lightly tapping on his goblet with a knife to get everyone's attention, Saint Philippe cleared his throat and lifted his glass, saying, "My dear friends, I am so happy that you have all come to my little masked party. Now that you have had a few hours to enjoy the music, it is time for you to unmask and sample the delicacies I have had prepared in your honor. After we have eaten our fill, the music will again commence to engage our eager feet. So, eat, drink, and make merry."

Everyone applauded and happily removed the feather-adorned masks that had only barely concealed their identities. Soon only the sound of clicking silver filled the room as they occupied themselves with the fabulous meal of lobster and crayfish swimming in butter, salads with thick tasty dressing, chicken in wine sauce, and beef in natural juices enhanced by a trace of burgundy wine.

Honey remembered the grand parties at her parents' home and the food that overflowed the tables. She also recalled the first years after her father's death when she and her mother had to sell the old place and move to New York. They had been hungry then until her face sparked attention and earned her modeling jobs and a very comfortable living. The groaning tables reminded her of her old poverty as well as the prosperity of the past.

At that moment, Honey decided that she not only had to discover her father's connection with the white house and its inhabitants, but she had to restore her family's home to its former glory. She would have to convince the owner to sell it to her, which would not be an easy task since he had moved away years ago. Friends of the family had written to Honey and her mother in New York to say that Mr. Morrison had left town about two years after purchasing their home. The heat and humidity of New Orleans and the constant fear of hurricanes and flooding had proved too much for him. He could not become comfortable with the idea that the levies that separated his land from the mighty Mississippi might break and bring on his ruin. At the time, her mother would not agree to return to New Orleans. Now that she was on her own, Honey would do whatever she could to reclaim her inheritance.

Honey surveyed the faces of Saint Philippe's many friends. Surely one of the many lawyers in the room would be able to track down Mr. Morrison and act on her behalf. She would have to ask one of them as soon as she could. Looking in Stephen Turner's direction, she remembered that Saint Philippe had said he was one of the brightest new attorneys on the New Orleans horizon. If he would agree to represent her, she would be able to see more of him at least professionally and maybe something would blossom between them personally. As soon as the music began again, Honey decided that she would position herself for the chance to speak with him about her concerns regarding the house and the white house.

She did not have long to wait because as soon as the waiters served the dessert and Louisiana coffee flavored with chicory, the orchestra once again began to play. As if reading her mind, Stephen appeared at her elbow. If possible, without his mask he was even more handsome. His deep brown hair reflected the candlelight, his eyes sparkled gaily, and his dimples played mischievously as he said with a teasing tone in his voice, "Honey, could you again find it in your heart to allow this humble barrister to trample upon your feet? If you could so incline your favors, I would love nothing more than to have the honor of being your partner for this waltz. Or perhaps, a more sedate stroll around the garden would be to your liking?"

"I would indeed love that stroll," Honey responded with a happy smile. "Saint Philippe's garden is not to be missed. The heliotropes and bougainvillea are trying to outdo the night blooming water lilies for supremacy among the flora. It is certainly a spectacle for the eye and a treat for the nose."

The glow of the moonlight struck them full force as Honey and Stephen walked through the porch doors. As she had promised, the fragrance of heliotropes and bougainvillea filled the air and mingled with that of the lilies. The sound of frogs singing on Lake Pontchartrain joined with the song of the nightingales and the hooting of the owls. The New Orleans night was just right for love.

Amidst the flowers, Saint Philippe had planted a formal boxwood maze that grew taller than the top of a man's head. He had envisioned it as the perfect place for lovers to sneak a discreet kiss or two. Over the years, more than one couple had gone for an after-dinner stroll and found themselves in the center of the maze. The lovely wrought-iron bench would beckon them to rest and chat. Once seated, the reluctant couple would be moved by the stars, moon, and privacy to declare their affections.

Honey and Stephen wandered along the twisting corridors until they reached the bench. Sitting amidst the branches, they chatted about the success of the party until Stephen asked, "What brought you back to New Orleans? You certainly could have enjoyed a lucrative career in New York. You did not need to return to your hometown to find prosperity, although I am sure from the increased clientele in Saint Philippe's shop that you are reaping the rewards of your labors."

"After my mother died, I saw no real reason to remain in the North. She had wanted to stay away from New Orleans because she found the memories of my father and their life together too painful. I wanted to live where he had and see the same things that appealed to him. As soon as Saint Philippe made the offer, I decided to come home. I left many good friends in New York, but I needed to be here where the accent is soft and the nights are gentle. Now I find that I have some unfinished business here," Honey responded with a tinge of sadness in her voice.

"If at any time you find yourself in need of legal assistance, I am more than willing to do whatever I can for you, Honey," Stephen commented with genuine concern. Honey could see that the blossoming affection she felt toward him was returned in equal amounts even if it had been given a boost by the lover's moon.

Delighted that Stephen had removed from her shoulders the burden of having to ask for his assistance, Honey replied, "As a matter of fact, I could use your help. You see, my father used to show affection toward the residents of a certain white house. I would like to find out what kind of relationship existed between him and the occupants, if that is possible. I met Jacqueline du Prix who says she's the daughter of the woman who owned the house. She is about my age. I was wondering if my father might have known her mother."

"This Miss du Prix of whom you are speaking is of a very old family. It is possible that your father knew them," Stephen commented with some hesitation. Honey felt that he was carefully selecting his words, and she understood why he felt the need to put forth so much effort.

"Saint Philippe says that a good many men knew her mother and grandmother and that Jacqueline is in the same profession," Honey said with a firm voice that reflected her determination to maintain her new friendship. "I don't believe him, but even if it is true, she is my friend. I have no intention of abandoning her. Perhaps I am being naive, but I will not hurt her that way."

Honey knew that stating her devotion to Jacqueline might mean that she would have to forfeit her relationship with Stephen, but she was willing to pay that price. If she were not true to her feelings about Jacqueline, she would have little if anything to offer Stephen in terms of true devotion.

"That's very noble of you, Honey, and a trait which I admire greatly in a person," Stephen counseled in a quiet voice that carried with it all the weight of his message. "However, as your attorney, I must warn you that many in this town will find such honorable feelings misplaced in dealing with women of Jacqueline du Prix's reputation. You must be prepared for the consequences of your actions even from those you count among your friends."

Stephen did not want Honey to make a mistake that might ruin her return to her rightful place in New Orleans society. Also, he found her green eyes thrilling and wanted to know more about her.

"Thank you for your concern, but I have set my course with full comprehension of its possible impact. Saint Philippe has been very helpful in making me understand that life is more conservative here than in New York, where the people have a tendency to be more liberal in their views. What is your opinion of my friendship with Jacqueline?" Honey asked, bristling from yet another well-meaning friend's efforts to dictate her actions.

Taking her hand, Stephen replied, "I would never advise you to abandon a true friendship; they are far too difficult to find. I merely wish you to be careful and to know what lies ahead."

Blushing deeply, Honey smiled into Stephen's gentle face and hoped that the moonlight would hide her uneasiness. Unlike Saint Philippe, whose main interest was his own reputation, she could tell from Stephen's eyes and expression that he was concerned only with her welfare. Honey found herself being drawn to him even more because of his genuine regard for her reputation.

Reluctantly extracting her hand from his, Honey asked, "Tell me about Jacqueline's family. Being with her felt so comfortable that I wondered if I might have met her at some time before leaving New Orleans for New York. My father was certainly drawn to the white house."

Carefully considering where to begin, Stephen said, "Jacqueline's family is indeed well-known in this city. The women in her family were recognized as the city's most elegant and gracious courtesans, so I have been told. During the day of this custom, there was hardly a man of substance or position in this town who had not had a relationship with a woman like them. When Susanna died, her daughter took her place. The legend goes that many wished that they could have kept company with Madeline, but she was most discerning and careful in her selection of admirers. She had to be mindful of her place in society and her reputation. She had to watch her finances, too, I suppose. It would not have profited her one bit to have entered into a relationship with a poor man even if she had loved him. She had to provide for her financial security against a time when she would be too old to work.

"I have heard the gossip that Jacqueline du Prix followed in her mother's footsteps. However, if she has, she did not need to for financial reasons, or so I understand. Her mother provided for her amply at her death. However, the city is very unforgiving and probably would not allow her to move into another social strata. There are others who are trapped in that life, too, I am sure."

"Then, I suppose Saint Philippe was correct in saying that my father was one of Madeline's associates," Honey conceded, speaking about memories that rushed to the surface, as real as if they had only just been made. "Still, I cannot believe that he would stop in front of the white house on Sundays with his wife and child with him unless the relationship went deeper than simply a . . . business arrangement. Yet, I must know the real reason for his sorrow on the last Sunday we drove there. He appeared especially distraught at not finding anyone at home. If I remember correctly, he stopped the car and ran up to the front door. After knocking for a long time, he returned to us and drove away. I think I saw tears in his eyes. I know my mother was crying. He became too ill to travel, and we never returned to the city after that. However, I would like to uncover as much as I can learn about the past."

"You must steel yourself against the fact that you may

never be able to uncover the truth about their relationship. They are both dead. Their secret might have gone to the grave with them," Stephen advised as he studied Honey's sweet, saddened face. He did not want to see Honey spend her time searching for answers she could never find.

"I know in my heart that the truth only waits for me to find it. I wouldn't feel so drawn to Jacqueline if our destinies were not intertwined in some way. There must be some record of my father's relationship with Madeline on file somewhere. My father was a generous man. Perhaps he helped Madeline obtain the mortgage for the house. If you'll help me, I just know we can uncover everything," Honey said firmly while placing her hand on Stephen's.

"We might uncover the facts, but there are some things that should be left alone, Honey, and this long-dead relationship of which you speak might be one of them," Stephen advised. He was afraid of the truth they might uncover and uncertain that Honey could stand whatever they unearthed.

"I'm not afraid of finding out that my father and Madeline were involved. I want to know to what depth the relationship reached. Now, please, will you help me? I cannot do it alone. You have all the legal resources at your fingertips. Please, Stephen, help me," Honey begged, strategically using his first name as a sign of their new intimacy. She fluttered her long lashes in a way that she remembered an older cousin telling her would work wonders on men.

Bowing over her hand, Stephen responded, "Honey, I am at your service."

As his mustache lightly tickled the back of her hand, Honey breathed a sigh of relief. With true appreciation and gratitude in her voice, she said, "Thank you, Stephen, I could never do this alone. I don't know the workings of the court system. It would take me months to uncover all the information I need. In the meantime, might I also ask you to search out information about my father's old home? We sold it at auction when we moved away, and now I would like to buy it back if it's available. I have heard from Saint Philippe that the current owner has badly neglected it and is at the moment not even residing in New Orleans. Perhaps he would be interested in selling it to me. If I'm to live here, I must make a home for myself."

"I'd be more than happy to look into that for you, Honey, but it is my obligation as your attorney and friend to tell you that you might want to look for a newer house. One that has been neglected can be extremely expensive to restore," Stephen replied as he studied Honey's expression of determination. He had a strange feeling that nothing he said would change her mind.

"I simply can't go on living in a hotel," Honey responded without any sign of hesitation. "It's very comfortable, but it is not my home. People will soon start talking about that, too. I have to be so careful to be seen alone as I enter the elevator or eat dinner as it is now, I feel as if I'm living in a goldfish bowl. No, I must have a home of my own, and I want to live in our family house. I'm counting on you to help me."

"Again, I'm at your service. I will do everything I can to get your house for you. In the meantime, I do believe I hear another waltz. May I have this dance, Miss Tate?" Stephen asked playfully as he rose from the bench and stepped toward her. Honey could feel her heart begin to pound at the prospect of being in his arms again.

"It would be my pleasure, Mr. Turner," Honey answered in the same mockingly formal tone as she eased into his outstretched arms.

Slowly they glided over the soft boxwood needles as the magic of the night enfolded them. Honey could hear her heart beating in her ears with every step. She felt pleasantly secure in Stephen's arms and enjoyed the closeness of him.

Feeling the same delight at being near her, Stephen looked longingly into her eyes. Seeing only a gentle smile of encouragement on Honey's sweet upturned face, Stephen lightly pressed his lips against hers. Their hands, hesitant at first, grew bold and explored the unfamiliar terrain as their bodies meshed as closely as Honey's wide hoopskirt would allow.

Fearing that they might be swept away by the tide of their emotions, they separated almost as quickly as they had united. Standing at arm's length from each other, Honey and Stephen struggled to regain their composure.

"Honey, I'm sorry, but I have never felt this way about any woman. I knew when I first saw you in Saint Philippe's window that my attraction toward you was quite special. Since that day in the market square when I tried to speak with you and you turned away, I haven't been able to put you out of my mind. I think I've been falling in love with you," Stephen said as he held her hands in his and gazed into her deep green eyes.

"You do not need to apologize, Stephen. I feel the same way," Honey confessed as she allowed Stephen to pull her once again into his arms. "Since I first saw you peering at me through the parted curtains, I have wanted to meet you. I had hoped you would attend this party so that we might have a few moments alone. I have been very careful about forming relationships with men. Living on my own as I do, I have been very aware of the need to protect my reputation. In fact, you are the first man whom I have allowed to enter my life. I have been afraid of being hurt. I saw firsthand how love can demolish a person. I watched my mother die from want of it."

"If you'll allow me into your life, I promise that I will do nothing to hurt you," Stephen whispered into her ear as they allowed the music to enfold them.

Honey wanted to believe him, but she wondered if the controversy over her relationship with Jacqueline would prove too much for their new love. Deciding to let time answer that question, she willed the thought from her mind. The night was meant for love and dancing, not worry.

Reluctant to leave the privacy of the maze but knowing

they must, Honey and Stephen smiled into each other's eyes
as the blush of first love spread over her cheeks. It was time
to return to the house before their absence became too lengthy
and attracted attention. As they walked toward the exit, Honey
hoped that the happiness that enfolded them would never end.

Five

The next day, New Orleans slept late with everyone recovering from the parties that had filled the streets with music until early Sunday morning. Honey, although exhausted, was too excited to sleep. Memories of the evening spent in Stephen's arms constantly played through her mind. She could still smell the aroma of his cologne and feel the rippling muscles under his jacket. The sound of his soft, gentle, baritone voice continued to echo in her heart. Honey was hopelessly in love, and she thrilled at the feeling.

Dressing quickly, Honey rushed to pull on her clothes. She and Jacqueline had planned to meet after church for a tour of the cities of the dead and she had overslept. Now that she had Stephen helping her uncover the relationship between their families, she felt even more determined than before that she had to maintain her contact with Jacqueline.

Dressed in a dark brown linen pants suit, Honey walked through the deserted hotel lobby. Her hair cascaded gently down her back in a thick braid. Passing the reception area, she did not encounter the customary crowd of residents with their animated conversation. A pianist usually played discreetly in the corner, but this morning the lid of the piano was closed and the instrument silent. The concierge who greeted her enthusiastically every day as she hurried to Saint Philippe's shop sat slumped in his chair. His crooked tie and the dark circles around his eyes told Honey that he had spent his evening and early morning on the town, too.

The tall white spires of the St. Louis Cathedral beckoned in the silent morning. Even the musicians who usually played on the steps of the cathedral looked tired as they waited for mass to end. Easing silently into the church, Honey slipped into one of the last pews and waited for Jacqueline to join her. They had planned to attend service together and tour the cemeteries on foot. Now, as she waited, the silence and the coolness of the church surrounded her as the sun streamed through the multicolored stained glass windows.

Instead of following the mass, Honey's mind took its own path as she thought about last night and Stephen. She had seen through the shop window that he was handsome and elegant, but now she knew that he was gracious and caring as well. He could have advised her against continuing her new friendship with Jacqueline, but instead he appeared to understand the bond that had been forged in only one afternoon. In his open, expressive face, Honey had been able to read the degree of his affection for her clearly displayed in his light brown eyes and had enjoyed knowing that her feelings toward him were returned.

Now, as she thought about him while the priest intoned the words that purified the altar, Honey felt someone slide into the pew beside her. Turning her head slightly, she saw that Jacqueline had finally arrived. Unlike the jeans and T-shirt she had worn last weekend as they strolled the neighborhoods around the white house, Jacqueline wore a simple navy blue skirt and jacket with a tailored white blouse. Instead of having her hair in big curls freely around her head, she wore the dark tresses carefully subdued in a bun at the back of her neck. She wore no makeup or jewelry except for a coral brooch on her lapel. She certainly did not appear to be the notorious courtesan that everyone claimed she was.

As the organ sounded the doxology, Jacqueline leaned over

and whispered, "I'm sorry that I'm late. I always pride myself on punctuality. I was unavoidably detained."

"Don't worry. I arrived as the cross was processing, myself. It seems as if we were both busy last night," Honey responded, trying to put her friend at ease. From the calm manner in which Jacqueline's hands lay folded in her lap, she could see that she really did not need to try.

The two young women were the first people out of the cathedral when the service ended. Quickly they linked arms and rushed away before the dowagers and keepers of morality in New Orleans, who frequented St. Louis Cathedral more to judge than to seek forgiveness, could see them. Rounding the corner, they laughed at their luck as they walked toward the cemetery.

Along the way, Jacqueline confided, "I was not late because I overslept. I had to cut some flowers for my mother's grave. I wanted you to see it properly adorned. I placed them there before the service. I suppose I misjudged the time it would take me to make the round trip. I had no idea that the St. Charles streetcar would be behind schedule today. Here comes one now. Let's run."

Trotting along the sidewalk, the two young women arrived at the stop just in time to board the car. Breathing deeply of the warm morning air, they settled into the already packed streetcar for the ride up St. Charles Avenue toward the cemetery.

"You needn't have gone to so much trouble because of me. I'm sure the tomb is quite elegant," Honey replied with pleasure that her friend thought so much of her opinion that she would go to such lengths to make a good impression.

From her childhood, Honey remembered Metairie Cemetery as one of the most beautiful and serene places in the city. Of all the cemeteries from which to choose, she was glad that Jacqueline had selected this one for their tour. When she was a child, she had been afraid of the massive marble statues and angels that silently stood guard over the tombs of the city's affluent dead. Now as an adult, she marveled at their structure and the cemetery's quiet grace.

As if reading her mind, Jacqueline asked, "Do you have any relatives buried here? My mom's grave is over that way a bit further. I come here at least once a month to put flowers on it. It's one of the most beautiful ones here, if I do say so myself."

"No, no one. My mother is buried in New York. One day I'll bring her body back and bury it at our home next to my father's, but that won't be for a while. I have to buy back the old house first," Honey replied as she read another inscription.

"Now that we're friends, you can help me decorate my mother's grave. We can do all manner of things together, like picnics in the park and concerts in the evening. I love the theater and the opera. I've never had a best friend before," Jacqueline said with a sweet smile on her beautiful face. She was almost childlike in her excitement about having a companion.

"Why not? Didn't you play with other little girls when you were a child?" Honey asked. She remembered the excitement of having children visit from the neighboring houses and could not imagine going through life without friends with whom to share gossip and secrets about boys.

"Maybe a few but they were never best friends. I would see girls in the neighborhood that I would like to meet, but their mothers would not allow them to come to our house. Some of my mother's friends brought their children over sometimes, but most of them did not have any. I lived a rather lonely life," Jacqueline commented in a matter-of-fact tone. She was neither bitter nor hurt by the circumstances of her life. She simply stated the facts as they existed without embellishing anything to gain Honey's sympathy.

As they wandered among the monuments and cypress trees, Honey took the opportunity to ask the question that she had wanted answered ever since their outing to the old-fashioned ice cream parlor. Taking a deep breath, she tried to word her inquiry in a way that would not hurt her friend's feelings. "Jacqueline, forgive me for asking, but I've heard some stories about you from many different sources. Naturally, I did not believe them. I wanted to ask you about them. I would like to know the truth from you. Exactly what did your mother do that caused the people of New Orleans to stay away from you?"

With dignity, Jacqueline responded, "I am sure that you are referring to the stories about my mother's line of work. You saw those people laughing last Sunday. The things we did or said did not amuse them; they were ridiculing me with their ill-mannered laughter. By now you've probably been warned about associating with me. As a matter of fact, I was somewhat surprised to find you in the cathedral. I almost did not come because I thought you might have changed your mind when the matrons of this city told you all about me.

"My mother and my grandmother were among the most beautiful, famous, elegant Creole courtesans in New Orleans. As a matter of fact, so were many of the other women in my family. They were light-skinned, almost white in appearance. They made their living as did many women of their complexion as kept women. They weren't prostitutes, exactly, since they only had one lover at a time. Still, they received payment in the form of money, property, jewelry, and clothing. Everyone assumes that I have followed in their footsteps, but they aren't correct. I have never entertained a gentleman in my house for any reason and certainly not that one. When my mother died, she left the house to me, along with a fortune large enough to support me for the rest of my life. She invested her money well in stock that has more than tripled in value.

"I told you that I had a lonely childhood, but I did not mention my older years. My mother sent me away to live with cousins as soon as she realized that New Orleans would not be welcoming or forgiving toward the daughter of a woman in her profession. From the time I was about eight until I was fourteen, I lived with them in Richmond.

"I missed my mother terribly. Every day I tried to think of some way to run away, but they watched me too closely. Finally, after much pleading and with a full understanding of the way my life would be if I returned here, I managed to convince her that I should be here in New Orleans with her.

"As soon as I returned home, people started talking about me, saying that I had come home to join her profession. They did not know that my mother was terribly ill. I nursed her night and day for the better part of four years until she died. She told me wonderful stories about the people she had met in her lifetime, and she spoke lovingly of the father I never knew although she did not identify him by name. I sat by her bed for hours simply listening to the sound of her voice.

"When she died, the whole house seemed to cry. I buried her here in the best cemetery in New Orleans. Only women friends came to the funeral. Her male friends sent flowers and unsigned notes of condolence. I closed up the house and went away to college for a few years, but I missed New Orleans too much. I never finished school. I simply couldn't stay away."

Honey wiped the tears from Jacqueline's face and linked arms with her friend. Softly she said, "People can be so mean sometimes. Isn't there some way that you can clear your name? They have to stop treating you this way."

"I've lived completely alone for almost two years now," Jacqueline replied softly. "They never see anyone coming into my house, but they still talk. I can't think of anything to say that would convince them that I'm different from my mother. They think that I am also a courtesan. I don't know of any way to change their perception. They don't want to believe that I can support myself without following in her footsteps. I've thought about leaving here, but New Orleans is home. I'll simply have to live with it for as long as I can. I keep hoping that one day they will change."

"No, you do not have to endure this treatment," Honey said as they continued their walk toward the center of Metairie Cemetery. "We'll have to think of some way to make things right for you. If we just put our heads together, I'm confident we can come up with something."

As she had expected, Honey was completely in awe of the structure of the cemetery. No one had been buried below ground. All of the bodies were interred in mausoleums of the best marble.

Breaking the silence that had enveloped them, Jacqueline pointed, saying, "There it is. That's my mother's monument."

Honey followed the line of Jacqueline's pointing hand and looked toward the vault bearing the name of Madeline du Prix. On the top, a marble angel strumming a harp stood with wings outspread. The sunshine sparkled off the radiant white-ness of the marble.

"It's lovely, Jacqueline. You've picked such a wonderful lo-cation and a beautiful monument. Tell me about the others around here. Do you know any of the history of the other families?" Honey asked. She had not been inside the ceme-tery since she was a little girl and was fascinated by the stories behind the monuments.

"My mother told me that many of the families were quite notorious." Jacqueline responded. "Some were highly placed in the government and others were successful tradesmen. Many are famous writers, too. The most impressive thing is not how they lived but the way in which they have been remembered. Let's look around a bit more before we leave."

As they strolled the grounds, Honey studied the different designs and statues that adorned the monuments. Although they were quite elegant, none were as strikingly beautiful as the one for Jacqueline's mother.

"Look at all the flowers and tokens people have left in front of that one," Honey commented, pointing to a large tomb on which people had inscribed "x" marks and left flow-ers and photographs.

Smiling, Jacqueline replied, "That's the grave of the famous voodoo priestess Marie Laveau. Everyone regardless of color or wealth or position was afraid of her."

"I don't understand. I thought she was still alive. I visited the Voodoo Museum and saw posters about her," Honey inquired as they walked toward the gate.

"Those are all descendants or followers who claim to have her power. Voodoo is alive here, but not Madame Laveau," Jacqueline responded as they left the tranquil city of the dead behind them.

Feeling hungry, the two young women returned to the main street and startled a sleeping cab driver by tapping on his window. Instructing him to carry them to Honey's favorite restaurant, they settled into the soft leather seat and listened to the sounds of the awakening city of New Orleans.

Olivier's was blissfully empty when they arrived. Although it was late afternoon, no one had ventured out of doors. With only the waiters to see them, Honey and Jacqueline enjoyed a delicious luncheon and private conversation. Dining on salads and crayfish, they shared stories of their childhood in New Orleans. Honey was again amazed by how closely her life paralleled Jacqueline's.

Finally unable to restrain herself any longer, Honey asked the question that had been on the tip of her tongue ever since Jacqueline told her of her mother's illness. Leaning forward, she asked, "Tell me about your father. Surely he came to your mother's funeral."

Jacqueline finished the last bite of her pastry before answering. She seldom spoke of the man she did not know and was unsure how to begin her answer. Looking into Honey's honest, caring face, she replied, "My mother never told me much about him. I understand that he was incredibly handsome. She said that he was kind and very generous with his money and his time. He often took her to parties and private dinners. He spent as much time with her as he could, considering he already had a family. Sometimes he would take her out for car rides, but usually she stayed home with me.

"I remember wondering why anyone would want to be a courtesan when it meant being alone so much. Her only real friends were other women like herself. She was never welcome in other parts of society. I suppose that was the reason I decided never to live that life."

"How strange it must have been never to have known your father." Honey confided as she watched the pictures of her father play through her memory, "I loved mine very much. He taught me to fish and ride horses. He used to drive us to church on Sunday. Many times we would stop to look at houses in your parish. He loved white houses with bougainvillea growing from the balcony, just like yours. I still miss him."

"When I was a child, a car stopped in front of our house at all hours of the day and night. The same gentleman always sat inside. Sometimes he would get out," Jacqueline said with a sad chuckle. "Other times, he would act as if he were waiting for a signal from my mother. I noticed that if she wanted company, she would open the shutters of the first-floor living room. If she needed solitude, she would keep them closed. I used to rush to my window upstairs whenever I heard the car stop. I would peek out carefully so that no one would see me. If the man left, I knew that I could go downstairs to be with her. I loved to have her read books to me. If the car stayed, I had to remain in my room."

Jacqueline's memories were not as happy as Honey's. The sadness she had experienced showed on her beautiful face.

Placing her hand over her new friend's, Honey tried to comfort her by saying, "You won't be alone anymore, Jacqueline. You have a sister now. I've been by myself most of my life, too. I had playmates, but the houses were many miles apart. I only saw them when our families met for barbecues. From now on, let's be each other's best friend."

"Are you sure you want to take that risk?" Jacqueline said

as she smiled into Honey's sweet, genuinely concerned face. "I've told you that everyone here thinks that I'm a courtesan, too. Your reputation will be ruined if you're seen with me. You're taking a terrible chance being with me now. Some of the people of this town are very unforgiving. Despite the population, New Orleans still operates as if it were a small town. The class system is very much alive and well. It's who you know as often as what. You really should be careful."

"I'm not worried about them." Honey responded. She was determined that nothing would interfere with this new and forceful friendship. "We'll have to make sure they learn the truth quickly. I'll speak with my attorney and Saint Philippe. They might be able to offer some suggestions. My attorney is also a good friend. I'm sure he will do everything he can to help us. No matter what happens, we're friends and that's all that concerns me."

The young women had been so engaged in conversation that they had not noticed the arrival of one of the dowagers of the community. Mrs. Maitlain was not only well-respected by everyone in town, she was also the most feared of all the gossips. If she condemned someone for even a minor offense, the person's name would be removed from the list of invitees at the next function. Likewise, anyone she praised would receive warm welcomes from everyone who wished to remain on her good side. She could make or break a person's reputation with one whispered word behind her fan.

Mrs. Maitlain was a very formidable woman in appearance as well as in her status in the community. Standing almost six feet tall and carrying a hefty bulk, she filled the doorway as she entered. She dressed in battleship gray and appeared to sail across the floor as she followed the maître d' to her table shaking the floor with each thud of her large feet.

By the time Honey and Jacqueline saw her, it was too late for them to escape. Mrs. Maitlain had already made her assessment of the situation and had formulated the context of the information she would convey to all available ears as soon as she had dined to her satisfaction on the best cuisine Olivier's could offer. She was especially fond of chocolate mousse. Since this was her favorite restaurant also and her customary day to dine with her sister, the chef had prepared a large vat of the dessert. As she studied the menu, Mrs. Maitlain knew exactly what she would order and what news she would share with her sister upon her arrival.

A few minutes later, the two young women sat horror-stricken as they watched Mrs. Collins navigate her equally impressive size around the chairs and tables. Cruising to their usual table, she eased into the chair and waited anxiously as her sister brought her up to speed on the latest gossip and her choice of entrees. All the time Mrs. Maitlain spoke, Mrs. Collins cast searing looks in their direction. She did not even slightly veil her contempt for both of them for their obvious impropriety. Without knowing either of them firsthand, she joined her sister in condemning them to the periphery of polite society.

Honey could hear Mrs. Collins say, "Well, my dear sister, this simply cannot be tolerated. They have always known their place and remained respectfully in it. I cannot imagine what has possessed these young women to behave so brazenly. They know that they are supposed to stay to themselves. I wouldn't think of attending one of their parties; therefore, they should not frequent one of our restaurants. Hussy!"

"That's not the half of it, sister. That Jacqueline has caused Honey Tate to become one of them. I warned Saint Philippe that she would be a bad influence and that he needed to steer Honey in the right direction. What a shame! She's from one of our finest Creole families, too," Mrs. Maitlain voiced with sufficient volume that Honey and Jacqueline could hear every word.

"Didn't I see her with your nephew last evening?" Mrs. Collins inquired. Her voice was filled with the fear that somehow her family name would be connected with one of the two young women.

"Yes, and with yours as well. As a matter of fact, she danced with all the young men from the finest families. We'll have to do something about this immediately. Come, my dear, let's go home. This incident has spoiled my lunch," Mrs. Maitlain huffed as she paid the waiter and steered her sister out of the restaurant.

"The old cow will have it all over town in half an hour that you were here with me. I'm so sorry, Honey," Jacqueline stated with genuine distress in her voice.

"Don't worry. I'll talk to Saint Philippe as we planned. Did you notice that she cleaned her plate although she lamented the ruined lunch?" Honey asked with a little laugh.

"Not only did she clean it, she practically licked it. There isn't enough left on it to wash off!" Jacqueline chuckled despite her worry for Honey's future and reputation.

Paying their bill, the two young women linked arms as they exited the restaurant. This time the driver was awake and eagerly awaiting their return. As the car pulled away from the block, Honey saw people staring and pointing at them. Mrs. Maitlain and Mrs. Collins had not wasted any time in spreading the news. Honey hoped that she had not overestimated the people of New Orleans and would be able to clear Jacqueline's name before her own was permanently damaged.

Six

Saint Philippe's shop was filled to capacity early on Monday morning as customers returned the borrowed finery they had worn to his party and gossiped about Honey and Jacqueline. From the number of busily wagging tongues, Honey concluded that Mrs. Maitlain and Mrs. Collins had succeeded in telling everyone in New Orleans society that they had seen Honey and Jacqueline together in a respectable restaurant frequented by only the best families. The social strata inhabited by courtesans was a restricted one and limited to only their own kind. Although they were financially well-established in New Orleans and lived quite luxuriously, they never had been and never would be ranked among the movers and shakers of the community. Throughout the history of society, the dowagers had acknowledged the existence of courtesans, but they continued to resist accepting them as equals. For one of their own to socialize with one of them was simply unthinkable and behavior worthy of punishment.

As Honey eased her way through the crush of bodies toward the dressing room, all eyes turned on her. She almost laughed at the speed with which the conversation stopped and the stares of burning criticism and condemnation darted toward her. She felt as if she were walking to the gallows after being found guilty of murder or witchcraft. She found it amazing that people could be so small-minded, petty, and judgmental as to condemn her without the benefit of a hearing. Little wonder they had unanimously decided that Jacqueline was a courtesan like her mother without even investigating the possibility that she was not.

Immediately Saint Philippe rushed to her side. His ordinarily carefully coifed hair was disheveled, his tie was crooked, and his vest was incorrectly buttoned. His usually bright, twinkling eyes were dull and rimmed in dark heavy circles as if from lack of sleep. His hands fluttered nervously. On what should have been a merry day of heavy sales volume as customers filled the shop to return borrowed finery and purchase more practical attire, he looked depressed and worried. He showed in his slow step and clipped manner of speaking that he was also very angry at Honey for putting him in this uncomfortable position. He hated being in the middle of controversy.

Touching her elbow lightly, Saint Philippe said, "Honey, I would like to speak with you for a moment if you please. Follow me to my office, my dear."

Honey knew that Saint Philippe never would have left the display floor with so many customers in the shop if he had not planned to discuss something of such importance that he did not want anyone to overhear the conversation. She followed his slumped shoulders and rapid step to the office at the back of the shop. She had only visited it one other time and that was the first day she had reported to work for him. That day she had been impressed by the way the sun streamed through the windows and reflected off the bolts of fabric and the drawings pinned to the walls, which created a rainbow of colors in the small office. Today, the little room did not look cozy, but oppressive and overly warm and cluttered.

Saint Philippe fell into his chair as if his legs could no longer hold him under the weight of the topic that pressed heavily on his shoulders and mind. Overnight he had changed from ageless to a very old man. Only Saturday he had been the vivacious Louis. Now, he looked more like the messenger of death himself. Honey wondered when he would pull out

his sickle and end their anguish. She hated to see her benefactor and employer looking so miserably unhappy, but she
could do nothing to make him feel better. No matter what he
said, how he pleaded, or to what extent he threatened, she
would not abandon Jacqueline.

"Honey," Saint Philippe began with tears in his eyes and
a quiver in his voice as his anger melted into profound distress, "how can you continue to visit this misery on me? I
warned you about being seen with Jacqueline du Prix. I told
you that your reputation would be ruined and that you would
take my poor establishment and me along with you. Now
look at what has happened. Everyone knows that you lunched
with that woman at one of the most respectable restaurants
in town. It would have been sufficiently degrading of your
position if you had visited one of the many cafés that cater
to her type, but to be seen in one of our favorites is simply
too much. What were you thinking? Do you care nothing for
my poor nerves that you would do this to me?"

Genuinely sorry for his distress but equally determined to
remain true to her course, Honey replied, "I have done nothing wrong. I simply visited a cemetery and lunched with another young woman who has been quite unjustly slandered
by the matrons of this city. Would you rather that I sneak
around with her? Jacqueline and I met in the cathedral and
lunched in a very public setting. I see nothing wrong in my
actions. The crime here is in the way the people of New
Orleans have treated her."

"What do you mean by accusing us of mistreatment?"
Saint Philippe sputtered. His indignation bordered on rage at
the idea that Honey would try to defend her misconduct by
placing the blame on the town. "We are very understanding
people and treat everyone fairly. I will forgive your poor manners and blame it on that woman. You have become rude and
insolent in a way most unbecoming of a young woman of
our circle."

"I do not mean to be rude, Saint Philippe. I am merely

stating a fact," Honey answered, quickly growing tired of having to defend herself and her friend. "Jacqueline is not a courtesan, but the entire town treats her as if she were one because her mother was. She has lived a very lonely life because of the choices her mother made. Unfortunately, New Orleans has not been willing to allow her to step outside of the shadow cast by her mother. The matrons assume that because Jacqueline lives well that she must have followed in her mother's footsteps. That is not the case. Her mother left her a considerable inheritance and the house. She wants for nothing, including the money to pay you for the fashions you secretly design for her."

"On what do you base this information of yours? What proof do you have of her innocence?" Saint Philippe demanded, irritated that Honey had thrown his business relationship with Jacqueline in his face. He continued to be reluctant to believe that the town had misjudged Jacqueline du Prix. It was much easier for him to think that Honey was misguided.

"Jacqueline told me herself that she lives on her inheritance. As her friend, I do not require more than her word," Honey replied, aware that her answer lacked the needed substance.

"That, my dear Honey, is not enough!" Saint Philippe said, rising from his chair. "People, especially desperate, lonely ones, can and will say anything to influence a new friend, gain power, or seek a higher position. I myself have exaggerated the truth to gain what I desired. I understand your loyalty and appreciate your devotion to your friend. I hope that I can count on your friendship when I am in need. But, when it comes to a matter of this seriousness, I must have more proof than the woman's word. Until you can provide some legal document that will clear Jacqueline's name, you are to stay away from her or suffer the consequences that arise from your deliberate disregard for my instructions. I simply cannot allow you to disrupt my life and the flow of business in this shop. Is that understood?"

Now that Saint Philippe had delivered his ultimatum, he felt much better and almost restored in spirit.

"Yes, Saint Philippe, I understand," Honey agreed. "I will get you the proof you need as soon as my attorney uncovers the necessary papers and arrangements. Until that time, I will proceed with the ultimate caution and discretion."

Honey had seen a side of New Orleans society that almost made her want to return to New York. She hated the idea that hypocrisy and prejudice still lived in her hometown.

"Good, then that is settled," Saint Philippe said as he shooed Honey from his office and toward the fitting room where he had personally set out his latest creation. "I knew that you would respond to reason once I had the opportunity to speak with you. I told Mrs. Maitlain and Mrs. Collins that you were a very responsible young woman. Your heart is too large for you to disregard the feelings of others for your own benefit. Well, hurry off now. You need to change your clothes. I selected an exquisite raspberry colored skirt and jacket ensemble for you to model this morning. I'll settle this matter with the ladies."

Saint Philippe's talented seamstress had finished sewing the outfit the previous week and had waited impatiently to introduce it that day while the women still glowed from the excitement of his masked party. Restored to his usual flutter of happiness by his successful talk with Honey, Saint Philippe hurried back to the display room and his gathered customers. Mentally, he could hear the merry clinking of the register.

As Honey changed into the outfit, she knew that Saint Philippe would share the details of their conversation with the matrons of New Orleans who waited in silence for a full report. He would embellish his portion of their discussion and exaggerate her reaction to his advice and her words of contrition as was his style in retelling any event. When he was satisfied that he had fulfilled the matrons' expectations of him, he would begin the parade of his new fashions as he had originally planned for the morning's entertainment before this nasty business with Honey had interrupted his day.

The ladies greeted Honey's return with polite applause as she walked through their midst. Wearing her usual composed expression, she stopped occasionally so that they might admire the splendor of the outfit and marvel at the luxury of the fabric and the perfection of the fit. Unable to read her face for the expected signs of penitence, they turned their attention to the fashions the other models paraded for their enjoyment and purchase.

Taking her place at the window, Honey blocked out their existence and concentrated on her plans for clearing Jacqueline's name. Now more than ever she was convinced that she had to ask Stephen to help her. She needed more than simply Jacqueline's word as proof that she was not a courtesan. She had to have financial records, wills, and court records to support her claim that she lived on her mother's fortune. Deciding that at lunchtime she would go to his office to speak with him in person rather than phoning, Honey mentally outlined the course she would follow in her efforts. She did not feel the passage of time as she concentrated on her plan.

The city was bustling with excitement as Honey left the shop for lunch. She blended with the foot traffic that made its way to the restaurants, piers, and stores along the banks of the river. No one seemed to notice her or the heat of the day as they pushed and shoved in their sense of self-importance and their need to move along quickly.

As she matched her stride with theirs, Honey heard someone in the crowd calling her name. Recognizing Stephen's voice, she stepped out of the crowd until he could catch up with her. Taking her elbow, he gently guided her into the nearest café and the last empty table.

Ordering gumbo for both of them, he said, "I stopped by the shop to take you to lunch, but I must have just missed you. I was hoping to see you today. I called at your hotel yesterday, but you were out."

"I was hoping to see you, too," Honey replied with a happy smile. She could still feel the pressure of his lips on hers. "I received the lovely flowers after I returned from my afternoon with Jacqueline. I went to mass and then she took me on a tour of Metairie Cemetery. She wanted to show me some of the tombs of the famous people buried there and her mother's as well. It is very lovely, with an angel perched on the top. I'm terribly sorry that I missed you at Saint Philippe's, but we're together now."

"I have heard about your afternoon as has probably everyone else in town. You really should be careful until this business is cleared up," Stephen advised. He also feared for Honey's reputation.

"That's one of the reasons that I wanted so desperately to see you today," Honey confided as she leaned closer. "Jacqueline said that her mother left the house and an income to her in her will. If we could circulate a copy of it to the right people, we could clear her name. Do you think you might be able to find it?"

"Probably, but you forget that even if we prove to all the right people that Jacqueline is not a courtesan, her mother most definitely was," Stephen commented, knowing that the city had a long memory and held on to some prejudices more forcefully than it did others. "She will not be completely free of this kind of treatment no matter what we do. It might be necessary to show that Madeline was not as notorious as everyone has wanted to believe. We might even need to disclose the identity of her lovers, if we can. Are you sure that Jacqueline is aware of this?"

"Of course she is, but she hopes that some people will be convinced by a minimum of disclosure and will not continue to hold her mother's profession against her," Honey replied as she picked at her food. "For that matter, she's thinking of my reputation and wants to remove anything that would create a scandal for me."

She really was not hungry. Her conversation with Saint Philippe that morning and the closeness of Stephen that afternoon had dulled her appetite. She was much too nervous to eat being in his company.

Lightly resting his hand on hers, Stephen said, "I promise to do anything I can to help you, but we must proceed with caution. There are many people in this town who might worry about what we could discover in Madeline's will. I am hopeful that she kept a record of the names of her admirers that might help our cause. Although everyone knew that she was a courtesan, no one wants the identities of her clients flaunted or printed in the newspaper. We will meet opposition at every step, especially the closer we come to uncovering the facts."

"Stephen, I knew I could count on you to help us. I told Jacqueline that my attorney would be able to uncover documents that would set things straight. You are the most wonderful man," Honey said enthusiastically as the warmth of his hand caused her cheeks to flush.

"As your attorney, I will begin my search of the court archives immediately," Stephen responded. He was glad to be of service and to see that Honey's affection for him had not dimmed in the sunlight. "By the way, I already did some investigation into the status of your old home. It would seem that the current owner has solicited the assistance of a friend of mine to represent him in its sale. He says that he will never return to the city because he finds New Orleans too hot and humid for his taste. I will submit a reasonable bid on your behalf this afternoon. I'll stop by the shop with any news of my success."

"Wonderful!" Honey gushed. "I had planned to visit the old place this weekend. Maybe it will be mine again by the time I do."

Leaving Honey at Saint Philippe's shop, Stephen again expressed his concern for Honey's reputation and promised a speedy resolution to the issue of Jacqueline's position in society. He smiled as he lightly kissed her lips and promised to call her later that afternoon with news. Waving good-bye, Honey stepped into the relative quiet of the shop to find that almost everyone had gone home. Happily, she saw that she was no longer the hot topic of discussion as the customers busied themselves with selecting accessories and bags.

Later that afternoon as she and Saint Philippe were leaving the shop, Stephen rushed up in a state of great agitation. Recognizing the need to leave the young people alone, Saint Philippe said his good-byes at the shop door and allowed Stephen to walk Honey home. He was not blind to the blush of a budding romance that colored Honey's cheeks and made Stephen fly to her side.

On the way to the hotel, Stephen nervously played with the coins in his pocket. Honey could tell that something important was on his mind, but she could not encourage him to share his thoughts with her no matter how many times she asked. As they sank into one of the sofas in the lobby, she decided she would have to wait until he felt comfortable bringing up the troublesome topic.

Watching the faces of people he knew well pass through the lobby, Stephen summoned up the courage to tell her of his discoveries. He started with the good news about her house and moved from there to the unpleasant information about Jacqueline's estate.

Fingering the chain of his gold pocket watch, he began by saying, "I contacted my friend and presented an offer on your behalf. I am pleased to confirm that you are once again the owner of Longmeadow house. All you need to do is go to settlement and that won't take long. The owner is so anxious to be rid of it that he has generously passed the key to you so that you might start remodeling it."

"Oh, Stephen, I'm so grateful. Thank you so much. You can't imagine how desperately I have wanted to call the old place home again. I'll drive out there this weekend. I can hardly wait," Honey interrupted enthusiastically. Her dream of Longmeadow was now a reality.

Clearing his throat, Stephen continued with a stoic expression on his tired face, "Unfortunately, I also have bad news. I have not been able to uncover anything that would substantiate Jacqueline's claims regarding her mother's fortune. Quite to the contrary, I have run into a great deal of opposition to my search as I expected. Even the partners in our firm have spoken out about my efforts on her behalf. They believe that Jacqueline might have fabricated this story to make herself feel better about the way she has chosen to live.

"Every upstanding family in New Orleans has heard about my efforts on her behalf, and they have circled their wagons in opposition. They have personally contacted my family and suggested that unless I stop this investigation into matters long closed, we will find our names stricken from the social register. Before the letters began to arrive, my parents requested that I stop these actions since they worried about the reactions of their friends.

"I am sorry that I have failed you in this endeavor, but I cannot jeopardize my family's name and position in the community. Perhaps we might begin again after this initial tempest settles a bit."

"But, Stephen, do you personally know anyone who has ever been associated with Jacqueline . . . professionally?" Honey responded with true dedication to her new friend. "She says that she has never even had a date because of her reputation, and I believe her. I think the people of this town simply want to keep the indiscretions of their private lives hidden at her expense."

"Perhaps you are correct, but at this point I will not be able to pursue the matter more fully. Feel free to employ the aid of another attorney if you would like, but I don't think he would have any better success. Too many people are working against us at the moment," Stephen said, remaining steadfast in his determination to conform to his family's desires.

"No, I don't want another attorney. You're wonderful. I do not doubt your ability. I just want to do more. What do you suggest we do next for Jacqueline?" Honey asked with worry clearly written on her beautiful face and clouding the radiance of her green eyes.

"Until the climate changes, there is nothing more that I can do for her. I would suggest that you distance yourself from her as Saint Philippe has suggested. Your reputation is in grave danger," Stephen explained. He spoke slowly and carefully in an effort to make Honey understand the full weight of his words and the seriousness of the situation. "They have been willing to excuse your behavior up to a point. However, now that you have been warned again, and I have been ordered to pull back from my search, they will not treat you with leniency if you continue your association with her."

"Do I understand you correctly? Are you saying that you'll turn your back on me, too?" Honey asked, although she already knew the answer.

"Our society has taken the matter out of my hands. My family name is at risk. As you are aware, family honor is vitally important in the South. I must act as my parents would wish," Stephen responded. His fingers no longer toyed with the gold chain, and his expression no longer concealed his emotions. His face reflected the torment that had ruined his afternoon. He knew that Honey's decision regarding Jacqueline could forever seal off any chance that they would have for happiness.

"Then, I suppose this meeting is over, Stephen. You see, if the tables were turned, you would not want me to abandon you. Therefore, I will remain true to my friendship with Jacqueline and find a way to clear her name without your help. I trust that you will send the bill for your legal services to my suite at your earliest convenience. Good night," Honey said in a very formal tone as she rose from her seat. Her knees felt rubbery at the loss of the only man she had allowed into her heart since her father's death.

Leaving Stephen standing in the lobby, Honey carefully climbed the stairs to the third floor and her suite rather than riding the elevator. Her eyes were so full of tears that she could barely see the lock and insert the keycard. As she fumbled with it, tears splashed on her trembling hand.

Rushing to the bedroom, she threw herself across the bed. Great sobs wracked her thin frame as the impact of her actions washed over her. She had remained true to a friend and lost a lover. The finality of the choice was almost too devastating to bear.

Wiping the tears with a crumpled tissue, Honey sat on the bed and thought. She knew that Stephen had done what any son would have in order to show respect for his family name. He had no choice but to follow the dictates of his parents and law firm. He had to protect both his name and his inheritance. She would have done the same thing if she had been in his position. Still, it hurt to have him turn his back on her because of her decision to be true to a friend. Honey had hoped the dilemma would not have resolved itself as it had. She had envisioned that Stephen would have success in clearing Jacqueline's name and that their relationship would flourish.

As she sat thinking over the latest events in her life, Honey noticed that someone had added a little doll that lay on a white, lace doily next to the Bible, rosary, and love potion on the table beside her bed. Fingering it lightly, she studied its intricately carved design. The little figure had been carefully wrought from carved wood and rubbed smooth to the touch. Turning it over in her hand, Honey could almost see the features of its little face although it did not resemble anyone she recognized. Having heard about voodoo since she was a child, Honey knew that the figure only needed to have human characteristics for its powers to work on those who believed in the ancient force.

Snuffing out the candle, Honey decided to rent a car the

next day rather than wait for the weekend. She could not suffer the indignities of the stares from the matrons of the city any longer. She wanted to see the house she had once shared with her parents and had not seen since she was a teenager. She needed to return to a place of harmony and happiness. Honey had to make a world where she could be at peace from the gossip and stares of New Orleans.

Seven

Early the next morning, Honey called Saint Philippe in his shop to explain that she needed to explore her old home immediately now that she had purchased it, and was taking a much-needed day off from work. She knew he would be disappointed by her absence. Saint Philippe had told her the previous night that he had already planned for her to model several new creations. Honey knew that, as usual, they would have looked fabulous on her but frightful on the women who would purchase them.

With a shrug of her shoulders, she brushed away the thought of work. For the first time in her adult, working life, she did not care about her responsibilities to the job. She had something important to do for herself. Modeling the gowns could wait until another day or one of the other women could model them.

Climbing into the waiting car, Honey forced away the thought of Saint Philippe and concentrated only on her return home. When she first returned to New Orleans, Honey had been afraid to visit the old home for fear that she had merely dreamed of its splendor in her loneliness and homesickness. So much of her childhood lay covered in the mist of memory that she could no longer trust her vision of reality. In her memory the house had been grand in size and appearance. Honey was afraid that the process of growing up would have reduced its size. She feared it might in reality be a humble shack.

Honey felt strangely liberated as she drove along the busy streets. She smiled to herself from behind the privacy of the windows as people tried to peer inside to see who rode by in the rented luxury sedan. The slightly tinted glass protected her from their prying eyes. She almost laughed when Mrs. Maitlain had to step aside quickly to avoid being run over. The formidable figure had been so busy talking that she had not noticed the car as Honey veered into the approaching traffic. Her face had puckered with anger at being disturbed in her gossiping with Mrs. Millcr. Honey fleetingly wondered if she was the topic of discussion.

Passing Saint Philippe's shop, Honey saw a cluster of men standing on the sidewalk. Carefully looking out, she spotted Stephen among them. Although impeccably dressed in a gray pinstripe suit, his face looked drawn and tired. Deep, dark circles outlined his eyes, and his shoulders slumped with fatigue. He looked as if he had spent a sleepless night. Honey hoped that his dreams had been as filled with visions of her as hers had been of him.

Leaving the city limits, Honey leaned back against the soft leather and breathed deeply of the sweet country air. Memories of running through the meadows and picking wildflowers and berries flowed through her mind as she passed open fields. All around her lay large homes and former plantations in various stages of repair. Some had been converted into historical monuments to the old South and added to the list of must-see sights of New Orleans. Tourists wandered over the lawns with maps clutched tightly in their fingers. Other houses showed signs of needing work. Dilapidated, crumbling fences marked many of the property lines. Her memories of home tugged at her heart and almost made her drive faster.

A lopsided sign greeted Honey at the mouth of the road that led to the main house. Studying its faded black letters, she read "Longmeadow House . . . a place of serenity and peace." After years in New York, Honey had finally returned home.

Honey could barely contain herself as the car made slow progress over the deeply rutted road. She made a mental note that the road was one of the first things she would have to repair now that she owned the homestead once again. She would have to plant lots of flowers around the main house to restore the gardens and begin plowing immediately since all the fields seemed to have returned to their natural, wild state. As far as she could see, nothing but weeds and brush met her eyes. Neglect had reduced the once-thriving farm to wild grass and scruffy trees. The meadows in which the most beautiful black stallions in the area had romped had gone to seed. They lay in overgrown abandonment, cluttered with wild saplings. Honey hoped the house had not been treated in such a shameful manner.

In the distance, she spotted the silhouette of the house rising in the glare of the hot, morning sun. Honey's heart began to pound wildly as the car drew closer. She knew the house still existed, but she did not know its condition. In a few minutes, as her eyes adjusted to the harsh, glaring light, she would see for herself.

Slowly, the car rounded the driveway and stopped in front of the house. Stephen had said that the house had sat vacant for some time, but Honey had not prepared herself for the sight that met her eyes. Vines of clinging ivy and Virginia creeper trailed up the sides of the house. Shutters slumped in disrepair, with missing slats giving them a toothless appearance. Slate from the roof was missing in spots. Windows were broken. Yet, although the paint on the rose-colored pillars had faded and chipped with time and neglect, they still stood strong and tall as they held up the three-story white house with its two balconies and spreading wings. Honey stepped onto the soil of home for the first time in years.

Stepping carefully and testing the weathered, rotting boards before putting her full weight on them, Honey walked onto the porch on which she used to play at her parents' feet as they sipped their mint juleps and watched the sunset. As the

flooring creaked under her feet, she quickly crossed the wide
expanse to the front door.

Searching her purse for the key that Stephen had given her,
she unlocked the door and tried to push it open. The hinges
were so rusted that at first they would not budge under the
pressure of her slight frame. Leaning her full weight against
it, she pushed until the creaking door slowly opened. Peering
into the darkness, she saw nothing as the smell of the dust
and mustiness of the closed-up house rushed to assault her
nose.

Flipping the switch of the flashlight she found on the front
porch, Honey slowly entered the quiet house as memories
flooded over her. When she was a child, the sound of happy
laughter and music had always greeted her at the door as a
guest visited in the living room or her mother played the
piano in the library. A fresh breeze always blew from the
back of the house even on the hottest day. Now, only the
sounds of mice scurrying away from her intruding feet
greeted her ears, and the heat and stuffiness of summer filled
the air.

Shivering at the thought of the vermin that inhabited her
house, Honey carefully picked her way toward the living room
to the right. The flashlight cast a shadowy glow on the scuffed
wood floors and the discolored, faded, mauve wallpaper. Black
stains darkened many places along her path, as if water had
puddled on the once glorious floors. No furniture blocked her
movement in the forlorn house. She remembered that a large
round table had once sat in the center of the foyer that was
now empty. Vases filled with flowers from the garden always
adorned the table and filled the air with a sweet fragrance.

Shining the light through the open living room door, Honey
was again greeted by emptiness. Not knowing where they
would live when they left for New York, and needing money
desperately, they had sold the house with all of its lovely furnishings. She was surprised to see that none of the heavy mahogany furniture remained. She supposed the previous owner

had taken everything with him when he left. Honey had hoped her mother's piano would still be in the library. Now, she no longer had that expectation.

Walking into the living room, Honey pushed aside massive cobwebs that hung from the chandelier. Dust covered the wall sconces and the mantel. Dried leaves lay on the floor in front of the window where they had blown through the broken panes. She could hear birds chirping in the fireplace, which told her that the screens had blown off and had never been replaced. Considering the condition of the inside of the house, she wondered if the chimney was even safe to use. She would add cleaning it to her list of projects, along with repairing and replacing the fences and the broken windows and painting the house.

Walking to the window, Honey pulled open the heavy, dusty drapes that ripped into tatters in her hands. Sunlight burst into the room, further illuminating the effects of neglect and decay. The once proud room lay cluttered with mouse droppings and trash. Honey's heart hurt from the sight. She was glad that her parents were not alive to see the destruction of everything they had held dear. Seeing the ruin, she was even more determined now than ever to restore Longmeadow to its original grandeur.

Retracing her steps to the foyer, Honey moved across the hall to her father's study. When she was a child, the shelves that lined the walls had overflowed with books. As she opened the door, she found this room empty too. Someone had stripped the drapes from the windows as well as the tomes from the shelves. Looking through the dusty sunlight, she could remember where her father's desk and chair had sat and where she had lain on the sofa reading one of her favorite books while he worked on his many law cases. Now, only emptiness and scattered sunbeams filled the room.

As Honey walked toward the sunroom at the back of the house, she was glad that Stephen and Jacqueline were not with her. She had told both of them so much about the house that it would have broken her heart even more to see the disappointment on their faces at finding the house in this dreadful state of disrepair.

Stephen. The thought of him only added to the weight that tugged at her heart. Honey had thought she would marry him someday, but now she was afraid that she would spend her life alone. She hated the thought that her existence might become as joyless as Jacqueline's. She did not want to be cut off from love and happiness because of the narrow-minded attitude of people in New Orleans society, but she would not abandon her friend. She had promised herself that she would find a way to win Stephen's love despite the objections of his family to her friendship with Jacqueline and his investigation into her past.

Shining the light down the dark hall, Honey pushed thoughts of Stephen from her mind as she entered the sunroom. Peering into the gloom, she saw a shadow in the corner. Rushing forward, she joyfully discovered that her mother's piano sat in front of the shuttered window, although the bench was missing. Placing the flashlight on the floor and opening the window, Honey lifted the dust-covered lid. She slowly ran her fingers over the discolored keys. Although the piano was sadly out of tune, it still played despite the neglect. At least one memory of her childhood had remained intact. She would be able to entertain herself during the long, lonely hours.

Now that Honey had found one element of her youth on the first floor of the desolate, unloved house, she was ready to climb the stairs to the bedrooms. She was sure that they would be as empty as the public rooms, but she needed to assess the damage that the years of disrepair had caused.

As she climbed the wide staircase, the banister shook in her hand and mice darted across the steps to disappear into large holes in the wall. With every step, she disturbed yet another cloud of dust. Her hands were caked with the gray, clinging powder. Dirt clung to everything. Cobwebs hung from the ceiling and the once glorious chandelier.

Oddly, despite the disheveled appearance, the house felt like home to Honey. She could hear the laughter in her memory and see the furnishings where they once stood when the house was in its glory. She took comfort from knowing that the old house was hers once again, or it would be as soon as she went to settlement. She promised herself that nothing and no one would ever take it from her. She would make it her home and live here with her husband and children . . . someday. If she was destined to live alone, then she would enjoy its solitude.

The thought of sharing her life with a loving husband should have been pleasant, but now it plucked at her heartstrings. She could envision Stephen sitting in the restored library with his feet resting on a stool while she embroidered a pillowcase with the names of their children. Their life together could be so happy in this house if only they could push past the interference of New Orleans society and Stephen's conformity to it.

Reaching the closed door of what had been her bedroom, Honey paused for a moment. The air was so thick with dust that she could feel her lungs struggling to extract sustenance from it. Strangely tired from the excitement of returning home, she needed to catch her breath and allow her heart to stop racing.

Feeling a bit less lightheaded, Honey turned the knob and opened the bedroom door. As she did, birds of every description flapped wildly at the intrusion. Some of them disappeared up the chimney. Others flew out the broken glass in the huge window. Still more bashed themselves against the walls in their confusion and fright. After they settled once again on the profoundly soiled floor, she dared to enter.

Sliding her feet slowly through the droppings, bodies, and feathers, Honey made her way to the window. Heedless of the birds that pecked angrily at her shoes and ankles, she threw open the sash to allow the fresh air to penetrate the fetid air. Although the weather was hot, she preferred the heat to the stench of bird droppings.

"What a mess!" Honey muttered to herself as she inhaled the refreshing aroma of the outdoors. "How will I ever return this house to the way it used to be?"

"You'll need a great deal of help," answered the voice behind her.

Spinning around, Honey came face to face with Stephen, who stood in the doorway. "I didn't hear you come in. I thought you were in town," she said with a mixture of pleasure and surprise in her voice.

"I couldn't let you come out here alone, not after seeing the condition of the old house for myself late yesterday. I stopped at your hotel, but the concierge told me that you had already left. I followed you out here. I hope you don't mind. I have cleared my calendar for the entire day," Stephen replied as he walked toward her through the angry flapping of birds' wings.

"I'm very happy to see you, Stephen, but aren't you worried about what the others might say? You're taking a big risk being with me, you know," Honey commented. She had to control herself from flying into his arms.

"I lied to my partners and family by telling them that I had an appointment in Natchez that would keep me away from the office all day. I had to see you alone and away from the prying eyes of New Orleans' well-meaning but nosy matrons," he responded in a controlled voice. Stephen forced himself to keep his distance although he wanted desperately to hold her.

"You needn't have put yourself to such trouble on my behalf," Honey said with her hurt feelings at finding the house decimated sounding in her voice. "I'm doing quite well on my own although I am happy to see you. As you can see from the mess that surrounds us, I will need your advice on finding the services of competent workers to restore this house. It's a shame that the previous owner did not take better care of it. This once was a glorious house, probably the most beautiful in New Orleans."

Moving closer, Stephen responded, "I know just the firm for this project. Anderson and Anderson restored the court-house, the mayor's home, and the art gallery. They shouldn't have any trouble with this restoration. Despite the daunting size of the task, this house could be restored to elegance in a matter of weeks with the right people doing the work."

"Do you really think they could accomplish the task so quickly?" Honey said as she struggled with the enormity of the task. "The chimneys all need cleaning and rescreening. The doors need planing and oiling. All the floors have to be scrubbed and waxed. The entire house needs fresh paint and paper. I haven't been into the greenhouse yet, but I'm sure it has been neglected as badly as this portion. From the road, I could tell that the barns and stables have practically fallen down. And let's not forget the miles of fences that have to be replaced and the well that needs cleaning before we can turn on the pump again. I can only imagine the family of frogs that must have taken up residence in there. Remember, that's one of the hazards of living in the countryside."

"Leave it to me. I'll get in touch with Jim Anderson right away," Stephen said with confidence as he dialed the firm's number from his cell phone. "Next week this time, you won't recognize the place. All you need to do is select the furniture you want and decide where you'll place it when it arrives."

While Stephen made the arrangements, Honey stepped gingerly onto the balcony. Surprisingly, the wisteria still entwined itself around the columns and bloomed as if the house were not in shambles. Bees darted hungrily from one bloom to the other as if nothing had changed.

"It's done," Stephen called from inside. "Jim will meet with you later today and start his crew immediately."

"Again, thank you for coming to my aid. This is rather overwhelming," Honey exclaimed, shaking her head at the waste as she rejoined him in her former bedroom. "I did not expect to find my house looking like home after all these years, but I didn't expect this. We sold a perfectly charming house to that gentleman. Just you look at what he allowed to happen to the place. I bet the roof leaks, too."

"It's a good thing that you haven't looked in the other bedrooms yet," Stephen remarked. "There's a large water spot in the ceiling of the master bedroom and a big stain on the floor. You don't really want to see any more of this, do you? I'm starving. I brought along a picnic lunch. Would you care to share the contents of my hamper with me?"

He was quite happy to have thought of something that Honey had not. She appeared to him to be the organized type who worked out every detail. It gave him pleasure to be able to do something for her that she had forgotten to do for herself.

"Lunch would be wonderful, Stephen. I am terribly hungry and thirsty. My hands are filthy. I hope you brought plenty of soap and water," Honey said as she allowed him to escort her down the stairs. She had seen enough of the dreadful treatment that her beloved childhood home had suffered in her absence. She was ready to put into play any suggestions he might offer for restoring it.

They found a perfect spot on the front lawn under a cypress tree and spread out their feast on a damask tablecloth on which they placed gold-trimmed china and sparkling crystal. Stephen had stopped at Olivier's rather than a fast food establishment for their lunch. The crayfish étouffée was divinely flavorful and the baguette was still warm from the oven. The wine was pleasantly sweet and slightly chilled. As they dined in silence, they looked across the expanse of green at the mighty Mississippi River as it rolled peacefully along.

As they ate their peach cobbler, Honey turned to Stephen and asked, "How do you plan for us to drive back to the city without someone noticing that we have been out together. I'm afraid there's no way around arousing suspicion and creating a scandal."

"I've got it all worked out. Jim Anderson wants to meet with you this afternoon, so you can stop there on your way back to the hotel. I need to stop at Tulane to pick up a book from the library. No one will be the wiser," Stephen said confidently as he wiped a touch of cobbler from his lips.

"And the next time we meet, what will you say then? How many believable stories will you be able to make up?" she asked tartly. Honey hated the idea of lies and deception. Someone always saw through the subterfuge, and the person's character was ruined anyway.

"I'll continue to fabricate them for as long as it takes us to clear Jacqueline's name. I hope that in a few more days or at the most a week I will be able to produce the proof of her innocence that you requested," Stephen replied confidently. He realized that even after producing the facts, many months would pass before the mindsets of the people would change.

"As much as I have enjoyed our afternoon together, I cannot allow you to put yourself in jeopardy for me any further. We really must think of some way to right the wrong that society has done to Jacqueline so that we might live our lives in peace," Honey said as she brushed the crumbs and ants from her burgundy skirt.

"I will restart my investigation tomorrow as soon as I get to the office, but I must move slowly and carefully. My father and other partners are watching me very closely right now and so are all the other men in town. Despite what you must think of me for progressing so slowly, I will remain vigilant," Stephen confided as he gathered the plates and returned them to the hamper.

"And what about us, Stephen?" Honey inquired as she folded the tablecloth and placed it on top of the plates.

"We'll find a way to be together. Nothing will keep us apart," he responded, enfolding her small hands in his.

"You mean we'll sneak around behind people's backs," Honey stated calmly as she studied his eyes for the affection she knew lived in his heart. "We'll steal moments together. No, that's not what I want. Our relationship has to mean more to you than that. It does to me. You have to put us ahead of your family's reputation. I have risked everything, my reputation, my place in society, and my professional future, for my friend. You should be able to do the same for me."

"Honey, I have loved you since I first saw you, but I can't go against my family. Stolen moments are all we'll have until I can clear up this mess," Stephen replied, with the ache in his heart reflected in his voice. "By moving slowly and without drawing attention to my efforts, I will be able to gain the information we need without upsetting the population of New Orleans. You must understand that I have to make my father believe that I have distanced myself from Jacqueline's life and yours until I can accomplish the task. Therefore, we must keep our relationship secret for a short time."

"Then, I suppose I'll have to find a way to convince you that I am more important to you than your family's pettiness," Honey replied as she pulled his face close to hers. "You are falling in step with their goals for you rather than striking out for what you want for yourself. I was of the impression that your plans for our being together were important to you, but I can see now that you still need a little convincing."

Pressing her lips against his, she kissed Stephen with all her might. There was little doubt from the warmth of the embrace and the strength of her arms that she meant to remove the thought of his family from his mind.

Stephen willingly succumbed to Honey's persuasive, bold caresses. He eased his arms around her lithe body and pulled her tightly against him. He could feel her heart pounding through her clothing with the excitement of their bold moves. He knew that she never would have initiated a kiss of such a sensual nature if she had not desperately wanted to make him understand her feelings toward him. For his part, he was very willing to allow her to exert her womanly talents in any way she chose. For the moment at least, thoughts of his family were far away as his body responded to the fragrance of her shampoo and the closeness of her womanly softness.

"Now," Honey said suddenly as she violently pushed him away, "I'm going to Jim Anderson's office. That's the last kiss you'll have from me until you decide who has the top spot in your life, me or your family's money. I won't play second fiddle to a purse full of money and neither will I sneak around like a common whore. That would make me as trashy as the kind of woman you and New Orleans unjustly condemn Jacqueline for being. When you make up your mind exactly which one of us you want, your precious inheritance or me, you'll know where to find me."

With that, Honey stomped away to the car, stirring up a cloud of dust in her wake. She left Stephen standing with an expression on his face that vacillated between puzzlement and agony. She did not look back as she climbed into the seat and slammed the door. Grabbing the hamper, Stephen watched as she sped out of sight, risking a broken axle or worse on the rutted road.

Eight

During her lunch break the next day, instead of strolling through the gardens or eating a leisurely meal with Stephen, Honey marched toward Congo Square with a purpose in mind. She had to find a way to make Stephen realize that she was more important to him than his family and his inheritance. She could think of only one way to accomplish the task. She would seek the help of the new Patrice Auguste, the descendant of the famous voodoo priestess.

Many had tried to push the practice of voodoo into the past, but it was still very much alive and well in parts of the South. New Orleans was no exception. In addition to the museum dedicated to its history and artifacts, practitioners still plied their trade in the squares, in private homes, and in temples dedicated to its activities. The original Patrice Auguste and her daughters had died many years before, but their followers participated in a thriving business.

The new Patrice Auguste lived in a house that looked like any other from the sidewalk, contrary to what Honey had been led to believe by New Orleans gossip. It was small and of the typical Creole style with decorative woodwork and touches of ironwork. As Honey walked up the steps, she saw that for all of the priestess's fame and notoriety, her house was in need of repair. The well-trod steps looked dusty, as if scrubbed in red clay, and appeared in desperate need of painting. Dry clusters of cut flowers dotted the stairs accompanied

by carefully placed charms and tokens. The door wanted a
good scrubbing to remove the fingerprints of the countless
believers who had sought her help in matters of the heart,
finances, and other dealings. Heavy wooden shutters covered
the windows to keep out prying eyes. Whatever magic Patrice
Auguste practiced in that house, she wanted the secrets to
remain within those plain whitewashed walls.

She had visited the voodoo museum and seen the depic-
tions of the great powers of Patrice Auguste. The portrait of
her in the museum showed her to be as handsome as the
original Patrice Auguste, who was a strikingly beautiful quad-
roon. Although she was a little frightened of meeting someone
who claimed to possess the power to control the actions of
others through the use of potions and spells, she had instantly
become enthralled at the possibility of seeing Patrice Auguste
in person.

When Honey was a child, she had known of women from
the town's most respected houses who secretly collected gris-
gris similar to the one displayed in the museum and the one
someone had left on her bedside table. They claimed that they
were only collecting a part of the great New Orleans tradition
to preserve it for posterity. Honey had overheard too many
passionate discussions in Saint Philippe's shop to believe their
protests.

Knocking tentatively on the door, Honey continued to study
the house and yard. It was not at all what she had expected.
The small house on St. Ann Street bore no resemblance to
the grandeur she had imagined it to possess. She had thought
that someone with the power attributed to Patrice Auguste
would have lived in more splendid surroundings. Obviously,
this Madame Auguste did not need the trappings of fame to
feel successful.

As the door creaked open, Honey stepped inside and prepared to meet the renowned woman. One of Patrice Auguste's
followers ushered her inside and, without speaking, she motioned toward a chair in the far corner near the hearth. A

well-worn sofa and two mismatched chairs were the only pieces of furniture in the room. Following the mute directions of the plainly clad woman, Honey crossed the thin carpet and took a seat in a chair with stained upholstery and rickety back that smelled of cat urine and cigar smoke.

The living room was equally as unimpressive as the exterior. Honey looked at the smoke-stained walls, the faded upholstery and drapes, and the crooked cross hanging near the doorway that led to the back of the house. She wondered how this woman could have risen to a position of importance and yet owned so few possessions. Disappointed by the lack of pretension, Honey picked up her purse in preparation for her departure. She could not imagine that anyone who lived in such relative poverty would be able to do anything to help her situation. Obviously, the Madame Auguste mystique was merely a tourist rip-off.

As she reached the center of the room, the door that Honey had assumed led to the dining room opened. "You came for my help, but you're leaving without seeing me. That certainly is curious behavior," a woman's voice said calmly, breaking the silence of the room.

Turning around to face her, Honey was immediately impressed by the woman's soft, light beige complexion, her piercing brown eyes, and her physical size. Although not a particularly large woman, Patrice Auguste cast a commanding presence in her towering head wrap that covered all but a few strands of escaping brown hair. Although not as beautiful as the original priestess, she was still very attractive.

Patrice Auguste was not dressed the part of a priestess. Honey had heard that she wore barely any clothing at all and always carried a basket of snakes, mummified babies, and skeletons, which she used in her magic ritual in her house. To Honey, this very attractive woman looked like many others she had seen in the marketplace, except for the force of her gaze. Her black cotton skirt and New Orleans T-shirt looked like those worn by ordinary people. Patrice Auguste's gaze was still and constant. She did not look away from her guest as she eased toward the spot where Honey stood transfixed on the faded, rose-patterned rug.

"I am Patrice Auguste, namesake of the famous voodoo priestess. What brings you here? You are definitely not of this neighborhood and you don't look like one of the tourists who flocks to my house," Patrice Auguste asked in a voice that was soft and smooth like the fur behind a cat's ear.

"I am Honey Tate, and I have newly returned home from New York. I have heard of your ability to cast spells and perform voodoo that can help a woman win the affection of the man she loves. I have come to purchase one of your special potions," Honey replied. She had not been able to move and had barely blinked since the other woman had entered the room. Patrice Auguste might not have appeared imposing, but she certainly possessed a demeanor that forbade anyone from leaving her presence.

"I was of the impression that you already had a bottle of one of my potions. One of the women at your hotel left a bottle beside your bed next to the Bible, the figurine, and the rosary if I am not mistaken," Patrice Auguste commented quietly as she sank into the straight-backed wooden chair that one of her assistants brought forward for her use.

"How did you know about the potion? I don't even know who left it. How do you?" Honey asked as she stared at the woman who now sat passively in her chair with her arms folded across her body.

"You don't need to know the identity of my follower. What is important is that you have not used the gift that she left for you. Do you not believe in the power of the gris-gris? Surely you must since you are here today asking for more of my special help," Patrice Auguste said as she studied Honey's fearful and somewhat concerned face.

"The only thing I know for certain is that the man I love is more devoted to preserving his inheritance than he is to me. He turns his back on me publicly because of my friend's reputation and his family's objections, but he wants to see me privately as if I were a courtesan. I will not allow any man to treat me in that manner. The airport shops sell gris-gris and potion; I thought you might also," Honey replied, keeping her gaze as steadfast as Patrice Auguste's.

"Your devotion to your friend despite the opinion of others is quite commendable. I have heard about the behavior of the women who consider themselves the pillars of New Orleans society toward you. They think they can control the lives of everyone who lives in this city. They even tried to tell me how to conduct my business, but they soon discovered that my power is stronger than the wagging of their silly tongues. The revenue I bring to this city from tourist money alone makes me a force of considerable financial value. Very well, I suppose you do need something more powerful than those get-together drops. It is sometimes difficult to convince a man that he owes a stronger allegiance to the woman he loves than to his wallet. I will help you, but first I have to know why you came to me," Patrice Auguste said with a calmness that Honey had never experienced before in anyone. It was as if she were speaking from the edge of sleep.

"I did not know where else to turn. I have used my own wiles on him, but he has continued to resist. I only have one female friend, and she seems to be as innocent of men as I am. I had no one else to ask. I thought of confiding in one of the hotel's maids, but I don't really know them and was reluctant to begin a conversation with them. I need to do something drastic to get his attention. If your potion works, I will be eternally grateful," Honey replied with great sincerity. She really was not sure why she had come to the voodoo priestess, but something had compelled her to venture into this part of town for the purpose of making Stephen love her.

"Very well. At least you are honest in your ignorance of my powers and in your need for my help. Other people would make up stories to conceal their desperation and their fears about being seen in my house. You do not seem to worry about that. I suppose if you can dine with the daughter of one of the town's most famous courtesans, you can visit a voodoo priestess. Wait a few more minutes. I will solve your problem for you," Patrice Auguste said as she rose from her chair and disappeared down the hall.

Honey stood incredulous. She could not believe that Patrice Auguste knew so much about her. She could not understand why anyone of her reputation would concern herself with the life of a woman newly returned to New Orleans and experiencing difficulty with the old guard. She was only one of the many desperately in love young women who struggled to win the heart of the center of her affection. However, Honey was the topic of much discussion in New Orleans, and she decided that Patrice Auguste must also listen to gossip.

Before Honey could collect herself, Patrice Auguste soundlessly returned to the living room. This time she stood so close that Honey could smell the smoky fragrance that emanated from her skin and clothing. The letters on the "Ya'll Come to New Orleans" T-shirt seemed to glow brighter with every breath. Patrice Auguste was even more beautiful than Honey had thought when she initially gazed on her from her seat in the shadows across the room.

"Here is a small mojo hand. You are to carry it with you all the time. I have conjured a spell that will make your young man love you and devote himself to you regardless of the consequences. That is what you wish, isn't it? Your problem is not unique, you know. I seem to remember another young woman coming to me many years ago. Go now and take this as a reminder of what I have promised. The next time you see your young man, whose name I believe is Stephen, he will be yours forever," Patrice Auguste commented, placing the small cloth bag in Honey's outstretched hand. She waved her toward the door and turned away.

"Please, let me compensate you for your skills," Honey said as she eased the mojo into her purse.

"No, this time my magic is free. Remember, it only works on those who think it does. Now go. I need to be alone to prepare for tonight's ceremony. You should come sometime. You would find it highly instructive if you were to come. Think about it. I always have room for one more. Good-bye," Patrice Auguste said as she left the room, taking with her the only energy in the sad, dark little house.

As Honey collected her things and headed toward the door, she heard a deep, chanting voice growing louder and louder. It emanated from the back of the house and appeared to pulse and swell in velocity until the whole house resounded with it. She was sure that the song came from Patrice Auguste, but she did not wish to stay around to find out. Chuckling to herself, Honey could easily understand how the tourists could be taken in by the thoroughness of Patrice Auguste's performance.

Clutching her purse, Honey retraced her steps until she discovered herself once more on the main street and on her way back to Saint Philippe's shop. Even though lunchtime had passed, the street still teemed with shoppers and workers rushing to their various appointments. She wondered if Saint Philippe would be curious about her long absence from his shop. Chuckling softly, she acknowledged that many of his customers would be very happy for her to have stayed away, although she would have removed a source of gossip if she had.

Slipping into the lovely red velvet dress that awaited her in the fitting room, Honey again took her place in the grand salon after tossing the purse containing the mojo in her locker. Standing silently and motionlessly at the window, she chided herself for having wasted her lunch hour at Patrice Auguste's. The place was obviously a tourist attraction. However, as the day lengthened, Honey began to wonder if she would see the effects of Patrice Auguste's spell on Stephen.

Although Saint Philippe did not question her absence, he did study her composed appearance and confident air. He

knew that Honey was a woman who liked to keep things to
herself and who always appeared very self-assured. Still, he
wondered what she had been doing that afternoon. It was not
like her to be away from the shop for long periods of time
without explanation.

Saint Philippe had noticed that young Stephen had walked
past many times during her absence and following her return.
He had peered through the window anxiously, as if searching
for her. He wondered if the young man had taken his family's
advice regarding Honey and now regretted his actions. Making a mental note to find out, he returned his attention to the
customer who was happily preening herself before his full-
length mirrors. The customer had desperately and vainly tried
to turn back the clock by donning a heavily brocaded jacket
and matching mid-thigh evening skirt in a vain attempt to
give herself an appearance of youth.

That afternoon, as word began to circulate that Honey had
purchased her family's old home and had hired the firm of
Anderson and Anderson to repair it, more customers than
usual flocked to the shop. All the women of society dropped
by to ask Saint Philippe in confidence about the financial
dealings of his model. Much to his distress, he could not
embellish the story except to repeat the information that
someone else had told him.

Saint Philippe knew that Honey had demanded a considerable fee for her work in the establishments of New York
and in his shop, and that she lived in luxury in the best hotel
in New Orleans. However, he had not been aware of the fortune that she must have possessed to be able to buy the old
homestead. Publicly, he clucked his tongue along with the
others who thought it disgraceful that an unmarried woman
of her age would consider living alone in that massive house.
Privately, he was again in awe of the determination and drive
of the young woman for whom nothing seemed impossible.

Honey appeared unmoved by the chaos she caused as the
rumors flew around New Orleans' best families. Her mind

was set on restoring her home and moving into it, and on winning Stephen's heart. None of the stares or loud whispers from Saint Philippe's customers could faze her as she stood frozen in one fetching outfit after the other.

She did notice, however, that more men than usual stopped by the shop window to look at her. She recognized all of their faces from the masquerade party and wondered at their boldness. She assumed that they fabricated for their own enjoyment all sorts of stories about the ways in which she had acquired the money to buy the house and effect the repairs. She doubted that any one of them thought that she and her mother had lived modestly and saved most of what they had made on the sale of the house and had augmented it with her wages as a model.

Undoubtedly, the men thought of other ways in which she could have come by this large sum of money. With slightly crooked smiles, they nudged each other and snickered that she probably traded her favors for her fortune. That assumption made, they could easily understand her attraction to Jacqueline and her deceased mother.

Honey read the town's opinion of her business dealings in the expressions on their faces and from the snatches of conversation she overheard in the shop, but she did not care what they thought or said. She had planned to buy the house long before she returned to New Orleans. She and her mother had shared the dream of one day living in that house again. When her mother died, Honey had decided she would find a way to purchase the house herself. Now that she had put her plans into action and the repairs would soon be underway with Stephen's skillful assistance, she did not care what the people of New Orleans had to say about her. She was living her dream.

Honey acknowledged to herself as she stared through the parted curtains that there was still one more thing that could add to her happiness if she could only obtain it. Since meeting Stephen, she had not been able to imagine spending her life with any other man. Not only was he tall, handsome, educated, and financially well-established in the community, he was witty, charming, kind, and gentle. She loved the sound of his laughter, the aroma of his cologne, and the deep rumble of his voice. She wanted him in her life as much as she needed Longmeadow House. Without both, she would not feel complete.

The afternoon had passed quickly, and dusk had arrived by the time the last of the customers had finally left the shop and she had changed into her own clothes. Honey had given up the little hope she'd had that Patrice Auguste's mojo hand would work when Stephen stormed through the door. His crooked tie, windblown hair, and dust-covered trousers told her he had just returned from racing his convertible along a dry road. She could think of only one place that he could have gone and that was Longmeadow House.

Throwing his baseball cap on the nearest table and with a quick nod to Saint Philippe, Stephen rushed to Honey's side. Clutching both of her hands in his, he knelt on the floor at her feet and said, "I don't care what the matrons of this city and my family whisper about you. I know the truth and that's all that matters to me. I must have you in my life. I love you, Honey, and I want to marry you if you'll have me. I've acted foolishly by allowing them to cast doubts in my mind. My behavior has been self-centered and driven by regard for my fortune rather than my love for you. I apologize for my shortcomings and beg you to forgive me. Please, Honey, say you will marry me and make me the happiest man in New Orleans."

As Honey was preparing to speak, a loud crash from the back of the shop disturbed the silence that hung between them. Looking toward the sound, she saw Saint Philippe standing with his hands over his mouth as a puddle of expensive perfume spread around his feet. Expressions of embarrassment, annoyance, joy, delight, and disbelief comically played across his elegant face as he witnessed this lover's tale enacted in his shop. Knowing him as she did, Honey knew that he took careful note of everything he saw and heard. Before the sound of the key in the lock had died in the night air, he would have informed everyone of the developments between the young lovers.

Turning her eyes back to the tortured face of the man she loved, Honey whispered her response softly. She hoped that the eavesdropping Saint Philippe would at least have to strain his ears to hear her say, "Stephen, I appreciate the earnestness of your proposal and the warmth of your affection. However, our relationship has been of a relatively brief nature. With all the controversy surrounding my friendship with Jacqueline and my purchase of my family's home, we have hardly had time to become acquainted with each other. We need more time to get to know each other. Perhaps during that time we might more fully learn each other's habits and find out if we are truly compatible. Although I have often thought of the rewards of marrying you and spending the rest of my life with you, I need to know more about you. I don't even know if you're neat or sloppy or what you like to read or if you enjoy the theater."

"Honey, I cannot survive without knowing that you love me too and that I can count the days until you will marry me," Stephen stated firmly. "I am fully aware of the gossip that surrounds you and my family's reaction to you, but I do not care any longer about the opinions of others.

"I have spent the better part of this afternoon at your home during which time I have supervised the hiring of men to begin the repairs. I have stood alongside Jim Anderson and picked only the most talented craftsmen from his crew. Nothing but the best will do for your home. Jim and I have met with the job foreman and outlined everything that needs to be done to make the house the grand place it was during your childhood residency. The three of us have planned the second phase that will restore the grounds to their former splendor as well.

"It was during that time that I knew that I could not continue without you. I realized that I was not functioning simply as your attorney, but as the man who loves you. I could hear your laughter in the living room. I could see you sitting in the sunroom at the piano. I envisioned you riding across the meadows. And I could see myself sitting on the porch in the evening with you as our children played at our feet the way you did at your parents'. I cannot give up that dream.

"Honey, I beg you. Don't make me wait for your answer. I will not be able to work or eat or think until I know your thoughts."

Honey could feel her heart break for love of Stephen, yet she could not bring herself to say that she would marry him. She had wanted him to propose marriage more than anything in the world. She knew that she would wander the silent halls of Longmeadow in despair if she did not have him to share the house with her. She, too, had imagined him in every room of the grand house. She had also seen their children playing on the porch in her mind's eye.

Since first seeing him in the market, dancing with him at Saint Philippe's party, and lunching with him, Honey had known that Stephen was the man for her. She had never been impetuous and had certainly never acted without considering all the consequences. However, when she first met him, Honey knew she had to have him in her life.

However, the slight weight of the mojo hand had grown heavy on her conscience. After visiting Patrice Auguste, Honey was even more certain that she did not believe in the powers of voodoo, but she had asked the most famous and powerful priestess to cast a spell on Stephen that would make him love her. She had thought that having him at any cost would be worth the price. Now she was not so sure.

As she looked into his stricken face and saw the love mirrored there, Honey wanted to have him willingly and of his own volition, not by the force of witchcraft. She wanted him to love her for herself and to be willing to face the hardships together because of their shared affection, not because of the efforts of a voodoo priestess. She needed him to come to their relationship as openly and freely as she did.

Honey concluded that she had to postpone her answer until she could visit the home of Patrice Auguste one more time. She would beg the voodoo priestess to undo her magic even if it meant losing Stephen. She had learned that she would rather not have him than to question his affection forever. Worse still was the thought that the spell might wear off and that he would leave her for another woman. In case the spell had worked, Honey wanted it removed so that she would know the reality of Stephen's love.

"But, Stephen, all I ask is one short week," Honey begged. "We need to know each other better before we can be certain that our affection is strong enough to weather the test of the years and the storms that we will encounter. I know that I love you, but we need the time to be absolutely sure of our commitment. Let's attend a few parties together and go on picnics. You can drive me out to the house and show me all the things you planned for the restoration. We might have lunch together and dinner. You know, I haven't eaten dinner with anyone since I returned except at Saint Philippe's party. Our last meal together was a picnic at Longmeadow. There's so much we can do together."

Stephen rose from his knees as Honey's words gave him hope that his desires would be fulfilled. Taking Honey into his arms, he said with a teasing, Old-World tone in his voice, "Very well, Honey, I will wait the week you have requested, during which everyone in New Orleans will see us and stop wondering about the nature of our relationship. At the end of the week, I will again ask you to marry me. I hope that you will agree the next time."

Before Honey could answer, Stephen drew her closer and, with Saint Philippe looking on, planted a tender kiss on her lips. For a few fleeting moments, New Orleans and its gossips

seemed far away. The smell of spilled perfume ceased to fill
the night, and the weight of the mojo hand vanished.

Coughing and loudly banging the dustpan against the
broom, Saint Philippe disturbed their heavenly moments. Giggling with embarrassment and happiness, Honey picked up
her purse and waved good night. Tipping his hat to the ever-
watchful Saint Philippe, Stephen followed. Linking their arms,
the young couple walked from the store. As Saint Philippe
swept up the last of the glass and sopped up the perfume, he
wondered whom he would contact first with this tasty tidbit.

Nine

Honey and Stephen spent as much time together as they could during the next few days. She took long lunch breaks so they could stroll through the parks and dine in their favorite restaurants and cafés. He ignored the advice of his family and escorted her to the theater and opera as well as to musical performances. They attended every party to which either was invited and reveled in being the most popular couple in town and the source of gossip at every table. They visited Longmeadow, which had taken on a new energy as workers painted, scrubbed, hammered, patched, and repaired everything that neglect had damaged. She had not seen the house and grounds this lively since before her father's death when money and manpower had been plentiful.

Honey knew the damage their association was having on Stephen's career, but she pushed the thoughts to the back of her mind. She and Stephen were so happy that the mean stares and loudly whispered comments did not faze them. When he was not engaged in his other workload, Stephen quietly investigated the connection between Jacqueline's mother and the men of New Orleans. He wanted a resolution to this annoying obstacle in their lives as much as Honey did.

Late in the week, while Stephen was pleading a case in court and unable to spend lunch time with her, Honey returned to Patrice Auguste's house. Again she sat under the watchful gaze of the paintings, but this time she did not feel afraid. Rising to her feet as the voodoo priestess entered the room, Honey stated her case without her former nervousness. Patrice Auguste listened as she said, "Please, madam, remove the spell you cast on my beloved Stephen. I thought that I would be happy with his total devotion, and I am. However, I find that I need to know if he truly loves me or if he is only responding to your power. Please, I will pay your price."

"No, my dear, I have enjoyed your visits. Let this be a lesson to you. Love must come of its own without interference or else we will not be happy with it. By the way, although I would never say this to the tourists who flock to my door, mojo only works if you believe in it. I did nothing to make Stephen fall in love with you. Now, go back to your work and leave me to mine," Patrice Auguste responded as she took the offered mojo hand and sailed out of the room.

Feeling greatly relieved, Honey left the little house on St. Ann Street and planned to return to Saint Philippe's shop by way of Jacqueline's house. She had not shared any of her news with her new friend and was desperate to tell her about the visit to the voodoo priestess and Stephen's proposal of marriage. She knew that of all the people in New Orleans, Jacqueline would be deeply interested in both.

The streets were almost deserted as Honey hurried along. With the exception of a mother pushing a stroller, she did not see anyone as she wound along the cobblestone walkways to Jacqueline's house. The city was so beautiful that afternoon that Honey was tempted to stop in one of the little parks for a rest. However, she needed to share her information and would not allow the sweet song of birds and the fragrance of flowers to deter her.

Reaching the steps, Honey gazed once more at the loveliness of the white house. Its stately pillars, blooming bougainvillea, ornate ironwork, and black shutters made it the most beautiful house in the neighborhood. Sitting at the end of the street, it commanded a view of all the other homes on the block. Unfortunately, its location allowed all the neighbors to see the visitors to the stately home as well. Honey could imagine that on more than one occasion the residents had peeked curiously from behind their curtains to see whose car had stopped in front of the house.

As she lifted the heavy black iron knocker, Honey inhaled deeply of the intoxicating fragrance of the abundant flowers that bloomed in Jacqueline's garden. She loved their profusion of colors and would have to plant some of the same kind around her home once the men had finished the reconstruction work. She wanted everything to be just as it had when she lived happily with her parents.

When no one answered her repeated knocks, Honey walked toward the back of the house and the sweeping porch. Once again she was impressed by Jacqueline's green thumb. She had never seen so many varieties of flowers and plants. She remembered her mother's gardens, but even they had not been as impressive as Jacqueline's. It seemed to Honey as if her friend had poured all of the love she had not been able to share with people into the flowers.

As Honey turned the corner, she discovered Jacqueline and her three helpers merrily ministering to the soil. They wore brightly colored jumpsuits that made them look at home among the blossoms. The women chatted contentedly as they added compost and rich black soil to the already dark earth in which the massive begonias and hollyhocks thrived. Honey could tell that a close sense of companionship had developed between the women based on the hours they spent amidst the flowers.

Almost reluctant to intrude on their work, Honey approached quietly, hoping that one of them would see her and invite her into their midst. As she walked across the lush lawn, she stepped on a little twig, causing it to snap under her weight. The sound startled the birds into silence and made the women drop their tools and look around at the intruder.

Looking up, Jacqueline said, "Why, Honey, I didn't hear

the knocker. We have been so busy working in this flowerbed all morning that I'm afraid we lost track of time. It must be after noon by the sundial and the length of your shadow."

"I hope I didn't frighten you," Honey replied as she smiled at Jacqueline's dirt-smudged face. "I knocked several times and thought I would check around here. Your gardens are exquisite. I'm restoring the old family house and gardens. You'll have to help me with mine as soon as the men finish their work."

"I'd love to," Jacqueline cooed as she tapped the soil around a newly planted petunia.

"The afternoon was too lovely to stay indoors, so I came to share some news with you," Honey added. "However, I see you're awfully busy. I should have sent around a note first, but I was so anxious to see you that I forgot to call ahead."

Even with her hair tumbling around her face in a casual cascade of curls, Jacqueline was still one of the most stunningly attractive women Honey had ever seen. She was as lovely and unspoiled as her flowers.

"Why don't you sit on that bench and tell me everything," Jacqueline replied, waving her trowel in the direction of the wrought iron bench nestled among the rose bushes. "We have only a little more to do. After I finish, we can have a little lunch. I've made a wonderful chicken salad with pineapples, sesame seeds, and a garnish of nasturtiums."

Allowing the heavenly fragrance of the flowers to envelop her as she shaded herself under the branches of the mimosa tree, Honey told her friend all the news of Stephen's proposal and her trips to Madame Auguste. If any of the ladies had been surprised by her confession, they were all too preoccupied with the flowers to express their emotions. Jacqueline muttered sounds of interest and words of encouragement in recognition of hearing Honey's story, but she never stopped digging around her flowers. To Honey, it appeared as if news from the outside world barely penetrated the cocoon of Jacqueline's garden.

By the time Honey had completed relaying her information, Jacqueline and her helpers had finished their work in the flowerbed. Gathering her tools into the basket at her feet and tossing her work gloves on top, Jacqueline rose and brushed the grass from her skirt. Turning to Honey, she said, "I think you were most brave in visiting Patrice Auguste. I have never been to her house although I have heard the stories of her powers. I'm sure you did the right thing in asking her to remove the spell from Stephen although I've never believed in those things."

"I found that I had no choice in the matter," Honey replied with obvious sadness and worry in her voice. "I could not bear the idea of going through life wondering if he really loved me more than he was devoted to his family and inheritance, or if he was simply bewitched. Just in case it worked, I had to set him free of her spell to find out if we had a future together. It would have been more than I could stand to wake one morning to find that the spell had lost its power and he no longer loved me." Honey did not need Jacqueline to tell her the chance she had taken.

Linking her arm through Honey's and leading her into the house, Jacqueline consoled, "I'm sure that everything will work out as you expected. Stephen undoubtedly loves you very dearly. I understand that Patrice Auguste's spells cannot work where desire and emotion do not already exist or on people who do not believe in them. I've been told that voodoo merely brings out the feelings and beliefs that we harbor deep within us. From what you have told me, Stephen was torn between his family and his love for you. If the voodoo worked at all, it simply removed his inhibitions and freed him to make his decisions without worrying about the consequences. He probably realized what a great woman he was letting slip through his fingers. Now that he has taken these steps, I am sure that he will continue to be true to you."

"I do hope you're right, Jacqueline," Honey offered, smiling. She happily and willingly acknowledged Stephen's importance in her life and his efforts on Jacqueline's behalf. "I would hate to go through life without Stephen. Did I remember to tell you that he has dedicated himself to clearing your name in this community? From the reactions of his legal partners and his father, I would say that he is close to uncovering the documented proof that your mother left this house to you along with an inheritance of sufficient size to support you. He is the dearest man. I cannot imagine my life without him."

"I am sure that Stephen will do his best for me," Jacqueline said as she led Honey up the wide expanse of stairs, where colorful landscapes and portraits decorated the walls. "Now, let's not talk about money any longer. I find that it is the cause of more hostility between people than anything else in the world. Why don't you come upstairs with me while I change? You can give yourself a tour of the house. It is a lovely home, even if it is haunted by sad memories."

Reaching the landing, Honey paused and stared in awe at the painting of the elegant woman dressed in a pale blue silk dress. In her hands she held a bouquet of white roses. Cascades of chestnut-colored curls fringed her oval face with its high cheekbones. Although lovely beyond description with soft brown eyes, the artist had captured a deep sadness in the woman's face.

"Who is this breathtaking woman?" Honey asked, unable to pull herself away from the portrait.

Turning toward her friend, Jacqueline responded quietly, "That's my mother. She doesn't look at all like a notorious courtesan, does she?"

"She's lovely. Why do you keep her portrait up here? Why isn't it in the living room for everyone to admire?" Honey inquired as Jacqueline returned to her side.

"This portrait hung in the living room when I was a child," Jacqueline responded softly. "Every time my mother's gentlemen callers visited us, they would linger in front of it. Often they would comment that I would be as beautiful as she was some day. I suppose I moved it up here when she died so that I would not have to see the object of their affection and the reminder of my unhappiness more than twice a day. I rush through this hall so quickly that I usually don't even notice it. Downstairs her face always greeted me when I passed the living room."

"You could have closed the door. That way you wouldn't have seen it at all," Honey offered quietly.

"I know, but the room is too lovely to close off, and this portrait is too commanding to deny," Jacqueline said as she quickly brushed aside the memories of her past and concentrated on the present. She was happy her friend was visiting her. She had so little company to enjoy. "I suppose I needed an occasional reminder of her sadness and mine to keep me on the right track. Come with me. I'll show you the rest of the upstairs. There's much more to see than my mother's portrait. The view from the windows onto the flowerbeds is breathtaking."

Merrily, Jacqueline led Honey through the many bedrooms. She opened the door to the nursery that had been her lonely playroom when she was a child. The toys had been neatly stacked in chests and on shelves until her children might need them. The armoires and closets were filled with dresses and little outfits in which to clothe a princess. The bed with its white silk canopy looked ready to welcome a sleepy little head. Honey could see through Jacqueline's sadness that she wondered if she would ever marry and have the family for which she yearned.

The main bedroom at the far end of the hall contained windows with a spectacular view of the stately magnolia and cypress trees as well as of the gardens. Looking down, Honey could imagine a quartet playing on the porch as guests mingled and chatted while sipping champagne and nibbling little sandwiches during the old days when people of society, both

black and white, had time for such pleasures. This was a
perfect room in which to curl up with a good book.

She could also envision Madeline entertaining her gentlemen callers in this room. The ornately carved, four-poster bed
with heavy satin drapes that matched the ones at the windows
looked inviting. Its thick, comfortable down mattress would
have served as a pleasurable background for a tryst. The
splendid sitting room to the side would have been the ideal
place to relax and become acquainted. Honey could easily
understand why Jacqueline had decided not to inhabit this
room after her mother's death. From the heavy brocade wallpaper to the thick carpet and the lingering fragrance of perfume, the room seemed to flaunt its past and dare anyone to
change it.

As Honey continued her tour of the house, she discovered
that even the smallest of the rooms had been tastefully appointed. The bed and chaise lounge had been covered in the
same fabric as the drapes, providing a delightful coordinated
array of flowers. Sunlight streamed into the room through the
window that offered a view of the smaller but no less lovely
side garden. Someone spending the night in this room would
awaken to the singing of birds and the tinkling of water in
the garden's fountain.

Coming full circle to the room nearest the stairs, her friend
pointed out the works of famous painters that lined the walls.
Even with her relatively untrained eye, Honey realized that a
fortune in art lay at Jacqueline's disposal if she ever wanted
to sell it. She hoped that over time she would be able to
adorn the halls of Longmeadow with the same lovely art the
way they used to be before her father's death and their poverty
forced them to sell everything.

As they entered Jacqueline's room, Honey was shocked by
its relative austerity. She had opted for a plain four-poster
bed without a canopy. There were no heavy drapes at the
windows, only gossamer-thin white curtains that billowed
with the breeze that brought the smell of roses into the room.

No carpets covered the natural luster of the beautiful oak floor.

The adjacent sitting room was as unadorned as the bedroom, with books and unfinished knitting, crocheting, and embroidering in baskets beside the chairs and chaise lounge. It looked to Honey as if Jacqueline had deliberately tried to make her room as uncomplicated as possible in comparison to her mother's highly decorated room.

"I will only be a minute," Jacqueline called from the bedroom as she hurried to change from her grass-stained gardening clothes.

"You need not rush on my account," Honey replied as she gazed onto the lovely vista of the gardens from the sitting room window. "I'm very happy here looking at the view. I don't think I've ever seen such brilliant colors."

"I work very hard in the gardens, and I thank you for appreciating them," Jacqueline responded as she slipped into cream silk slacks and rose blouse. "They are my comfort when all else fails. Are you hungry? I'm absolutely famished."

"I'm starving and can hardly wait to taste that salad," Honey said as she pulled herself away from the window. She could imagine the face of the lonely child watching her mother from the safe distance of this window as she entertained men in the gardens below.

"This suite of rooms has been my home since I outgrew the nursery. It afforded me a good view of the gardens and the street. Lunch should be ready and waiting in the dining room," Jacqueline said as she once again linked her arm through Honey's.

Passing the portrait of Madeline, Honey was once again struck by the beauty of the regal brunette with the mane of chestnut-colored hair. She could easily understand how Jacqueline's mother had snared the hearts and affection of so many men. Yet, she questioned the cause of the sadness that the painter had captured in the lovely eyes and wondered if it was more than just the isolation imposed on her by society.

The meal was every bit as tasty as Jacqueline had promised. They began with a flavorful soup made of blackberries and blueberries, followed by the chicken salad with nasturtium garnish. After that, they dined on the lightest chocolate mousse Honey had ever eaten. Jacqueline was thrilled to see her friend enjoying her food with such relish.

During the meal, they chatted about fashion and Honey's hopes for her future with Stephen and the restoration of Longmeadow. With sadness in her voice, Jacqueline commented, "I cannot really plan my future. I don't know what will happen to me. I suppose that I will continue just as I am today, but I hope Stephen will be able to find documents that will give me a rosier picture. If not, I might travel to Europe. At least there no one will have heard of my mother. I am fluent in French and Italian. I should be able to get along quite well."

"Oh, no, Jacqueline! I cannot bear the thought of losing your friendship. I am sure that Stephen will uncover something that will make everything look brighter," Honey replied with not only concern in her voice but fear that her friend might actually leave New Orleans.

Placing her hand on Honey's, Jacqueline replied, "I would hate to leave here, too, now that I have you as a friend. However, you will soon be busy with your family. You won't have time to visit me and share your secret thoughts, and I will be alone once more. No, unless Stephen can help me, I will have to take action that might remove me from New Orleans. But, let's not think of that now. Let's enjoy our afternoon instead."

After lunch, they adjourned to the sunroom where Jacqueline entertained Honey with her skill on the piano. Honey applauded loudly and shouted "Brava!" when the little concert ended. Not wanting to return to Saint Philippe's shop, she happily sat through an encore. She enjoyed Jacqueline's company immensely and pushed away any thought of separation from her friend.

Spying an album among the books on the living room shelf, Honey asked, "Might I see some of your family photographs?"

"Of course, but they really are not very interesting," Jacqueline responded as she pulled down the heavy book. She was so happy to have companionship that she would have shared anything to keep Honey from leaving her.

Flipping through the book, Honey cooed at Jacqueline's baby pictures and laughed at her antics while playing dress-up in Madeline's shoes, pearls, and boas. Jacqueline blushed red as she pointed out the photo of her in her first party dress. With her hair piled on top of her head in soft curls, she had looked remarkably like a younger version of her mother, but with an interesting mixture of features that reflected her father's contribution to her heritage.

As they reached the end of the volume filled with pictures of women in elegant attire, Honey hesitated as she formed the question that lingered at the surface of her mind. Although she knew that Madeline had alluded to the identity of Jacqueline's father in conversations with her daughter, she did not want to embarrass her friend by asking her about him. Honey had hoped that Jacqueline would bring forward any photographs she had of him while they were enjoying the old prints together.

After they closed the book, an awkward silence developed between them. The unasked question seemed to occupy a space on the sofa. Realizing that neither of them would broach the subject, Honey prepared to leave. Rising, she turned to her friend and said, "I've spent a delightful afternoon playing hooky from Saint Philippe's shop. It is time that I returned. Thank you for the delicious luncheon and the enjoyable time. When I have restored Longmeadow to its former splendor, you will have to pass a nice long visit with me. I could use your expert advice on flowers."

Joining her as they walked to the door, Jacqueline said, "Nothing would give me more pleasure than a long stay in the country. I would be delighted to help you plan your garden. I hope the soil is as fertile there as it is here."

"My mother had great success with flower gardens. Maybe I will, also. Again, thank you for the lovely afternoon," Honey replied as she bit back the question that still lingered on the tip of her tongue.

Reluctantly opening the door, Jacqueline asked, "Do you think we might spend some time together again soon? I do so enjoy your company. I feel a wonderful kinship with you that I've never experienced with anyone else. Perhaps you and Stephen might come around one evening for dinner. I've found a wonderful recipe that I'm dying to try out. This weekend would be perfect if it would fit into your plans. As you know, the city is throwing a big Midsummer's Eve celebration beginning this Friday afternoon. It's not quite as big a bash as Mardi Gras, but there will be partying in the streets as usual and a parade. I won't be going out that night, but I would love it if you could come by for dinner on your way to one of the parties."

"I would love it, Jacqueline," Honey bubbled, happy at the invitation and the thought of showing off her friend to the city of New Orleans. "I had completely forgotten about this weekend. Why don't you come with us? I'm sure Stephen wouldn't mind. He would love to escort two women to the party."

"No, I don't think the gentle folks of the city are ready to welcome me into their homes yet, but I'll expect you and Stephen at eight o'clock," Jacqueline conceded graciously as she escorted Honey as far as the end of the walk.

"We'll see you on Friday then," Honey called over her shoulder as she walked toward the street. Waving good-bye at the corner, she watched Jacqueline disappear into the big white house and close the door.

Suddenly, Honey felt as if someone were watching her.

Scanning the nearby houses, she thought she saw a curtain move at the upstairs window of the large brick colonial on the corner, but she could not be certain. Shrugging off the feeling, she continued her trip back to Saint Philippe's shop. If someone were watching her leave Jacqueline's, the news would quickly reach her ears as the gossip flew around New Orleans.

Ten

By the time the weekend came, everyone was talking about Honey and Stephen. All of New Orleans' Creole elite had heard a version of Saint Philippe's story of Stephen's moving declaration of love and his proposal. They also knew that Honey had asked for some time to consider his offer. The matrons were aghast that he had so willfully disobeyed his parents' orders regarding the topic of forming a relationship with this friend of the courtesan's daughter who was in all likelihood one herself. They were equally insulted that Honey, whose reputation was in tatters, would need time to ponder the possibility of uniting with one of the best families in town when she should feel proud that Stephen would have her.

The men, as they played billiards in their clubs, openly discussed Honey's apparent lack of virtue despite her hesitation to marry Stephen. Surely any woman who would cavort with an assumed courtesan must be of loose morals herself. Several wondered if she was faithful to Stephen when he was not around. Others who enjoyed making crude remarks questioned the price of her favors.

Stephen's parents made it known that they disapproved of this alliance but were helpless to stop their grown son from throwing away his future. They told all of their friends they were concerned about Honey's ability to judge people's character. The wife of a prominent attorney needed to surround herself with friends who were as above reproach as she.

Despite the wagging tongues, New Orleans society had never been happier. As the social elite prepared for the solstice parties, they invited Honey and Stephen to all their parties in the hopes of acquiring more gossip and for fear of insulting them if the stories proved false. Every hostess lamented her fate as she joyously sent around the one invitation that assured the success of her party. No one dared decline an event to which the couple had been invited for fear of missing a chance to exchange tidbits of overheard conversation.

Honey was aware of the scandal that surrounded them, and she acknowledged that she could do nothing to stop others from talking. She would not abandon her friendship with Jacqueline, even if doing so would remove the stain from her own reputation. She certainly would not stop seeing Stephen.

As the days passed, Honey forgot to wonder about the power of the mojo hand as Stephen's love for her became more obvious with each passing day. No matter what the consequences, he would not remove himself from her company. Therefore, they tolerated the prying eyes, the simpering smiles, the wicked winks, and the whispering. The parties and picnics gave them the chance they needed to be together.

Saint Philippe was almost beside himself as the criticism of Honey's continued friendship with Jacqueline spread throughout the city. As much as he enjoyed the attention and the increased number of customers in his shop, he worried that his reputation would be affected along with hers. However, he had not as yet decided to sever his relationship with her. Instead, he resolved to take his lead from Stephen's family. So far, aside from grumbling about their disobedient son, his parents had done nothing to distance him from Honey. She was, regardless of her poorly conceived friendship with Jacqueline, a member of one of the best old families in town.

And the Crescent City loved to embrace its own. At every opportunity, the people of New Orleans threw a party, cooked mountains of food, and dressed to the nines to celebrate anything and everything that would bring them together. The weekend celebration of summer solstice was no exception. Colorful bunting hung from every tree and lamppost. Jazz bands, string quartets, marching bands, and orchestras tuned up for the three days of fun and festivities.

All of the restaurants in town forgot their rivalry and teamed up to produce food fit for a king and queen. From mouth-watering gumbo to succulent shrimp, New Orleans chefs surpassed their usual level of perfection to provide tasty treats that would satisfy even the most discriminating palates.

In every shop in town, seamstresses and designers worked overtime to prepare the elaborate costumes for the masquerade parties and parades, and the gowns for the formal social gatherings. They used bolts of fabric, vats of dye, yards of thread, and baskets of sequins to create the unforgettable outfits that would become part of the city's history as soon as the events ended and everyone returned to their normal lives.

No one had idle hands with a weekend of activities scheduled. Florists were busy making bouquets and nosegays, augmenting gardens with flowering potted plants and decorating tables and banisters with sprays and ropes of hearty, fragrant blossoms. The floats themselves required tons of flower petals and miles of ribbon.

Even animals did not escape the excitement of the preparations. Horses were groomed and their manes plaited in preparation for their role as the bearers of handsome soldiers in re-enactment costumes. Dog acts practiced endlessly to master that last impressive jump that would wow the spectators and garner applause as their float passed the appreciative crowd.

Honey found her days filled with wonder as she watched New Orleans change before her eyes. She felt as if she were observing the preparations for Christmas, as fresh coats of paint covered any signs of aging and windows sparkled from fresh washing. She watched as flags fluttered in the breeze, people chatted happily in the streets, and life took on an excited atmosphere.

When Honey was a child, her parents had brought her into town so that she could watch the parades and attend the parties. However, she missed all the hectic preparations by living in the country. Now, she found that the chaos of getting ready for the weekend was almost as exciting as the festivities themselves. She saw people from all walks of life come together to make the weekend a success. No parish was exempt as the parties flowed from the main downtown area to the river and beyond.

The night of the solstice masquerade party, Honey dressed carefully in Queen Elizabeth regalia. She wore a fawn-colored dress with a skirt that was so wide at the hips she had to walk sideways through even the widest doorways. The multilayered ruff of the dress stood stiff and tall as it covered her bosom and straightened her neck. She fashioned her long hair in a style that hugged her head and coordinated perfectly with the pearl encrusted cap. A spicy pomander hung on a satin rope from her waist. After dusting her face with powder, Honey looked very much like the stately head of the British royal family.

Stephen greeted Honey as she walked down the stairs, and he gaped in appreciation of her beauty. He was not alone in his reaction, as every eye turned toward her. Everyone in the lobby spontaneously broke into applause and whistled at the magnificence of her costume and the radiance of her smile that was only for him.

For his part, Stephen wore an outfit like Sir Walter Raleigh would have worn on a court visit to his queen. His stockings were sparkling white and his waistcoat a rich burgundy brocade. A family crest embellished the deep navy jacket and added a touch of color. His soft white shirt with ruffled collar and cuffs completed the look and gave the impression of being straight from the late 1500s. Stephen had covered his thick brown hair in an elegant barrister's white powdered wig, which he had borrowed from his father for the evening. A rapier once used in fencing competition from his college days hung from his waist.

Saint Philippe walked past as the handsome couple climbed into Stephen's car. As was his custom, he was again the French King Louis. This time, however, he wore a sparkling silver blue outfit that brought out the color of his eyes. As he tipped along in his heels, he looked very much like the troubled ruler of France.

"Might we give you a lift, Your Majesty?" Stephen said, waving from his seat in his open car.

Looking with regret at the empty space in the car and down at his already aching feet, Saint Philippe replied, "No, thank you, Stephen. You are very kind to ask, but I must stop at the shop first. Besides, aren't you off to dinner before the party? Everyone dines out first, you know."

"Oh, yes, we are, but we could drop you wherever you would like to go on our way," Stephen responded cheerfully.

"How dear of you, but no. I only have another block to go. My feet are already killing me. I don't know how I'll make it through the night. Have a good time, you two. You do make an adorable Elizabeth and Raleigh," Saint Philippe replied as he continued to pick his way down the sidewalk in shoes that pinched his feet at every step. Biting back their laughter at the comical picture, Honey and Stephen made themselves comfortable for the short ride to Jacqueline's house where Honey knew that a wonderful meal awaited them.

As the car pulled in front of the white house, Honey gasped at the splendor of its beauty. In every window, an electric candle burned brightly, inviting them to take comfort from the night. The house looked awash in a subtle yellow glow and sparkled from the many bulbs of the chandeliers. The fragrance of night-blooming flowers perfumed the gentle evening breeze.

Putting her hand lightly on Stephen's, Honey asked, "Would you mind terribly if Jacqueline accompanied us tonight? It's so terribly sad that she never attends any of these functions. No one would even recognize her until the unmasking and by then she would have had a wonderful evening. Might we invite her to come along with us?"

Bowing over her hand, Stephen placed a gentle kiss on the little white glove that Honey wore to complete her costume. "If it would make you happy to have Jacqueline along, by all means invite her to come with us. You're right that no one will recognize her until after midnight. We can leave early to save her the embarrassment."

"Oh, Stephen, you're so understanding. Thank you, my dear," Honey enthused with great sincerity. She had been waiting for signs of a decline in his devotion now that Patrice Auguste had removed her spell. This latest kindness was a definite show of his true affection. Honey was beginning to believe that her suspicions were correct and that the spell had never worked. Stephen was very familiar with the possible consequences of their association with Jacqueline. Simply being seen in front of her house could mean that they would be the center of gossip in the morning. Bringing her with them could cause their ruination.

As Jacqueline opened the door, the sound of soft violins wafted out from the living room to greet them. Behind her, the hall was awash in a gentle pale yellow glow that softened the corners and cast shadows on the walls. The plain yet elegant jade satin evening shirt and slacks accentuated her figure. Honey briefly wondered if she had made a mistake in formally introducing Stephen to this lovely creature. She did not want any competition for his affection.

"Good evening and welcome to my home," Jacqueline said formally, stepping aside so they could enter. An evening breeze carrying the mix of fragrances from the garden cooled the house despite the warmth of the day. Jacqueline's home seemed to have been spared the steamy solstice.

"Jacqueline, you look absolutely stunning!" Honey cooed as soon as she laid eyes on her friend. "That outfit is too lovely to wear only for dinner. Join us at the party. Stephen would simply love to escort both of us."

Showing them into the living room, Jacqueline replied, "I think that would be out of the question. It's much too risky for you and Stephen. What if someone were to recognize me? No, I'm perfectly happy entertaining my dear friends in my own home. It's not every day that Queen Elizabeth and Sir Walter Raleigh come to visit. After Stephen clears my name in this community, there will be plenty of opportunity for me to attend parties. Besides, if I really wanted to go out, I could go to any number of the parties given by my mother's friends, but I prefer to stay home."

"Not tonight, Jacqueline," Stephen argued as he poured glasses of red wine for all three of them. "I insist that you accompany us. No one will recognize you unless we stay for the unmasking. We can leave before the magic hour. I would not feel comfortable accepting your kind hospitality and leaving without you."

"Well, I suppose that I could find a mask in my mother's things, I'm sure," Jacqueline agreed reluctantly. "She loved to attend parties and give them, too. I remember the nights that her guests overflowed from the house into the gardens. Maybe someday I will be able to host one of those grand galas. All right, I will go with you. I do hope we won't all regret this decision. But for now, shall we adjourn to the dining room? I can't wait to hear your reactions to the food I've prepared."

Jacqueline hoped that no one would suffer for her acquiescence. She had been so careful to hold herself away from the prying eyes of New Orleans that she worried about the consequences of mingling with them now. Yet, she could see that her friends very much wanted her with them. She had so few friends that she hated to decline their kind invitation.

The three friends chatted amiably over a sumptuous dinner of crayfish salad on fresh tropical fruit, peach soup, roast pheasant with pecan and mushroom stuffing, ratatouille, and chocolate truffle mousse for dessert accompanied by all the appropriate wines for each course. Honey did not recall ever eating a meal prepared with such skill and attention to the melding of flavors. Perhaps it was the solitude with which Jacqueline lived that caused her to pour all her love and attention into whatever she did, whether it was preparing food or arranging flowers.

After dinner their conversation naturally turned to Stephen's efforts to clear Jacqueline's name. "Do you think you will be able to uncover a copy of my mother's will?" Jacqueline asked as she poured their coffee in the living room.

"I don't know if that would help us very much," Stephen replied with confidence as he sipped the delicate after-dinner wine. "What I'm looking for is something that would connect her with prominent men in this town. That's what would do the most to show how your mother acquired the fortune she left you. I must be close because almost no one in the office will dine with me. That's a sure sign that I'm on the right track. I don't think it will take me much longer to uncover the name or names of her wealthy patrons."

Stephen did not tell the ladies that he had received a number of anonymous letters in which the authors had expressed their dissatisfaction with his efforts on Jacqueline's behalf. Several had contained threats of a financial nature if he continued with his efforts. Since falling in love with Honey and taking on this cause with a fervor that surprised even himself, he had decided that nothing would slow his progress, not even suggestions of ruination.

"That is wonderful news. I never guessed that you were so close to solving Jacqueline's problem," Honey replied as she looked at him with an expression of complete adoration and pride on her lovely face.

"Ladies," Stephen urged as he checked his pocket watch, "as much as I enjoy being the center of attention from this wonderful company, I really think that we should be on our way. The hour is getting late."

"Oh yes," Honey chimed. "Let's hurry, Jacqueline. Quickly, we must find a mask for you."

As the ladies scurried off, Stephen was left to sip his coffee alone in the living room with only the quartet for company. Contentedly, he reflected on the mystery behind Jacqueline's fortune, the men in her mother's life, and his own involvement in uncovering the truth. He acknowledged that his love for Honey played a large part in directing his efforts and steeling his spine against the attacks of his detractors. Any other time, he probably would not have risked so much for a client. At any point in his investigation, he could have stopped his hunt and saved himself the harassment by his colleagues. He could simply have told her that he had not been able to uncover anything. With everyone in town being on needles and pins concerning what he might unearth, he knew that no one would challenge him.

However, because of Honey's infectious belief in Jacqueline's honesty, Stephen had found himself engrossed in the hunt for truth. He could not pull away. He could not distance himself from the need to uncover the facts regardless of the personal risk. Actually, for the first time in many years, Stephen felt alive and excited about a case. He relished the hunt and laughed at the risk. This element of excitement was what drew him to the practice of law in the first place. Over the years, the humdrum had replaced the novelty of the hunt. Jacqueline's case had returned the old intrigue to the law.

Muttering to himself as he drained the last of the coffee from his cup, Stephen said, "If I go down in a blaze of infamy, I can always retire to Honey's house as a gentleman farmer for the rest of my life."

Pouring a brandy, Stephen returned to his seat and waited for the women to join him. It was getting late, and he was anxious to see how their charade would play out. He could imagine the expressions on the faces of the men of New Orleans society when they discovered they had danced with the daughter of one of the town's most well-known and elegant courtesans. He wondered if any one of them might actually be Jacqueline's father.

Upstairs the women applied the finishing touches to their ensembles. Honey checked her close-fitting little cap to make sure that no tendrils of hair had escaped, while Jacqueline tried on several of her mother's gowns and ornate masks. Finally deciding on one that had been fashioned with a great upsweep of feathers that matched the dress into which she had changed, Jacqueline turned to Honey for inspection.

"How do I look? Do you think anyone will recognize me?" Jacqueline asked. She was not yet comfortable with the idea of associating with people who scorned and ridiculed her behind her back for something that was beyond her control. She looked breathtakingly beautiful in a wine red dress with narrow skirt and long train. Her shoulders were bare except for the light play of feathers that fringed the top of the dress. She had piled her hair on top of her head in a cascade of curls that set off her long, graceful neck and high cheekbones.

"You look stunning . . . simply stunning. And who will you say you are when someone asks? I'm Elizabeth, Queen of England, Scotland, Ireland, and assorted other territories," Honey replied with a happy little curtsy.

"Well, since everyone is so busy talking about her and since this is a night for mischief, I thought I would go as the topic of discussion . . . Madeline du Prix," Jacqueline answered with a wicked glint in her eyes.

"Oh, how wonderfully devious!" Honey laughed as she hugged her friend and linked her arm through Jacqueline's. "No one would ever guess that you would impersonate your mother at a masquerade party. How funny and how appropriate! Wait until we tell Stephen."

At the head of the stairs, the women stopped and looked at the portrait of the real Madeline du Prix. Jacqueline looked even more like her notorious mother with her face made up and wearing the revealing red dress. She certainly did not resemble the woman who had shown Honey around the cemetery or who had worked in her garden among the flowers only a few days ago. She stood with her shoulders back and her head held high as if defying anyone to challenge her. As they walked down the steps, Honey decided that she found this side of Jacqueline's personality only a little less likeable than the quiet submissive one. Her friend was a woman of many faces, and Honey could tell that she would like all of them.

Stephen stood with his mouth and eyes wide open at Jacqueline's transformation. She had metamorphosed from a lovely garden flower draped in lush green into a woman of the world whose face and figure would definitely turn heads.

"I certainly am a lucky man tonight. There won't be many men in town who will be escorting such lovely women. Shall we go, ladies?" Stephen asked as he placed his hands on their elbows and propelled the women toward the door. So far, the evening was proving to contain more surprises than he had expected.

The summer solstice masquerade party was second only to the Mardi Gras party in attendance and outpouring of food and drink. Everyone who was anyone in New Orleans society attended the party at the mayor's residence, leaving those people unfortunate enough not to be invited to the social event of the summer having to content themselves with the lesser affairs. Torches flickered on the sidewalks to illuminate the pathway into the mansion. Everyone sparkled in sequined finery.

To Jacqueline, the night was especially enchanting since she hardly ever ventured out into society. The last time she did, the reception had been anything but hospitable as the denizens of New Orleans had turned their backs on the young woman of twenty some years who had only returned to nurse her ailing mother. Since then, Jacqueline had been very careful in selecting the places she would visit. Mostly, she kept her appearances to the confines of church, the cemetery, and Saint Philippe's shop. Even the latter she only visited by special appointment after hours when none of his other customers would see her.

Alighting from the car, Honey and Jacqueline surveyed the assembled cream of New Orleans white, black, and Creole societies. Neither of them had ever seen so many sparkling diamond necklaces and stickpins. Although Honey had attended Saint Philippe's party during the spring season, this one made his appear small and inconsequential by comparison. The costumes were more elaborate than any of the ones the guests had worn to his affair. Feathers and sequins appeared the norm on everyone. Even the men came attired in brightly colored outfits. She had originally thought that Stephen's Sir Walter Raleigh costume was a bit showy, but now she saw that it was in keeping with the fashion for the evening.

As Stephen guided them inside, Honey heard the enchanting sound of orchestral music. From the strength of the melody, she could tell that the mayor had hired more than a simple quartet to entertain his guests. She was not at all surprised to discover that the heavenly sound came from a full-sized orchestra. It occupied the north end of the ballroom into which they had been ushered by valets attired in black velvet jackets and breeches.

The ballroom had been festooned with garlands, flowers, and bunting. Chairs discreetly arranged around the perimeter of the room provided the only seating in a space that had been specifically designed for dancing. Sparkling crystal chandeliers glittered overhead and twinkled as if keeping time with the music. The doors opened onto the porch from which guests could obtain cooling refreshments and on which they could refresh themselves by the bubbling fountains. Fortunately, the sweltering heat and humidity of late June had given way to a cool breeze that ushered in the fragrance of flowers when the stars began to shine. Everyone relished being able to put aside their everyday lives and assume the personas of famous people. Even more, they thoroughly enjoyed being able to mingle under the stars rather than in the confines of an air-conditioned house.

As the masked guests mingled, Honey could tell that Jacqueline's appearance had already begun to cause a stir. She watched as men jockeyed into position and requested places on her dance card. Honey wondered what all of these dandies from the best families in New Orleans would say if they discovered that this gorgeous woman who had chosen the costume of a courtesan for the evening was in fact Madeline's daughter.

Saint Philippe was one of the men who made it his business to acquire a spot on her card. Stepping forward in his too-tight shoes, he bowed grandly in the manner of Louis and said with his usual flourish, "My dear young woman, I would consider it an honor if you would grant me just one waltz. I am overwhelmed by your beauty and find myself almost speechless or else I would declare my undying admiration for you in far more eloquent terms. Surely your escort is remiss in leaving you here alone to be pounced upon by strangers and suitors. With your leave, I will defend you to the death if necessary."

Graciously inclining her head, Jacqueline replied playfully, "I would be most honored to have you as my squire, Your Majesty. I am sure that your noted personage would keep the wolves at bay. Unfortunately, many other gentlemen have already snagged the first waltzes."

Feigning heartbreak and insult, Saint Philippe retorted, "I shall have to take steps to remove the obstacles in the way of my success with such a lovely young woman. Surely everyone knows that the king always has the first dance with all women new to our court. Very well, I will have to settle for the fourth waltz since no others are available to me. Might I say, my dear, that I am at a disadvantage in that you know my name, but I do not know yours. With whom do I have the honor of conversing?"

"I hope, Your Majesty, that my name will not be too shock-

ing to you, although I have often found that men consider
knowing me to be quite exciting," Jacqueline replied with a
smile tickling the corners of her perfect mouth. "You see, I
am known far and wide as Madeline du Prix, one of your
most loyal and willing subjects."

"Madeline du Prix?" Saint Philippe said, pulling himself
to his maximum height of barely five feet three inches. He
was quite appalled at her selection. "My dear, do you think
it is a good idea to masquerade as a woman of her reputation?
Surely you could have thought of someone more appropriate
for a young woman of good family."

"I hope I have not offended you, Your Majesty," Jacqueline
responded with a quiet elegance as the dimples played in her
cheeks. "I thought that, since the lady in question is deceased
and notorious and this is the solstice during which all manner
of things can happen, my choice was quite ingenious. It's
actually quite well-conceived when you think about it."

"Well, when you explain it that way, I suppose I can see
the humor and the appropriateness, Mademoiselle. You certainly are dressed the part. As a matter of fact, that dress is
very familiar to me. Could it have—?"

Before Saint Philippe could finish voicing his question,
Stephen stepped forward and interrupted, saying, "Mademoi-
selle, I believe that this is our dance. If I remember correctly,
I am the first on your card."

"You are indeed, sir. Your Majesty, if you will pardon me,"
Jacqueline replied with a nod to Saint Philippe as she linked
her arm through Stephen's.

"That dress and that woman are vaguely familiar to me,"
Saint Philippe commented to Honey as they stood on the side
watching the dancers enjoy the first waltz.

Honey was quite amused at Saint Philippe's confusion as
they watched Stephen and Jacqueline dance the first waltz.
If it had not been for the need to protect Jacqueline from
inquisitive minds as much as possible, she would be twirling
around the floor in Stephen's arms instead of standing with

Saint Philippe at that very moment. However, she delighted in watching him struggle to identify both the woman who pretended to be the notorious courtesan and the dress that she wore.

Honey said as she teased his ego and encouraged him to lead her onto the floor, "You should feel flattered that one of your older creations still lives. You have created so many lovely gowns in your long career, I daresay that you see them again and again. Your work is legendary. No woman can consider herself well-dressed without one of your creations in her closet. Although it has withstood the test of time well, that is obviously an old dress from someone's attic, handed down to the next generation. My friend probably borrowed it from a woman who could no longer wear it.

"That's enough fretting. Isn't the music divine, Saint Philippe? Shall we dance? You haven't asked me and my feet are itching to waltz."

"My feet are killing me, but I cannot disappoint a woman with the good taste to enjoy my fashions even if I do pay her to model them," Saint Philippe consented as they eased into a somewhat halting version of the waltz. "I see that your own costume incorporates many of my styles although I do not remember designing that little hat you are wearing."

"I must confess that I made it myself from a drawing in a history book," Honey sighed as she followed his slow steps and watched Jacqueline enjoying Stephen's skillful dancing. "Have no fear, I have no intention of entering either the millinery or the fashion business. After tonight, I will put it away forever."

If Jacqueline had not been her friend and if she had not almost dragged her to the party, Honey would have felt a bit jealous of Jacqueline's beauty, grace, and charm. As it was, Honey checked her emotions and resisted the temptation to wonder at Stephen's enthralled expression as he guided Jacqueline around the floor. Honey made a mental note to provide as much opposition as possible to the time Stephen and Jacqueline spent alone together.

When one waltz ended and another began, Stephen returned to Honey's side as Saint Philippe tipped away on tender feet. After kissing her hand playfully, Stephen watched as Jacqueline disappeared into the crowd on the dance floor with another admirer. She was certainly the most popular woman at the party as she pirouetted in the sparkling red dress with its many feathers and abundant sequins.

Taking Honey into his arms, Stephen danced around the perimeter of the floor to avoid some of the crush of people. Easing into the twirling, turning revelers, Honey pouted teasingly, "You certainly seemed to be enjoying yourself with Jacqueline. I was beginning to think that she had bewitched you."

"No, I was simply filling her in on the latest developments in her case," Stephen laughed, thoroughly pleased with the hint of jealousy in Honey's voice. "As you remember, I went to her house to interview her a few days ago. She was so different there among the flowers. She was quiet and reserved. She did not seem capable of understanding the complexities of dealing with this situation. Tonight, she is very much aware of the obstacles I could encounter in clearing up the confusion. I think it must be her involvement in this charade she's enacting. She seems to have assumed some of her mother's confidence as well as her identity. Look at the way she's flirting with Jason Martin. You would think that she made her living being a coquette."

"Don't say that!" Honey scolded playfully. "She's only having a good time. I'm glad that Jacqueline could step out of her self-imposed imprisonment long enough to enjoy this evening. Her success tonight will only make the gossip more juicy when the town discovers who she really is. She's giving an award-winning performance." Honey was genuinely happy for Jacqueline's success now that Stephen was safely in her arms.

Pulling her closer, Stephen whispered in Honey's ear, "You're always eager to wish everyone the best. Well, I hope this evening turns out as you've planned. As a matter of fact, I think there's something that you and I have to discuss before the evening is over if I'm not mistaken. It seems to me that you promised me an answer to my proposal by the end of the week."

"Oh, Stephen, let's not discuss that right now," Honey laughed as she steered him away from the topic that had been foremost on her mind all week. "Let's dance and dance. Later we can take a walk in the garden and have our serious talk. As Elizabeth to her Raleigh, I order you to enjoy yourself and to put all important matters out of your mind." She had already decided her answer, but she wanted to wait until the appropriate time to tell him. A quiet stroll in the garden would give them the opportunity to be alone.

"Whatever you wish, Your Majesty. I will always be your devoted servant and will anxiously await your answer. My happiness is in your hands," Stephen responded as he quickly placed a kiss on Honey's cheek.

Honey had never attended a more exciting and elegant party. Everyone appeared to be having a wonderful time, whether engaged in dancing or gossiping about those who danced. They all wondered as to the identity of the woman with the dazzling figure who had charmed all the men in the room. More than one person approached Honey and Stephen for hints as to her identity, only to be turned away. They would not deprive Jacqueline of the pleasure of disclosing her secret. They simply said that their friend was masquerading as Madeline du Prix because of the recent stir in town concerning her.

Much to Honey's surprise, the evening slipped away as one waltz blended into the other and joined a tango or a foxtrot. Periodically, the band added a little big band sound for the older crowd. Of course, jazz and Motown figured prominently in many of the selections. She and Stephen were so busy on the dance floor that they never managed to have their quiet moments alone. When they were not dancing with each other, each of them was engaged with a demanding partner.

As the unmasking time approached, everyone gathered in tight little clusters to watch as those they suspected of being friends hidden under horse's heads and juggler's masks disclosed their identities. Most of the unattached men hovered around Jacqueline. She had told everyone she was Madeline du Prix and now they all wanted to learn her true identity. Many were already so hopelessly enthralled with her that they did not care who she was. She could have been the notorious courtesan for all they cared.

Although Honey and Stephen had promised an anxious Jacqueline that they would leave before midnight, they now stood on the sidelines and waited for her to join them in their departure. She had grown confident and almost bold as the evening had progressed, causing them to wonder if she would want to leave early.

Seeing them, Jacqueline nodded her head almost imperceptibly and slipped away from her adoring partners on the pretext of needing to visit the powder room to refresh her makeup before the unmasking. As the sea of people parted in disbelief, she linked her arm with theirs. The three friends eased out of the ballroom and into the gardens. At the sidewalk they climbed into Stephen's car and stole away into the night, leaving everyone guessing as to the identity of the mystery woman who had exited their lives without leaving a trace.

"Oh, I had a lovely evening!" Jacqueline giggled excitedly as the three revelers happily chatted together. "I had forgotten how wonderful it was to be among people. I haven't attended a party since my years in Richmond. Thank you both for insisting that I accompany you. When all of this confusion has cleared up, I will give a grand party and invite everyone. Several of those young men were quite interesting."

"Don't start sending out the invitations yet, Jacqueline. I

still have much to do to satisfy this community," Stephen warned as he watched her mounting excitement.

As the car stopped in front of the white house and Stephen helped Jacqueline exit, she said in her usual subdued tones, "I am not naive to the ways of the world and New Orleans, Stephen. I know that you might never clear my name. Still, it's lovely to dream. Good night, my dear friends. You have risked much for me tonight and given me memories to dream on for a long time."

Honey and Stephen looked at Jacqueline's retreating back. In just a matter of moments the humility and temerity they had come to know as the characteristics of her personality had replaced her confident air. Gazing at each other, they expressed without words the hope that they would be able to do something to liberate her permanently and in so doing provide themselves with peace and freedom.

Eleven

The next day Stephen picked Honey up as the noon cathedral bells began to ring. To them, it seemed as if the entire town was still asleep as they drove through its quiet streets. Even the cathedral bells pealed more slowly as they leisurely wound their way along the path that rambled beside the river.

Alone in the car, Stephen laid his hand on Honey's and said, "I thought you might like to visit the old homestead today. You'll be impressed by the amount of work the men have accomplished."

"Do you think I'll be able to move in soon?" Honey asked with a sigh. "I am so tired of living in a hotel. I never imagined that the lack of privacy would be so great. Someone always seems to be watching my every move. I know that some of the curiosity stems from the fact that I'm Saint Philippe's model, but most of it comes from my association with Jacqueline. I need to live someplace where I can have time to myself to enjoy being alone."

Living in a fishbowl had been difficult on Honey these past months. All of New Orleans had appeared interested in what she ate and with whom, what she wore, and how she acted. She had not enjoyed any privacy even in her suite because someone had felt at liberty to place voodoo items on the table beside her bed.

"I'll let you be the judge of the progress, but I think that you'll be pleasantly surprised," Stephen replied with a smile.

He was determined to hold the information close to his chest even under the gaze of Honey's bewitching eyes.

They rode along in silence for the rest of the trip, enjoying each other's company, the song of the birds, and the fragrance of the flowers. They saw no one in the fields, and they passed no other trucks or cars on the road. Even the Mississippi seemed to be enjoying the Sunday respite from its travails as hardly any boats disturbed its mighty waters. The city that never slept had finally decided to rest.

As they approached the house, Honey felt the old surge of happiness that had made her heart beat fast every time she returned home as a child. Seeing the tall cypress, the miles of fences, the green pastures, and the freshly plowed fields reminded her of the time when her father was alive and her days were filled with happiness. Looking out at the wide vista, Honey hoped that her world could be that content again. Gazing at Stephen sitting at her side, she thought that just maybe it would be.

Already Honey was impressed by the changes in the house over the last week. Fences that had been falling down and in need of paint now stood proudly along the perimeter fields. Some outbuildings that had formerly been in ruin had been restored for use as storage barns for farm equipment. Everywhere she looked, Honey saw the signs of new life.

Honey had to blink twice to make sure she was not dreaming as Stephen pulled the car in front of the house. Not only had the mansion been painted and the windows washed, but also someone had planted flowers along the walks and around the lattice of the foundation. Daisies, marigolds, black-eyed Susans, bachelor's buttons, and even her mother's roses had miraculously appeared in the gardens and flowerbeds where they had lain hidden from view until someone stripped away the weeds and wild grasses. Butterflies and bees once again flittered among the blooms.

"Oh, Stephen, it looks like home again," Honey sighed as she allowed him to escort her up the newly painted front steps onto the porch. Everything sparkled as if waiting for her to return.

"See, I've placed rocking chairs and settees out here for us to sit on while we watch our children playing in the yard," Stephen said as he squeezed her hand and looked lovingly into her happy face. A soft blush added sparkle to Honey's cheeks.

"If only my parents were alive to see the house looking new again," Honey remarked excitedly as Stephen unlocked the front door. This time it did not squeak as he easily swept it open. "They would have loved to see it restored. As soon as this business about Jacqueline's mother is cleared up, I'll give a big party to welcome her into New Orleans society, just like in the old days. Everyone will come just as they did when I was a child and my parents gave parties."

"You mean we'll give a big wedding party, don't you?" Stephen chided softly as he pulled Honey into his arms. "I've waited patiently, Miss Honey Tate, for your answer, and I'm usually not a patient man. I love you, Honey. Will you marry me? I can't wait forever for you to come to your senses, you know."

"How could I possibly say no to someone who loves my home as much as I do. Of course I'll marry you, Stephen. I would be proud to be your wife," Honey replied as his lips pressed softly against hers.

As she melted against him, everything except that moment seemed far away and very insignificant. For the first time in years, Honey felt secure and safe. The memories of the poverty could not touch her as long as he stood between her and the harshness of the world.

As they walked through the hallway, Honey blinked back the tears of happiness. Each room had been freshly painted. The floors had been newly stained and waxed. The windows glistened without a sign of a crack or spiderweb anywhere to be seen. Instead of smelling musty and unloved, the house had the delicious aroma of lots of strong soap and water. The only thing the rooms needed now was the furniture she had ordered last week from the warehouse, not wanting to wait for a customized job. As soon as it arrived, Honey would be able to move into her old room again and out of the hotel.

Even the room that had been so ravaged by birds and their foul-smelling droppings was bright and clean. As the sun shone through the large window, Honey decided that her former room would make a perfect nursery. Looking at Stephen, she could tell that he had read her thoughts perfectly. Standing in front of the window with the sun at his back, he looked as if he were part of the house and belonged there just as much as she did.

"Honey, there's something that I really must tell you about myself," Stephen began in a sober tone as he gazed into Honey's beautiful face. Her green eyes sparkled with the reflected love and the overflowing happiness that filled her heart.

"No, Stephen, not now. Let's not discuss anything serious today. Today is for walking barefoot through the fields and picking wildflowers," Honey said, stopping him with a finger lightly placed against his lips.

Laughing at her feigned scowl, Stephen said, "All right then, let's do it. I saw a fine patch over there by the river. We'll pick a few and then go back to town. It's getting late, and Sunday or not, I have an important errand to run."

"An errand?" Honey pretended to whine. "You mean that you're going to leave me on a beautiful day like this?"

Grabbing her hand, Stephen replied, "Some things just can't be helped. Let's go!"

Rushing down the stairs and into the light, they ran to the meadow where black-eyed Susans bloomed with wild abandon. Sitting on a patch of thick grass that grew among them, she waited as Stephen filled her arms with the bright flowers with the dark centers. Honey laughed at the sight she must have made with flowers overflowing onto the skirt of her dress.

Lying beside her, Stephen smiled as Honey spread some

of her flowers over his shirt and trousers. Capturing the hand that stroked the runaway lock of hair on his forehead, Stephen lightly kissed each delicate finger before moving to the tender skin on the slender wrist. His lips tickled like the brush of a fuzzy caterpillar as they continued their journey up Honey's arm until they reached the elbow. Stopping at the cuff of her sleeve, Stephen linked his arm around her neck and pulled her toward him.

Sighing softly, Honey leaned forward to join her lips with his. The sensations flowed through her body and caused her head to swim as she gave herself up to the feelings that she had for so long held in check. Since the first day she saw him, Honey knew that Stephen would fill the void in her life perfectly. The confident manner in which he stood, the determination with which he tackled problems, and the gentle way in which he held her hand told her that he could offer her a lifetime of happiness.

As their mouths linked in long-suppressed passion, Stephen's hungry fingers struggled with the buttons on the front of Honey's dress. He wanted desperately to caress the warm, soft flesh, yet he was careful not to appear too eager and rip her clothing. His ardor increased as he loosened first one and then another of the little guardians of Honey's ripe, womanly body.

Now, as she tasted the sweetness of his kisses and felt his impatient fingers agonizing against the pearl buttons, Honey almost forgot the one thing that prevented them from moving forward with their plans for a life together. Suddenly, reality flooded back, wiping out all thought of personal pleasure. They had to clear Jacqueline's reputation or else abandon her, which was something that Honey would never think of doing. Jacqueline had befriended her when everyone else in town only considered her a novelty. Honey would not turn her back on her now.

"Stephen, stop. We can't," Honey said breathlessly.

"Why not?" Stephen groaned as the passion burned within

him. "There's no one to see us. We're far enough from the road that no one driving up would see."

"That's not it. It's just that I can't be completely happy with my friend still imprisoned by rumor and unhappiness," Honey said as she sat up and fastened the top buttons on her dress.

"I'm working on Jacqueline's problem as hard as I can, Honey. I don't see what that has to do with this moment," Stephen rebutted as frustration began to cool his passion.

"My mind just isn't on anything else right now," Honey replied as she gently stroked his furrowed brow. "I'm sorry, my love, but I just can't."

"All right," Stephen sighed as he adjusted his clothing. "Let's get married right away. There's no reason to wait any longer. In a week's time, the repairmen will have finished the house. You can have your grand wedding right here. Jacqueline can be your maid of honor and all will be forgiven."

"In a house without furniture? Stephen, be realistic," Honey stated firmly. "Besides, we still have not solved Jacqueline's problem, and I don't think that getting married with her at my side will quiet the wagging tongues. I feel this strange kinship with her, almost as if we were sisters. I'm sure that you will do everything in your power to set things right."

"But, Honey, this waiting puts too much strain on a man. This is not fair to me," Stephen objected, sitting upright and looking longingly at Honey. She was by far the most beautiful and exasperating woman he had ever met. Any other woman in the New Orleans social elite would have rushed to make her wedding arrangements, but not Honey. She was not impressed by Stephen's family connections, his place in the social register, or his finances. This left him feeling very frustrated. She had her own agenda. At times he could not understand what had drawn him to this strong-willed woman.

"Darling Stephen, I know you would not want us to begin our happiness while our dear Jacqueline lives in misery. As soon as you have righted society's wrong to her, we will marry," Honey said with a final nod of her head.

"But that could take weeks!" Stephen moaned.

"Well, I suppose you'll just have to get used to taking cold showers," Honey replied as she gathered a bouquet of flowers to decorate her hotel suite. She paused briefly to cast a quick look at Stephen's tortured face. "Saint Philippe says that they are good for the soul. Mama used to say that they toughened a man's resolve. Think of how strong you'll be if it takes months to solve Jacqueline's problem."

"If you don't mind my saying so, my dear Honey, you're all wet on this one. I'll be a shriveled up, frustrated prune of a man and that's all," Stephen grumbled as he followed her toward the waiting car. His desire for her made it difficult for him to walk.

Laughing, Honey patted him lightly on the cheek and said, "The time will pass very quickly, my dear. Before you know it, we'll be sitting on the front porch rocking and watching the sunset together while our children play on the lawn."

"Let's hope I don't turn to stone before then," Stephen replied sullenly as he put the key in the ignition and turned on the car. He certainly had his work cut out for him and considerable obstacles in his way.

Neither of them spoke much on the trip home. Each was occupied with plans that needed to be put into place. Mentally, Honey was placing the furniture in her newly refurbished house while Stephen struggled with the task that had plagued him for weeks. His desire to taste the sweetness of Honey's luscious body continued to torment his mind and body. Although he had not told Honey, Stephen sensed that if he could find just one more piece of the puzzle that was Jacqueline's heritage, he would have the way to remove the stigma forever.

Leaving Honey at the hotel to take a nap as the late afternoon sun shone through the cypress, Stephen hurried to his office. He knew that his father and partners would not be

there to bother him since only either the very young or the
very obsessed worked on Sunday. The older, established gentlemen preferred to sit on their porches sipping mint juleps
or to play leisurely rounds of golf. They had learned that the
practice of law could always wait until Monday.

But they were not as driven as Stephen. They did not have
the fire and passion of youth spurring them forward and making them want to uncover the truth and right the wrongs of
society. They did not have Honey Tate waiting for them and
holding off their honeymoon night until her friend's honor
had been restored. The thought of lying in her warm embrace,
of inhaling the heady perfume of her soft skin, and of tasting
the liberated wantonness of her kisses drove Stephen to work
at fever pitch. He had to succeed or perish from the flames
that burned within him.

Searching through his desk, Stephen found the folder that
contained a collection of photographs of well-known men in
New Orleans society. Among them were pictures of his father,
the mayor, two congressmen, and several other leading businessmen. What made the collection unique was not that it
was of all men, but that each of the men was posing with
the same beautiful woman. Unfortunately, he did not know
the name of the woman and had never seen her in town. He
also had never met Jacqueline's mother, the infamous Madeline du Prix. With luck, he had stumbled upon photographs
of her in the company of the men who vied for her favor.

Tossing the folder into his briefcase, Stephen hurriedly left
the office and climbed into his car. He did not call Jacqueline
to see if she would be at home, knowing that she seldom left
the safety of her house. If his intuition was correct, he had
stumbled upon evidence that, if investigated to its fullest,
could lead to the identity of her father and the clearing of
her name.

Pulling to a screeching stop in front of her house, Stephen
ran up the short flight of stairs and knocked impatiently at
the door. When no one answered, he remembered that Honey

had told him about Jacqueline's love of gardening. Rushing around to the side of the house, he found her bent over a lush bed of flowers, meticulously picking out any intruding weeds.

"Excuse me, Jacqueline, but . . ." Stephen began when no one responded to his discreet throat clearing.

"Oh, Stephen, you startled me," Jacqueline responded, dropping the little claw-shaped tool she held in her gloved hand. "I didn't hear you drive up. I've been tending my flowers all day with just my thoughts to keep me company. It is a glorious day for late June, isn't it? Thank you again for a lovely evening. I only wish I could have been brave enough to disclose my identity. Shall we go inside? I can tell from the serious expression on your face that you have not come to see me for a social call."

As she linked her arm through his, Jacqueline led Stephen into the cool quiet of the living room in which every vase contained some of the fruits of her labor. He did not think he had ever seen flowers this lovely anywhere other than in a florist's shop. He could completely understand why Honey wanted to plant beds all around Longmeadow after witnessing Jacqueline's green thumb in action.

Pouring a glass of iced tea for each of them, Jacqueline indicated a comfortable sofa near the window with a good view of her gardens. She watched intently as Stephen opened the briefcase and extracted the bulging folder. As he spread the photographs on the table, she stared with fascination as her mother's image appeared before her.

"Do you know this lady?" Stephen asked as he followed her gaze.

"Yes, that's my mother," Jacqueline responded without hesitation. "She's rather young and the quality of the photograph leaves much to be desired, but I am sure that the woman in those photographs is she."

"I was hoping you would be able to identify her," Stephen commented. "I found these in my father's office. It appears that he and another particular gentleman in this town were acquainted with her well enough to be photographed with her. Do you remember ever seeing either of these men with her? Did you ever see them visit her here at the house?"

Resting heavily on the sofa back, Jacqueline responded, "Both of them look familiar, but I was very young when my mother entertained these gentlemen. She sent me to Richmond as soon as I was old enough to understand the nature of the relationships. Once I returned, she was too ill to see anyone. Which one is your father?"

"This one," Stephen pointed. "The other is Honey's. Both were very prominent men in the community," Stephen explained as he slowly turned over every photograph, looking for previously missed labeling. "From the expressions and poses of familiarity, I would assume that your mother and our fathers were well-acquainted. I'm actually surprised that these photographs were ever taken. I'm even more shocked that they were never destroyed. My father made a concerted effort to hide them at the very back of his file cabinet in a very battered envelope. I came across them while searching for information on your mother's estate. He does not know that I have seen them. I'll replace them as soon as I return to the office so that he will never suspect."

"Did you find anything about her estate in your search?" Jacqueline asked. She was very distressed at the sight of the photographs, not because she did not know about her mother's past but because she had never seen it presented in such a casual manner. She had not expected to see her mother sitting on sofas with her admirers, posing with men kneeling at her feet, or being accompanied by one of them while she played her beloved piano.

"Oh, yes, I did," Stephen responded as he pulled a copy of the will from the pocket of his briefcase. "I guess I forgot to mention it in my rush to identify the woman in the photographs. I have the information right here. Unfortunately, she does not mention the name of her benefactor. She only says that she wished to thank the man who made her life so financially comfortable."

Taking it with shaking hands, Jacqueline read the words that confirmed what she had long been trying to prove to the people of New Orleans. She did not have to work as a courtesan or in any other capacity in order to support herself. The generosity of one of her mother's male admirers had made her financially independent for life.

Covering her face with her hands, Jacqueline cried tears of relief. As soon as Stephen publicized the will, she would be free. For the first time in her life, she would be able to walk through the streets of the town without hearing the snide comments of the other women and seeing the leering expressions on the faces of the men. She would never be able to change what her mother did, but at least now no one would think that Jacqueline had followed in her mother's footsteps.

Being one of those men who could not stand to see a woman cry, Stephen pulled the sobbing Jacqueline into his arms. "Jacqueline, don't cry," he begged. "The ordeal is almost over. You should feel relieved. Please, my dear, no more tears."

"You don't know how much this means to me, Stephen," Jacqueline wept into his jacket front. "I've been ostracized for so long. I won't have to stay alone any longer. You and Honey have solved the mystery of my inheritance and set me free."

At that moment a voice floated toward them from the garden, calling, "Jacqueline? Jacqueline? Where are you? I didn't knock thinking that you would be in the garden. Where are you?"

Before Stephen and Jacqueline could separate, Honey popped into the living room. Quickly, expressions of disbelief and surprise mixed with pain flickered across her face.

"Oh my, please excuse me," Honey said with great dignity and difficulty as she retreated toward the door. "I guess I've found both of you. Stephen, it certainly is a surprise meeting you here. I thought you had work to do in your office. I can see that you definitely have your hands full. Well, if you will both excuse me, I'll leave you alone. Good-bye."

"Honey, wait a minute," Stephen pleaded as Jacqueline looked on with big, tear-filled eyes. "This is all very innocent, believe me. I found some photographs that Jacqueline needed to see and a copy of her mother's will. You told me to solve the problem with the city's understanding of her circumstances as soon as I possibly could, so I rushed right over here. I'm only consoling Jacqueline because she started crying from the shock. Please believe me."

"I want to believe you, Stephen, but you certainly are in a compromising position," Honey answered, softening her reaction when she saw the stricken expression on his face. "Perhaps I should take a look at those photographs myself. They might help your case a bit."

"Oh please, do look at them, Honey," Jacqueline interjected, handing the pile of photographs to Honey. She could not bear the idea that her friend would think that she and Stephen had betrayed her. Honey was her only friend in the whole world, and she loved her like a sister. "The pictures are quite informative. No wonder all the families in town wanted Stephen to abandon my case. They must be afraid that other photos like these exist, hidden in other file cabinets."

"Yes, Honey, you really must look at them. You'll find your father and mine among them," Stephen added as he looked over her shoulder and pointed at the familiar faces.

"That really is my father!" Honey exclaimed. "This photograph must have been taken right before he died. He looks the way I remember him."

"Why, I think I saw a picture of him in my mother's dresser," Jacqueline said as she hurried from the living room and mounted the steps two at a time. "As a matter of fact, I'm sure that I did. She's wearing this same dress. Wait just a minute while I get it."

Returning the photographs to the table and pulling Honey into his arms, Stephen whispered, "You didn't think that I could be interested in any other woman, did you? Your jealousy is cute but unwarranted. I love you now and will love you forever. Nothing will ever come between us."

Snuggling deep into his arms, Honey replied, "I know you love only me, Stephen. But for a moment when I saw Jacqueline in your arms, I almost believed that you had changed your mind, considering your frustration earlier today. I believe you, my dear, when you say that you've been true to me."

Calling from the foyer, Jacqueline entered the room waving the photograph she had pulled from its hiding place under several yellowing handkerchiefs. "Look, I said I had one of your father and I do," Jacqueline said as she returned to their side. "It was taken on the same day. You can tell by their clothing. I wonder about the nature of their relationship."

"Other than the obvious one, you mean," Stephen asked as he examined the picture before handing it to Honey. "I don't know that we will ever find out. Does it really matter? We know that one of Madeline's suitors amply provided for her future and yours. Isn't that enough?"

"No, it's not," Honey interrupted quickly. "The town might be satisfied with that information, but I want to know why my father drove by here on Sundays and why he cried the last time we sat in front of the house. I have to know why he was so emotionally attached to your mother. She must have meant more to him than only being his love interest."

Regardless of what they needed for public consumption, Honey had to know the truth about the relationship between her father and Jacqueline's mother. She had a feeling that something more than a business relationship existed between them.

Something in the way the two people in the faded photograph looked at each other told Honey that they shared a deeper, more binding relationship. She could almost see love written on their faces. The expression was totally different from the one on Madeline's face when she posed with Stephen's father, who was just as young and handsome as her own. Honey was convinced that Stephen had not discovered all there was between these two handsome people. She watched silently as Jacqueline slipped the copy into the old photograph album rather than returning it to the drawer upstairs.

Shrugging his shoulders under the pressure of the demands of the two women, Stephen reluctantly agreed as a smile at the thought of being alone with Honey played across his handsome face. He quickly gathered the photographs and his briefcase and said, "I'll do my best. Considering all the information I've pulled together, the rest should be easy to uncover. In the meantime, I must return these photographs to my father's office before he discovers them missing. Besides, I have to be leaving now before anyone becomes suspicious about my comings and goings. I don't usually go to work on Sunday afternoons. If you're ready to leave, Honey, I'll drive you back to the hotel."

"I'd love that, Stephen. I really don't feel much like walking back to the hotel alone. Good-bye, Jacqueline," Honey said as she exchanged farewell kisses with her friend.

As they rode past the house at the end of the block, Honey once again saw the curtains at the upstairs bedroom window move. She wondered what news the unseen resident would spread around town tomorrow morning. With a silent chuckle, Honey knew she would find out as soon as she walked into Saint Philippe's shop in the morning.

Twelve

As soon as Honey entered the shop, a tense hush fell over the crowd of women whose faces wore expressions of consternation, scorn, and disapproval. Saint Philippe stood in the midst of the venomous mob looking ill-at-ease and nervous as he constantly fingered the chain of his gold pocket watch and chewed on his lower lip. Glaring at him, Mrs. Whitestone gave him a forceful shove forward when he remained rooted to the floor despite her angry whispers into her ear.

Staggering from the push and almost falling on his face, Saint Philippe tumbled toward Honey. His face was contorted in a mixture of fear, agony, and anger. He almost looked as if he would strike her if he could summon enough energy and will.

Honey stood her ground as he approached. She had known that a confrontation might happen if people discovered that the beauty who accompanied them to the party was Jacqueline. However, she had not anticipated that the crowd would be so large and so furious. Searching her mind in preparation for combat, she found only one thing that could have pushed them over the edge.

She did not have long to wait for confirmation of her suspicions. As Saint Philippe began his halting comments, Honey knew immediately that she had been correct. The town was not only insulted that Jacqueline had been among them, it was furious that she had involved one of the most upstanding families in her blatant disregard of their feelings and sense of morality.

"Honey, I have tried to be understanding of your affection toward Jacqueline du Prix although I have long thought that your relationship with her was at best self-destructive. I have been your supporter and often your defender. However, after the spectacle of Saturday evening, I can no longer in good conscience stand at your side against others. You paraded that woman for all of New Orleans to see. You thrust her among us as if she had a right to be in our company. You totally disregarded our express wishes to remain as far from that common courtesan as we possibly could. You failed to recognize that it is not the tradition in this town to fraternize with whores.

"I'm not naive about the relationship that certain gentlemen have with women of her type, but they have the decency not to bring them into our social circle. They know that courtesans are to remain within their own clique and not fraternize with the rest of us. They have their place, but it is not at our social functions. Why, she danced with all of the most eligible young men. I was even caught in the spell of her charm. Women of her kind are very skilled at luring men, you know, even confirmed bachelors like myself.

"What you have done is beyond the limits of our tolerance and well outside the dictates of our standards of decency. And to compound matters, you not only placed your reputation at risk by associating with her, you also tried to ruin that of the son of one of our most prominent families. By dragging Stephen Turner into this unholy relationship of yours, you have placed him and his family in an untenable position of associating publicly with women of ill repute. You used his affection as a tool to flaunt your disregard for our traditions. I understand that you even visited that voodoo priestess so that she could conjure a spell on him. There is no limit to how low you will stoop to get exactly what you want. You needed his help and got it any way you could. And to think that I welcomed you into my heart and my shop.

"If you feel so little for the land that gave you life, why did you return to New Orleans? I wish I had never seen you in New York. You should have stayed there where you could live as you please. However, in our little community of friends, we must live according to . . . to . . . custom. At least that way, you would never have had the opportunity to flaunt this woman in our company," Saint Philippe sputtered as the last of the wind left his sails. He looked spent and quite exhausted as he and his customers waited for her response.

"Saint Philippe," Honey began in a slow, patient manner, as if speaking with a child. She surveyed the assembled crowd of angrily twitching women. "I do not in any way regret Saturday evening. Stephen and I invited Jacqueline to the masked party so that she would not have to continue to spend her evenings alone. She has been unjustly labeled in this town and made to suffer because of your collective narrow-mindedness. She is not a courtesan, and I have documents that prove that her mother, Madeline, did indeed leave her with the financial resources with which to live without seeking employment in any profession. When Stephen thinks that the time is right to go public with the facts, as her lawyer, he will take the necessary steps.

"I did visit Patrice Auguste, but I am not the only one in town who seeks her out for advice. I understand that Mrs. Withers over there used Madame Auguste's special brand of counsel when she discovered a note from another woman in her husband's jacket pocket. And you have visited her also, if my information is correct. So you see, I'm simply doing what so many others have done. The only difference is that I don't slink around to do it.

"Not that it is really any of your concern, but Stephen loves me and not because of a spell. His affections bloomed quite freely and without the assistance of Madame Auguste's gris-gris or potions, although someone left them on my bed-side table. We plan to be married very shortly. If Stephen had his way, we would have set the date already for this Friday. I have begged him to wait until we could share our happiness with our friend, Miss du Prix.

"As for your other accusations, I have done nothing that should not have been done long ago. I did not return to New Orleans to set it on its ear or to right this dreadful wrong. However, I cannot turn my back on someone who has suffered so greatly at this community's hands. I came home to a world I remembered from my childhood as a place of peace and tranquility, only to find that this dreadful prejudice had over-taken my society. You have convicted and imprisoned Jac-queline unfairly and without benefit of trial. The day will come when you will see the error of your ways.

"Until then, I can see that my presence is no longer de-sirable. Therefore, if you will excuse me, I will remove myself from your company. Saint Philippe, kindly forward my wages to my attorney's office as per the terms of our contractual agreement. Good day to all."

Turning on her heels, Honey walked out of Saint Philippe's shop with her head held high. She felt no shame in her ac-tions, knowing that the greater offense would have been to slight Jacqueline simply because of unfounded rumors. Be-sides, she knew that Stephen was only moments away from clearing her friend's name and exposing the foolish behavior of the people who prided themselves on being the crème de la crème of New Orleans Creole society.

Returning to her hotel, Honey found that the same frosty treatment awaited her there. As she approached the desk, the manager said with all formality, "I trust that Miss Tate has made plans to take up residence in her own home now that the repairs have almost been completed. I have just received word that a major client will be arriving in town tomorrow and will need accommodations in this hotel. As is his custom, he would like the best rooms, which you now occupy. Knowing that the construction crew has worked wonders and your home is all but ready, I called him to say that I would be more than happy to make the arrangements. I do hope that you have enjoyed your stay in our hotel."

Not wanting to make a scene with the eyes of everyone in the lobby glued to her, Honey replied, "The suite has served me well, Mr. Reynolds. My furniture will be in place this Friday. Until then, I am sure that I can find temporary quarters with my friend Miss du Prix. I will pack my things immediately. Thank you for your attention to my needs. Good-bye."

As she climbed the stairs to the third floor, Honey paused on the landing to catch her breath and to eavesdrop on the conversations from the lobby below. Although she was sure of their comments, she needed to hear them for herself. She had experienced a morning that would take the breath from any woman.

Now as she calmed her pounding heart, Honey listened as the guests whispered amongst themselves. Catching snippets of conversation, she heard, "Can you believe that she's actually going to move in with that whore? Her parents must be turning over in their graves because of all this. My, my, I certainly hope my daughter never behaves in this shameful manner."

Honey quickly called Jacqueline to ask if she could spend a few days with her before packing her things into the huge, heavy trunks. She had bought several lovely outfits since working for Saint Philippe and would miss the opportunity to purchase his creations. However, Honey knew that once this business with her friend was finally settled, she would be welcomed with open arms and open cash register in his shop again.

After packing for hours, Honey looked around the room one last time. As she listened to the midday tolling of the bells at St. Louis Cathedral, she watched as several bellboys hauled her heavy trunks to the stairs. Preparing to close the door, Honey found that she had left the gris-gris items on the night table along with the rosary. With a smile, she dropped the beads into her purse and pulled the door closed behind her. She left the little bottle of potion on the table for the next occupant of the suite. As she walked through the silent, watching lobby, Honey stopped at the manager's desk to leave the keys. She would call Stephen from Jacqueline's to tell him of her change in residence. Stepping into the sunlight, she left the gossiping tongues to their feast.

Getting out of her car, Honey was once again struck by the beauty of Jacqueline's elegant white house. In addition to the architectural splendor of the columns, the porticos, and the verandas, the house seemed to exude warmth and charm unlike any other on the street. She decided that it must have been Jacqueline's inner loveliness that emanated from the very structure of the house.

"Honey, you've finally arrived. You took so long that I was becoming concerned," Jacqueline called as she ran down the steps to meet her. With Honey on one side and Jacqueline on the other, the two women managed to drag Honey's luggage to the first bedroom on the right.

"I hope I'm not putting you out any. It's so generous of you to take me in on such short notice," Honey commented as the two women linked arms and returned to the first floor.

"Nonsense, Honey. I have all this room and no one with whom to share it. How could I not welcome my best and only true friend? Stay as long as you like. With you in the house with me, every day will feel just like Christmas. I've already planned special meals for dinner every night, and I'm planning to use only the best china and silver. We'll have a party every day!" Jacqueline beamed as they crossed the threshold and closed out the prying eyes of New Orleans.

"I promise I won't stay long. Unfortunately, my furniture will not arrive until Friday, assuming that the construction remains on schedule. There's nothing I can do to speed up the process. I'm afraid that I'll have to stay with you until then," Honey said as she surveyed the other heavy trunks and suitcases that they would have to stow somewhere.

"Don't be silly, Honey. Stay as long as you like. You're almost a sister to me. I'm looking forward to having you here. We can have long talks in the garden, play the piano together, go to the movies, and discuss books we've read. I've so missed being able to share my thoughts with another person. I should have insisted on it earlier. Living in that impersonal hotel could not begin to compare to walking through my gardens. However, I was afraid to make the offer because of my reputation in this town. Why, this will give me the opportunity to share my gardening tips with you. I couldn't be happier," Jacqueline chirped contentedly.

Jacqueline had been alone since her mother's death and looked forward to having another woman with whom to share her thoughts. The fact that Honey was her own age made her company even more agreeable. Besides, she was so genuinely appreciative of everything that Honey and Stephen had done for her that there were no lengths to which she would not go to show her gratitude.

"Well, as long as I won't be in your way. I was quite flabbergasted when the manager all but told me to get out. He said that a longstanding client needed his regular rooms, but I knew that something more lay behind his words. The hotel lobby was filled with tension this morning," Honey replied as she accepted the glass of cool, refreshing iced tea.

"Tell me everything. I've been dying to know what happened ever since you called. This business didn't happen because of me, did it?" Jacqueline asked as she settled herself on the sofa next to Honey. Her lovely face was puckered with concern.

Kicking off her shoes and making herself comfortable, Honey said, "As we anticipated, the town did not take kindly to our little stunt at the masquerade party. I'm not certain who revealed your identity since we left before it was time to remove our masks. I can only suspect that your nosy neighbor at the end of the street saw us arrive for dinner and then leave as a costumed threesome for the party. That busybody must have phoned everyone she knew with the news. At any rate, it is done now. Everyone knows that our dear friend accompanied us to the party and that Stephen is working on your behalf to restore your reputation. Have no fear. Everything will work out perfectly, you will see. Stephen is on the verge of disclosing the contents of your mother's will and the identity of your father."

"Oh, no! I feel just awful," Jacqueline moaned as tears of bitterness, anger, hurt, and concern for her friends tumbled down her cheeks. "I never should have gone to that party with you. I knew something like this would happen. I should have followed my intuition and stayed here. I've caused my dearest friends considerable trouble. I only hope that the wrong can be undone with the publication of the documents that Stephen has discovered."

The women hardly had time to collect their battered feelings before Stephen burst through the living room door. His tie was crooked and his clothes dusty, much like the day he had traveled from Longmeadow in a hurry to show Honey the changes he had begun on her behalf. Honey could tell he had been rushing through the dusty streets. Plopping himself in the chair beside them, he immediately pulled a new folder from his briefcase. Smoothing his hair and straightening his tie, he leaned back and smiled into their bewildered faces.

"Good afternoon, ladies. Lovely weather for the end of June, isn't it? The humidity is not too oppressive and the heat is bearable. Altogether I'd say that we're having a lovely summer," Stephen said as they studied his flushed face for signs of heatstroke.

"Stephen, what are you babbling about?" Honey asked when she had convinced herself that the heat was definitely not Stephen's problem. The gentle breeze from the garden removed that thought from her mind.

"I thought I made a perfectly coherent comment regarding

our fair New Orleans weather," Stephen commented with a mischievous smirk on his handsome face. "I must admit that it is much cooler in this part of town than it is in the business district. Down there, people are bumping into each other in an effort to be the first to tell the latest gossip. By the way, have you heard that Honey Tate, formerly of New York and recently returned to the bosom of her friends in New Orleans, used voodoo to win the heart of one Stephen Turner of the famous law firm of Turner, Turner, and Turner. I cannot reveal the name of the eyewitness who saw her cavorting with the voodoo priestess, Patrice Auguste, but I have it on best authority that she was spotted leaving the renowned woman's humble residence. Had you heard that bit of gossip, ladies?"

"Yes, I went to see Madame Auguste. You were acting so funny there for a while that I didn't want to take any chances," Honey retorted, sticking out her tongue at her friends and rolling her beautiful eyes. "I asked her for help, which she willingly gave me, and for free, too. She said that the spell would only work if I believed in it. Anyway, I returned the next day. I decided that I'd rather not have you in my life at all if I had to resort to voodoo to trap you. So there. I admit it. What else have you heard? I was desperate. Honestly, you'd think I committed murder or something rather than paying a very generous woman a professional call. No one would even whisper if I had spent the same time with a doctor. Besides, whoever saw me there was in that neighborhood for the same purpose and has absolutely no right to talk about me."

"It's a good thing I didn't know what you had done," Stephen chuckled as he placed a kiss on Honey's lips. "I might have married you on the spot if I had known. Instead, I let you talk me into waiting until your furniture could be delivered. I am not convinced about the effectiveness of Patrice Auguste's spells."

"Oh, sit still! What else did you hear?" Honey demanded, laughing at his stiff behavior and formal language.

"Oh, only that you and Jacqueline have corrupted my morals," Stephen laughed.

Honey retorted with a little giggle, "It never ceases to amaze me that women are always the corrupters. We bring on the downfall of kings, princes, and even presidents of the United States. Such power!"

"Enough of that, you two. You're acting just like children," Jacqueline interrupted with a stern tone but a big smile on her face. "We have serious matters to discuss. What have you uncovered? You didn't come here to tell us the latest gossip among the Creole upper classes."

Jacqueline loved the pleasurable interaction between her two best friends. She had lived alone for so long that this happy exchange made her feel warm all over.

"You're absolutely correct, I didn't come out here to relay the latest gossip although I must say it lends itself to some interesting stories," Stephen replied as he sobered from their horseplay. "I made some inquiries at the hall of records and managed to uncover a copy of your birth certificate. An old friend owed me a favor and agreed to do some digging on his lunch hour today. He said that the ink has faded a bit, but if we work hard at it we might still make out the father's name. I brought a magnifying glass with me."

Stephen's discovery had brought him so much pleasure that he could hardly contain himself. He almost felt like gloating as he handed Jacqueline the official-looking envelope. He had worked hard on her behalf and felt as if he deserved the praise he knew she and Honey would heap on him.

"Stephen, you're wonderful! You found it. And to think you kept us waiting while you teased me," Honey chided him lightly as she placed a sweet kiss on his cheek, making him beam with pride at her happiness. Turning her attention to her friend, she continued, "Jacqueline, what does it say? Read it to us."

"Oh my, I'm so nervous I can hardly open the envelope," Jacqueline said as she handed the parcel to her best friend.

Her hands trembled uncontrollably and her face had taken on a sickly pallor, almost as if she would faint. "Honey, you read it to me please. I've wanted to know my father's name all my life. Now I find that I can't bring myself to look at it."

"The ink is awfully faded. I can almost . . . no, I need more light. Perhaps if I turn on this light, I might be able to read it easier," Honey said as she rose from the sofa, leaving Jacqueline wringing her hands nervously.

Straining her eyes to make out the letters, Honey turned the paper until the light illuminated it just right. As the words came into focus, she blinked several times before turning to Jacqueline and Stephen. She could feel the color drain from and rush to her cheeks in alternating waves. Her knees felt weak and her head spun from the discovery.

"Oh, my stars! No wonder my father always looked so sad when he lingered in front of this house. Remember, I told you that he stopped the car and knocked, but no one answered. Jacqueline, you're my sister," Honey cried as tears streamed down her face for the sister she had found and the mystery she had uncovered.

No one moved or spoke as Honey's words lingered in the pleasant summer air. Even the songbird whose melodious notes had filled the room through the open French doors seemed to grow still as the three friends stared unbelieving at each other and the paper that Honey held in her fingers. The women knew they had felt an uncommonly strong attachment, but they had not imagined that a blood link existed between them. Now they looked on each other as more than friends. In a matter of minutes, they had each discovered a sister who had been lost to them for more than twenty years.

Reaching into her purse, Honey extracted the small photograph of her parents she had pulled from the night table when she packed to leave the hotel. Pulling the intricately detailed silver frame from its velvet pouch, she gazed into the smiling face of her father. Remembering the photograph album that

Jacqueline kept on the bookshelf, she quickly crossed the expanse of room to the wall of shelves. Scanning the spines of the myriad novels and books on gardening, Honey pulled the one she wanted from the bottom shelf. Holding it firmly in her hands, she quickly returned to the sofa where Jacqueline sat motionless.

"It's true, Jacqueline. Look at these two photographs. I remember thinking when you showed me this photograph that something more existed between my father and your mother than simply a business relationship. Your birth certificate proves it. Look at the way they smile at each other. Now look at this photograph of my father. Compare the two pictures. There's no doubt that this is the same man in both of them, although yours is a bit faded.

"Now I know why my father looked so sad when he drove past here and why my mother hated to be in this neighborhood. He regretted being separated from you, but he could do nothing about it since he was married to my mother. My mother knew about you and the relationship that my father could not deny with your mother. She probably felt very betrayed by him. They must have concealed their pain from me because I was a child," Honey concluded as she sank onto the sofa beside Jacqueline and they quickly clasped their hands together.

Looking from one to the other, Stephen could see their resemblance now that he had their father's photograph in his hands. He had noticed before that the two women were the same height and overall size. Now he could see that their features appeared dramatically similar. Although Honey was an auburn-haired beauty with green eyes and Jacqueline had dark brown hair and a medium complexion, their noses and mouths were very similar and very much like their father's. Something in the way they held their heads to the side while thinking through a problem made them look very much like sisters.

"What do we do now? Should we take out an advertisement in the local paper and announce to the world that we are sisters? How do we let everyone know about my mother's will? That's really what clears my name even more than discovering my father's identity," Jacqueline said. Then, turning to Honey, she inquired, "How do you feel about this news? I would rather live here alone for the rest of my life than to cause you any pain. Does it bother you to know that your father had an . . . affair with my mother and that I'm the child of their union?"

"I'm proud to call you my sister," Honey responded, tightening her grip on her newly found sister's hand. Ever since the day I first met you, I've known that a bond existed between us, and now I know why that feeling was so strong. You're the sister I never had. I'm happy for everyone to know that my father loved Madeline and you and that he provided for your future so that you would not have to live as your mother did. When my mother died, all of my family went with her. Other than you and Stephen, there's no one about whose opinion or good thoughts I care one bit."

Honey was so happy to have the answers to Jacqueline's past and to have family again that she would stand against all the gossips of New Orleans to defend their connection if she needed to do it.

"Then it's settled," Stephen said as he prepared to make his departure. "I'll return to the office and put everything in motion. Wednesday's edition of the paper should contain all the important information. I'll leave you two ladies to talk. I can only imagine that I am in the way. I will see you both later this evening."

"Why don't you join us for dinner, Stephen? Honey and I will whip up something special," Jacqueline laughed as she offered the invitation. "We are almost sister and brother, after all. Just think of it, as soon as you two marry, I will have gone from being a lonely only child to being one of three in only a matter of a week."

"No, Jacqueline, not today," Stephen responded as he

scooped up his briefcase and dashed toward the porch doors. "There's too much for me to do yet. I still need one more puzzle piece. You see, there must be something else that my partners in the firm do not want me to uncover. My father must really have something hidden that he doesn't want me to unearth considering the photographs that I found buried in his old file cabinet. I will see you tomorrow. I need to finish my work before someone moves things out of my reach. I'll see you later."

For the first time since Stephen brought them the news, the sound of the birds in the garden began to filter into the living room. As they watched Stephen's retreating back, both women thought the late afternoon sun had never been lovelier and the birds had never sung more sweetly.

Looking at each other almost shyly, Honey and Jacqueline did not know where to begin. They each had so much to share about their separate lives in order to combine them into a singular family memory that neither of them knew how to start the conversation. For the time being, they were content to sip their iced tea and gaze into the garden where the butterflies and bees were gathering the last nectar of the afternoon. There was no rush to open their hearts all at one sitting. They had the rest of their lives to reconstruct their family.

Thirteen

Wednesday morning everyone in town was talking about the article in the newspaper about Jacqueline's mother and Honey's father. On the sidewalk below his office window, Stephen could see people gathered in clusters with the newspaper open in their hands, and his phone had not stopped ringing. By mid-afternoon, Stephen had been called into his father's office for the sternest discussion he had ever experienced with the elder Mr. Turner, Esquire.

Sitting across the mahogany desk from his father, Stephen waited until the sour-faced man stopped the incessant tapping of his pen on his outstretched palm and turned his small, piercing, black eyes in his direction. From his father's expression, he knew that he should remain silent until the older man began the conversation. Instinctively, Stephen sensed that something more than simply the article lay at the bottom of his father's irritation.

Clearing his throat as he lay aside his pen, Mr. Turner began speaking slowly and with great emotion in his voice, "It would seem, son, that despite my wishes, you were determined to drag long-buried information about Madeline and Jacqueline du Prix into public view. Most of us had hoped that when Madeline died everything would be buried with her. There are secrets, son, that should remain silent. Every town has them, and this one is no different. In fact, New Orleans might have more than its fair share of them. We've always been a daring bunch. Historically, we've had to be to make a life here on his watery site with the threat of annihilation always at our backs.

"In the case of Madeline du Prix, the relationship with Morgan was personal and private until prying eyes opened it to examination. Morgan was a good man. He cared for his wife and daughter. When he found himself drawn to Madeline du Prix, he naturally provided for her, too.

"Madeline was a beautiful woman, and one of the most elegant courtesans of her time. She had previously enjoyed the company of one of New Orleans' most upstanding businessmen, who had already established her in a comfortable townhouse in a good neighborhood. All of the men of our age vied for her favor. Morgan was the lucky one because she returned his affection.

"As soon as Madeline became pregnant with Morgan's child, he insisted that she sell her house, invest the money, and move into the one he purchased for her. I advised him not to act too hastily in his dealings with Madeline. I worried that my friend would find himself in an untenable relationship, one that would threaten his household. He was very much in love with her, almost to the point of distraction. I feared that she would use him for the security that a man of his wealth could give her, but not return the affection.

"However, on that score, I was incorrect. A very deep love developed between them. Madeline was as devoted to him as he was to her. She doted on their infant daughter, also, and constantly lavished her attention on the child. Any time anyone saw Madeline, the child was with her.

"Morgan considered it to be his duty to provide for the woman who had given him a beautiful baby daughter and who made his life a pure joy. He would not have anyone say that he did not treat Madeline as well as he did his wife.

"Besides, Morgan received a tremendous amount from his relationship with Madeline. She was more than his lover. She had a remarkably sound head on her shoulders and advised him on financial matters. She suggested that he invest his money in real estate rather than exclusively in the family home.

"To his credit, Morgan followed Madeline's advice, but not soon enough to prevent his wife and child from suffering from the effects of his death. His efforts at providing financial security for both of his families proved to be insufficient. Fortunately, the mortgage on Madeline's house was paid in full and her invested monies were secure due to her own efforts. Josephine's investments were, unfortunately, not sufficient to stave off the financial difficulties. Sadly, Morgan's insurance premium had not been large enough to cover the extravagances of his lifestyle.

"Morgan was so in love with them that he did the unspeakable; he paraded his second family in public. No one ever took his courtesan, or mistress as your generation calls them, and his illegitimate children to public functions except for Morgan, who could not bring himself to ignore his love for Madeline and the child. Naturally, everyone talked about his impropriety. I tried to stop him from committing this egregious error, but he would not listen to me. Morgan was my dearest friend, but there was nothing I could do to convince him.

"Naturally, the stories of his other family reached Honey's mother. The poor woman at first did not believe them, but after being told by many of her friends about her husband, she was forced to accept rumor as truth. When she confronted him, Morgan admitted the extent of the relationship. He confessed to the heartbroken woman that he loved them both. She cried and begged him to abandon Madeline with such fearful passion that he reluctantly agreed.

"You see son, poor, tormented Morgan feared public outcry at his treatment of his wife, so he stopped seeing her. Steeling himself against his wife's tears, Morgan took to driving past the white house after mass on Sundays, hoping for a glimpse of Madeline.

"Sometimes in his desperation, he would stop at the house with Honey and her mother in the car. I understand from a neighbor that the poor wife sat dejectedly with tears streaming down her face as her husband knocked on Madeline's door. Why she did not answer, I don't know. Although she attended the early mass every Sunday, she always returned home directly after the service. Perhaps she was in the garden. It really doesn't matter now. She did not open the door, and Morgan drove away in tears himself. He would never see Madeline and his daughter again.

"Morgan thought he had taken care of everything. He had not counted on the gossiping women and the assumptions they would make about Madeline's fortune. Madeline never divulged his identity to the child and endured the unjust criticism in silence.

"As Jacqueline has undoubtedly told you, Madeline's health began to deteriorate. We saw very little of her as she remained almost exclusively in her house where she could enjoy her memories. Her daughter returned to New Orleans to care for her, but not even the devotion of her child could save her. I believe that Madeline died of a broken heart and for love of Morgan.

"So you see, son, you've opened a real can of worms here. If you had only listened to me, we could have thought of another way to handle this matter. We might have spared everyone the pain of the old memories."

Stephen sat quietly while he allowed his father's retelling of the story of Morgan and Madeline to settle around him. He was quite moved by the hopelessness of the devotion that had grown between two people who should not have loved. Thinking of Madeline, Stephen marveled at the strength of the woman who had endured the unjust criticism and managed to raise Morgan's child. He felt increasing affection for Jacqueline, who had survived the ostracism to become a lovely, generous woman.

Stephen also felt great compassion for Honey and her embattled mother. Josephine had been deprived of the exclusive love and devotion of her husband and had died a withered woman. Poor Honey, without knowing the cause of her mother's behavior, had endured the lonely woman's ways without complaint. Everyone had suffered from Morgan's infidelity.

"I don't understand what you mean, Father. Jacqueline had repeatedly asked for help only to be turned away. What would you have done, prefabricated a story to silence her and keep your friend's name under wraps? That would not have been fair to either Jacqueline or Honey. They needed to know about each other. In many ways, they are the ultimate victims. They deserved to know the truth," Stephen challenged in a voice that barely controlled his anger at his father's perpetuation of the lie.

Stephen watched as his father rose from his chair and walked to the window. He did not know that his father could not see the thinning crowds through his tears. Stephen watched him brush his hand impatiently in front of his eyes as he turned and said, "There's more that I haven't as yet told you. I suppose you should hear it from me before it hits the paper, too, now that you have opened the old wounds."

"What is it? I don't think I have ever seen you so unhappy," Stephen asked. He was genuinely sorry for subjecting his father to the unpleasant memories that darkened his brow, yet he did not regret exposing the truth of Jacqueline's life.

"All these years, I have held this secret with the help of my long-suffering wife. Now, it is time that I disclosed it. Since you wish to know everything about Madeline, there is more that you must hear. Son, Madeline was your mother, too," Mr. Turner replied as he studied his son's face for signs of anger or hatred. His poor, tired face had completely clouded with emotion alternating between the fear that Stephen would turn from him in disgust, and relief that he no longer had to carry the secret.

For a long moment, Stephen sat in silence as his father's

words penetrated his confused mind. He had been prepared to discover that Jacqueline and Honey shared the same father, but now he had to process the new information that his mother and Jacqueline's were the same person. In a matter of minutes, Stephen had discovered that the woman he had cherished as his mother was not related to him at all. Further, he learned that he had a half-sister who had a half-sister who was about to be his wife.

"My mother, the woman I've loved all my life, isn't my birth mother at all," Stephen stated as the reality of the relationships settled over him.

"That's right," his father answered slowly. "My wife, out of love for me and because we were childless, offered to adopt the son Madeline had by me. Madeline was very young at the time of my relationship with her and was not ready for the responsibility of raising a child. I had been supporting her in the townhouse I mentioned to you a few minutes ago for about three years when she became pregnant. I had all but given up on ever having children and had put the thought of having an heir out of my mind. Your mother and I had been married for six years and had tried unsuccessfully to have a child. Madeline's news was like music to my ears.

"Your mother had known about my continued relationship with Madeline, having confronted me with her suspicion of my infidelity a few months earlier. Unlike Morgan's wife, she did not demand that I give up Madeline, although she was terribly hurt that I would have a relationship with another woman.

"When I told her about Madeline's pregnancy and her inability to raise the child, my dear wife showed her love of me by offering to make you her son. Since that moment, I have been a model husband. Over time, as you grew up, she forgave me. We have enjoyed a wonderfully happy life together.

"Your mother has given you a good life, Stephen, and could not have loved you more if you had been her own baby.

She nursed you through every childhood illness. She stayed up for many nights when you had the flu as an infant. She carried you from room to room after you broke your leg. She doted on you and she still does. You must never turn your back on her now that you know the whole story. She has been afraid that you would discover the truth of your heritage, too.

"So you see, Stephen, I wanted to spare your mother's feelings as much as I wanted to conceal the truth. That is the least I could do for her after all these years of love and devotion. Sadly, it's something I should have thought about many years ago. She has been an exemplary wife and mother. You could not have had better. Now that you know all the truth, what will you do with it? What is your plan?"

Rising and placing his hand lovingly on his father's slumped shoulder, Stephen replied without hesitation, but with a touch of bitterness in his voice, "First, I'll tell Honey and Jacqueline my news. Honey deserves to know the truth about the life of the man she plans to marry. She might not want me after she hears that my mother was a courtesan. I do not condemn you for the way in which you have lived, Father, nor will I turn from the only mother I have loved all these years. However, I must be fair to Honey. Our future is at stake, and she has already suffered enough."

"Stephen, please try to forgive me," the old man pleaded. "I only wanted what was best for all of us: you, Madeline, your mother, and myself. I cared deeply for Madeline, but she was not of my social circle. Our lives could never have been united. When I met your mother, I fell in love with her. She was like me. Yet, I was weak and could not stop seeing Madeline. My relationship with Madeline and her subsequent pregnancy gave me the son I wanted so desperately. Your mother's loving heart gave you a good, stable home. We've given you every financial opportunity in life, son. Please don't break your mother's heart."

"Don't worry, Father, I won't do anything to hurt my

mother," Stephen said as he rose from the chair in which he had passed the strangest afternoon hours of his life. "She has given me more love and devotion than any child could ever deserve. Madeline gave me life, but Christina raised me. She will always be the woman I love as my mother. However, I will from now until forever acknowledge the other also. What you have done in concealing my true identity from me will forever live with you. I neither blame nor absolve you of this deception. At any rate, I need to see Honey. I hope that she will understand. You see, I love her very much and have asked her to marry me. I cannot imagine life without her."

Making speedy progress through the streets of New Orleans, Stephen arrived at Jacqueline's door just as she and Honey were sitting down to an early supper. From the expression on his face, they could tell that much troubled his mind.

Rushing to his side, Honey guided him to the chair beside hers. Anxiously, they waited until he caught his breath from the breakneck trip. Unable to contain herself any longer, Honey put into words the question that had hung in the air between them. With great concern in her voice, she asked, "Stephen, has something gone wrong? We have stayed here all day waiting for you to call. Tell us quickly, Stephen."

Taking a gulp of the offered water to clear his throat, Stephen said as he looked from one to the other, "Everything went exactly as I expected with Jacqueline's case. Everyone has read the newspaper article about her life and her fortune. They have spent the greater part of the day discussing every nuance of it, based on the number of phone calls to our office. I am sure that your news will continue to be the topic of discussion at every dinner table tonight just as we expected it would be. Tomorrow morning, New Orleans will look at you differently. Perhaps our little circle will even begin to open its arms to you, if you still wish to become a member of this group after you hear the rest of my news. We will have to wait and see. We have done all we could on Jacqueline's behalf.

"I have made an even more startling discovery today. As you both know, my father has been opposed to my efforts on Jacqueline's behalf. I have long suspected that he and others of his generation were desperately trying to cover up the realities of their relationships with women like Madeline. When I found his folder of photographs, I knew that I was on the right track. However, I never imagined the degree of my father's involvement with her. I never suspected until today that there was much more that lay under the surface.

"My father called me into his office this afternoon for what I thought would be a strong reprimand for going against his wishes and pressing your case, Jacqueline. I was prepared for his displeasure as both my parent and my law partner. However, as a grown man, I must decide for myself which cases I will present to the courts. I was prepared to stand behind my convictions. Many of the people of New Orleans have treated you terribly, and I had to do something to rectify the situation.

"Instead of scolding me, he unburdened his heart to me in a way that he never has. You see, my father is a very closed man. He shares very little with his family almost to the exclusion of allowing others into his life. Yet, he shared a confidence with me that he has kept private for a lifetime although I am aware now that his closest friends have also known this unspoken truth about my father's relationship with Madeline. All these years, my father has been hiding something from me for my protection and for that of my mother. He confided in me that the woman who raised me is not, in fact, my birth mother. My birth mother is Madeline du Prix. Jacqueline and I are half-sister and brother."

The deafening silence enfolded Honey, Stephen, and Jacqueline as they sat in the dining room blankly staring at each other. No one moved or turned away as time stood still. Honey and Jacqueline slowly digested Stephen's words as the reality took shape and spread over them. Honey and Jacqueline were the daughters of Morgan Tate, although of different mothers. Stephen and Jacqueline were the children of Madeline, yet their fathers were not the same. Fate had joined Honey and Stephen in love and Honey and Jacqueline in friendship. The people who had been deprived the company of each other as children had serendipitously as adults found their way to a shared happiness despite the efforts of their parents to keep them apart.

Leaning heavily on the chair back, Honey was the first to find her tongue. Although she was shocked by the news, she was more bewildered that their parents would have tried to conceal their genealogy. "Goodness," she exclaimed, "what a mess! It's very difficult for me to believe that our parents thought they could pull off this subterfuge indefinitely. Could they honestly have thought that we'd never meet?"

Smoothing his hair nervously, Stephen replied, "When your father died, Honey, he took the secret of Jacqueline's financial security with him. My father as his friend would never have divulged the truth of his relationship with Madeline because, if he had, he would have needed to admit his own involvement with her. When Madeline died, they buried the secret with her. My father breathed a huge sigh of relief thinking that I would never need to know the truth. What my father had not anticipated was that you would return from New York and meet Jacqueline. No one would have suspected that a woman from one of New Orleans' finest Creole families would have become friends with the daughter of one of the town's most well-known courtesans. Ironically, Madeline was not really infamous for her profession but for the fact that she loved only two men in her lifetime and produced children by both of them.

"When you met Jacqueline and refused to give up your friendship with her despite the unified efforts of everyone in our circle, you set a downward spiral of events in motion. To be true to your friend, you had to clear her name. To do that, you had to expose the identity of the man who had provided her with financial security. In making his name public, you uncovered the name of her father and your birth connection with her.

"My discovery of my father's hidden folder added to the destruction of this carefully concealed cover-up because I now had proof that he, too, had at some time in his life befriended Madeline. He knew that it was merely a matter of time before I unraveled the entire story and exposed him. He was her first lover, and she was very young at the time. My mother's willingness to forgive his infidelity and to raise Madeline's child caused him to become a model husband and father. Honey's father entered the scene not long after that. Falling deeply in love with Madeline, he set her up in this house. The combination of her ability to manage her finances and his contributions to her living expenses left her financially secure for life.

"So you see, Honey, our secrets are finally in the open. You thought you were simply clearing Jacqueline's name. You did not know that you would uncover the identity of a sister and her brother."

Jacqueline sat quietly with tears of happiness running down her soft cheeks. She had spent so many years alone that she could hardly believe her ears. Struggling with her emotions, she exclaimed tearfully, "I'm so happy! I've gone from being an only child to having a sister and a brother almost overnight! Honey, you've not only cleared my reputation, but you've given me a wonderful family. Oh, my! What will happen now to your legal practice, Stephen? What will people say when they learn about your birth mother's identity? People can be so mean-spirited and unforgiving."

With an almost sad smirk and a slight shake of his head, Stephen replied, "It seems that the older generation already knows the truth about me. I'm probably among the last to know the truth. Frankly, I'm not going to worry about this at all. I'm too busy trying to establish myself and make a living to care."

Honey thought about everything she had heard as she poured each of them another glass of iced tea while the condensation rolled down the crystal pitcher and dripped onto the table like tears, "Now I understand why everyone was so nervous about my questions regarding Jacqueline's family background. All those important men worried that, if I could uncover those photographs of our fathers with her, someone else might discover the same information about them. There are probably sealed envelopes all over town of other men with their courtesans. I wonder how many of them have well-kept secrets."

"We will never know," Stephen concluded. He felt much more at ease now that Honey and Jacqueline had overcome their initial shock. Yet, he still wondered about his future with Honey. Strangely, Stephen discovered that although he was courageous about some things, he was afraid to broach this topic.

"Well, what do we do now?" Jacqueline asked with a big happy smile on her face. "The way I see it, we can either continue our lives, or we can burst out with a big party or a good old-fashioned barbecue to celebrate the three of us finding each other."

"A party? I thought we were having a wedding. I've already unpacked my mother's dress. Now that the remodeling is almost finished, I want to hold the most elaborate wedding this town has ever seen," Honey replied with a teasing tone in her voice. She had sensed Stephen's concern that she might withdraw from him. She had waited until just the right time to set his mind at ease. That moment appeared to be perfect.

Turning toward her, Stephen could not hide the joy that filled his heart. Falling to his knees at her feet and taking her hands in his, he restated the question he had asked two weeks before. Stephen begged playfully and formally in the grand old style saying, "Miss Honey Tate, would you do me the honor of bestowing your hand in marriage unto this most unworthy specimen? I love you more than mere words could ever say."

"Mr. Turner, nothing could make me more happy than to become your wife. With our sister as witness, I happily agree to marry you," Honey replied as she allowed Stephen to pull her into his arms.

For the moment all thoughts of Jacqueline, Madeline, and New Orleans were forgotten as the lovers pressed their lips together in mutual affection. For the first time since Honey returned home, her life felt as if it were on a clear, true course with Stephen at her side to help steer past the obstacles. In her heart, she knew that from that moment on everything would work out just fine for them.

"Excuse me! Well, I'll just go outside where it's cooler," Jacqueline commented as she pretended to be shocked by their lingering kiss.

Laughing at her discomfort, Honey and Stephen slowly released each other. They had much to plan and only a week and a few odd days in which to pull together the wedding to which all of New Orleans Creole society would be invited. As they settled in the dining room once again to make their initial plans and finish their forgotten meal, the big question remained dangling in the air between them. They wondered, if they invited everyone who was anyone in New Orleans, would any of them come?

Fourteen

The next morning as the town continued to buzz about them, Honey and Jacqueline began the wedding preparations. Sitting on the porch after breakfast, they decided that, although restored, Honey's house would need some help to look its best for the wedding. After deciding on the color for the bunting and the tent, Honey turned the rest of the planning over to Jacqueline.

In Jacqueline's mind only massive amounts of flowers and ribbons would add the appropriate feeling of festivity to the restored mansion. She quickly jotted down the kinds and varieties of flowers she would order from the florist as soon as they made their trip to the market. They would need masses of them for the tent in which the ceremony and dancing would be held and for the house from which the bridal party would receive its guests.

Next on the list was the menu. Jacqueline suggested that they use her favorite caterer, whose skill had been amply tested. Deciding on a traditional barbecue made the planning simpler, although the number of guests added its own level of complexity. Jacqueline knew that they would have to rise above this challenge since Honey was determined to invite every member of every prominent family in town. This wedding would not only be the union of Honey and Stephen, but Jacqueline's introduction to New Orleans.

After the two ladies completed the initial arrangements,

they prepared themselves for the trip downtown. Jacqueline dressed with more than her usual attention. She knew that everyone would be examining her from head to toe. She arranged her dark hair in big curls with more than her customary care. Her mauve linen suit showed off her figure to perfection as she surveyed her reflection in the mirror. Satisfied with what she saw, she joined Honey in her bedroom.

Honey knew that, as the catalyst behind the upheaval in New Orleans's society circle, she would also be under scrutiny that morning. She decided that a white silk suit trimmed in black piping at the collar and down the front would complement her perfectly. Besides, Saint Philippe had designed the dress specifically for her. Her attire would please at least one person in the critical town.

After finding a dreadful stain on the front of her mother's wedding dress, Honey had decided to ask Saint Philippe to tailor one of his creations to her measurements. If he refused, there were plenty of designers in town who would jump at the opportunity to fashion something for her use even on such short notice.

Walking through the upstairs hall, Honey stopped in front of Madeline's portrait. Turning to her sister, she said, "Don't you think you should move her painting back downstairs?"

"Perhaps you're right. It's a lovely painting, isn't it? Mother was a beautiful, elegant woman. Now that I know that the car I heard outside my window was my father's, I suppose I should feel differently about her. We can move it when we come back from shopping," Jacqueline agreed as the two women eased down the stairs and out into the sunlight.

Blending with the swarming masses on the sidewalks, Honey could feel the eyes of everyone studying them. Some of the older women tightened their plump bodies so they would not touch either of them as they walked past. Many other women dropped their eyes so that they would not have to look directly at Jacqueline. The younger women smiled and waved merrily as they passed, showing that the gossip and the newspaper article were of no importance to them.

Honey and Jacqueline followed the flow of shoppers through the various stores. After visiting the engraver and ordering enough invitations to paper New Orleans for a week, they entered the largest of the local florists. With Jacqueline's help, Honey ordered every potted gardenia, fern, jasmine, bougainvillea, and miniature cypress the poor overwhelmed man could deliver by the next Friday, before moving to their next task.

Stopping in front of Saint Philippe's shop, they looked through the window at the pleasant gathering of customers. Honey could almost hear the happy ringing of the cash register and see Saint Philippe's smiling face as the customers left the store with packages under their arms.

At that moment Saint Philippe turned around and spied them through the window. His eyes grew wide as he clutched dramatically at his chest and slumped into the nearest chair. As the women who ministered to him followed his gaze, Honey saw mixed emotions play across their faces. It was clear that the women were uncertain how they should behave.

Pushing open the door, Honey and Jacqueline stepped into the shop under the watchful gaze of Saint Philippe's customers. Only the swishing of the ceiling fan broke the heavy silence as they walked into the midst of the shoppers. Mrs. Maitlain and Mrs. Collins occupied dominant positions beside Saint Philippe's chair. They alternated between fanning him with a folded newspaper with such force that his hair blew out of place and whispering instructions into his ear.

"Good morning, Saint Philippe," Honey said with a happy smile despite the frowns that greeted her entrance. Jacqueline stood bravely at her side as the women stared at them with hostility and curiosity.

"Well, well, good morning, Honey and Jacqueline," Saint Philippe stuttered as he pushed his fragile frame to a standing position.

"As you probably already know, I am getting married a week from Friday at my newly restored home," Honey responded with dignity and eloquence. "I had planned to wear my mother's wedding dress, but, unfortunately, I discovered yesterday that there's a dreadful spot on the front of the skirt. Since I'm now without a dress, I thought I might buy one of yours. I remember modeling a stunning gown when I first returned to New Orleans. I hope it is still available in my size. I would love to mark the most important day of my life by wearing a design crafted by the most influential designer in the South."

Jacqueline looked on in awe at her sister's ability to ignore the hostility that filled the salon, when she felt like running away. She hoped that Honey would quickly conclude her business with Saint Philippe before the women forgot to be well-bred ladies.

Saint Philippe straightened his shoulders at the words of flattery that he felt were his just rewards for possessing a flawless eye for fashion, magnificent taste in fabric, and unwaveringly exquisite skill in construction. He enthusiastically pulled Honey into his arms in a warm embrace and ignored the expressions of annoyance that continued to flicker across the faces of Mrs. Maitlain and Mrs. Collins.

Cooing like a mother hen over the return of her wandering chick, Saint Philippe gushed, "Of course I have the dress. No one else but you in this town would be able to do justice to its beauty. You are the only one with the figure and the appreciation for artistry to wear such a stunning gown. As a matter of fact, I think you're wearing one of my creations now. You do have such divine taste."

Standing back just a bit, Honey smiled coyly into his beaming face and asked, "Do you think you might be able to create something special for my sister, Jacqueline, also? She will be my maid of honor, you see. I want her to look absolutely stunning. Since you have designed outfits for her for other occasions, I can think of no one else who could make her look almost as breathtaking as the bride."

"My darling, Jacqueline," Saint Philippe replied as he pulled her toward him and disregarded the shocked expressions on the old women's faces and the sucked-in breaths that hissed like teapots, "of course I have the perfect dress to accentuate your divine figure. Don't I always keep your measurements in mind when I select the fashions to display in my shop? I would be hurt if either of you ladies asked anyone else to provide the gowns for this wonderful wedding."

Stifling a laugh, Honey took a quick glance around the room. Several of the younger women had stepped closer in order to become part of the discussion. They were quite curious about the dress that Honey would wear since they had planned to ask Saint Philippe to design their wedding gowns, too. However, the older women of New Orleans society maintained their folded-arm postures of disgust that Honey and Jacqueline would dare come into their midst.

Clapping his hands, Saint Philippe called to his assistant, "Lucy, bring the bridal dress that Honey modeled two weeks ago. It's hanging in the back in the white velvet bag. Ask Mandy to help you carry the blue crushed satin I just finished last evening. It's still in the workroom. Don't just stand there! Hurry!"

Turning his attention back to Honey and Jacqueline, Saint Philippe escorted them to chairs beside his ornate desk. The composure with which he poured champagne into the delicate long-stemmed flutes and offered it to his guests belied his nervousness. A casual spectator would have thought that the appearance of the two women had not caused a stir in the shop. Saint Philippe, under the spell of Honey's flattery and desire to purchase his creations, had forgotten that only a few minutes earlier he had been in a faint and under the care of the town's disapproving busybodies.

The gowns quickly appeared and, to Honey's delight, they were more beautiful than she had anticipated. Although she had modeled the wedding dress, she was now looking at it from the perspective of the bride rather than as an employee. She could appreciate the detail in the seed pearl designs and the lace bodice much more clearly now that she could envision herself as the proud woman wearing the stunning creation on her special day.

Now, with everyone watching, Jacqueline applauded the exquisite blue dress that he displayed for her approval. She had always enjoyed her clandestine visits to Saint Philippe's shop. She would stop by after hours every time he called to tell her about new designs and the private showing he had arranged for her.

As Saint Philippe expectantly looked on, both women enthusiastically agreed that these gowns were the only ones in town that would ever prove satisfactory for Honey's big event. He was so thrilled with their acceptance of his fashions and their appreciation of his craft that he almost danced around the salon. However, despite his show of enthusiasm for Honey and Jacqueline's patronage, the gossips remained steadfast in their beliefs that the two young women did not belong among them. It would take more than fashions to sway them.

Continuing to ignore the looks of hostility that the matrons shot in his direction, Saint Philippe rubbed his soft chubby hands together and said, "It would make my old heart beat with joy to arrange final fittings for each of you. Honey, this dress only needs the most minor of alterations to make it fit you perfectly. Jacqueline, I designed this one with you in mind. I will have both of these marvelous works, if I do say so myself, ready for you by next Thursday. I will bring them out myself. Now hurry and try them on. I'm anxious to see you in them."

As Honey and Jacqueline slipped into the fitting room and the gowns, the women in the main part of the salon immediately began buzzing like a disturbed beehive. The old women discussed everything about them, from the clothes to their boldness in appearing at Saint Philippe's shop. They only paused briefly in their critiques when Saint Philippe returned to scold them about their voices. As soon as he retired to the back of the shop again, they returned to their attacks with the same vigor and venom.

Although Honey could not hear all of what they said about her or feel their burning eyes, she knew they blamed her for the downfall of Stephen's father and the embarrassment of his mother. Regardless of how they felt about her, Honey felt that their anger was a fair price to pay if it would give peace to Jacqueline after her years of silent suffering.

Honey had already overheard one of the women say with a lewd smile that Stephen undoubtedly got his handsome looks and charm from his mother's side of the family. If anything, he was even more mysterious and appealing as the son of a courtesan than he had been as the offspring of a respectable woman.

Leaving the shop, Honey could feel the sigh of relief propel them forward. The hostility of the old guard had been so palpable that she wondered if any of them would attend her wedding. They might not be able to forget what they considered to be her breach of etiquette and social morés. She wondered if they would remember that hers had been one of the most respected families in New Orleans and that by snubbing her, they would be committing a horrible social faux pas themselves.

Regardless of the actions of the townspeople, Honey and Jacqueline were determined to have a good time shopping. After they finished their fittings at Saint Philippe's, they stepped across the street to arrange for the photographer to take the wedding pictures. He was a gruff older man who had been well-acquainted with Honey's father and Madeline. As they chatted about the poses that would most appeal to Honey and arranged the time for her sitting on Thursday afternoon, they talked about the old days when men like Morgan Tate and Edward Turner kept mistresses and no one thought anything about it.

Scratching his beard, Mr. Sullivan said, "I think I might even have some photographs that I shot of your father, Honey, and your mother, Jacqueline, at a party. Madeline threw wonderful parties. She always had plenty of food and drinks. I could always count on hearing some great music, too, mostly hot jazz.

"That's where I met your father and Madeline. They were quite an item in their circle, if I remember correctly. No one thought that he would ever leave your mother, Honey, but everyone knew of his devotion to Madeline. She was not only one of the most beautiful women in New Orleans, she was one of the nicest. She went out of her way to do things for other people. I guess when you're a good person at heart you can take the ugliness other people throw at you.

"Anyway, I'm glad that this town knows about your parents. It's time some of these folks got off their high horses. I've got pictures around here that would make a number of them shake in their boots if I ever showed them to anyone. But, you see, a photographer is something like a doctor. I would never tell anything I know or show any of my pictures to people who don't need to see them. That's the way I am, I guess.

"Don't you worry your head about anything, Honey. I'll be there on time next Thursday afternoon for your portrait sitting, and then I'll come back for the wedding and take a few extras of you and Stephen. I believe in doing it up right."

"Thank you, Mr. Sullivan. I'll see you in a week," Honey replied as she started to walk from the cool shop into the heat. Jacqueline hung back a little for one last word with the knowledgeable photographer.

Turning toward him, Jacqueline said, "Thank you, Mr. Sullivan, for the kind words about my mother."

"Think nothing of it, Jacqueline. Madeline was a lady regardless of her profession, more than many of these uptight society women who won't give a working man the time of day. Tell Honey not to worry about her wedding being a success either. Everyone will come, out of curiosity if nothing else. Mark my words, they'll all be there next Friday," Mr. Sullivan replied as he moved toward his darkroom.

Arriving home exhausted from all the shopping and crowds, Honey and Jacqueline had just put their feet up and poured a soda when Stephen phoned to invite Honey to dinner that night with her future in-laws. Hanging up the phone, Honey felt her knees grow weak and her mouth become dry. She had felt stage fright as a model but never had she experienced anything as severe as this reaction to a dinner invitation at which she would be the main course.

Sinking onto the sofa, Honey looked with despair at Jacqueline and cried, "I knew I had to meet them at some point, but I had thought I could postpone the big moment until the wedding day. How should I act? What if they don't like me? After all, I am the one who caused all this upheaval, you know."

"Don't worry about a thing, Honey," Jacqueline offered as she hugged her sister. "They'll love you just as you are. I know you're concerned, but you shouldn't be. When they understand how much you and Stephen love each other, they'll forgive everything that has happened."

Rising from the sofa and pushing her tired feet back into her shoes, Honey replied, "I hope you're right. We'll find out soon enough. Well, come help me pick out my dress for this evening. I want them to see Stephen's fiancée looking her best."

As Honey and Jacqueline walked up the long, winding stairway, Honey's mind was already rehearsing some of the pleasant conversation she would offer at dinner. She knew that Stephen's parents would be judging her, probably no more so than any other in-laws would, but she felt the added pressure of the recent events on her shoulders. She needed to be ready to fill in the silences.

When Stephen and Honey arrived at his parents' house, his mother and father greeted them. The diminutive woman warmly embraced Honey and kissed her on each cheek while his father showed a stately reserve and offered only a handshake. Turning to her son, she admonished him saying, "Why Stephen, you should have brought Honey to see us long before tonight. To think your wedding is in only a week's time and this is the first time I've met my new daughter."

"Well, Mother, you know we have been rather busy lately," Stephen responded with a chuckle at his mother's very typical reaction to meeting her future daughter-in-law. "Honey has been occupied with her modeling and in renovating the family house. We'll have a lifetime for conversation and shared dinners after next week."

"Come with me, Honey, while the men chat a little. I want to have a minute alone with you," Christina Turner commanded with a smile as she waved her son into the living room where his father already sat sipping a bourbon and water.

Closing the library door behind them, Mrs. Turner stood for a moment composing her thoughts. Her hands shook as they fingered the cuff of her sleeve. Her pinched face mirrored the emotions that tugged at her heart as she said, "Honey, I have several things to get off my chest. In a household of lawyers, I don't have many opportunities to speak, so please do not interrupt me until I finish.

"I want you to know that I am very pleased with my son's choice in brides. I realize that many people feel that your inquiries have caused more harm than they have good, but I'm not one of them. The secrets that have been hidden for so long needed to come into the open. It was time that poor Jacqueline learned the truth about her family.

"It was most unfair of some of the more outspoken women in this city to condemn the child for the mother's behavior. I'm very relieved that Jacqueline is now free from the assumption that she belongs to her mother's profession.

"For too many years, I've lived with the fear that someone would maliciously leak the information about Madeline as a way of ruining Stephen. Now that everyone knows that she was his mother, I can rest easily for the first time since he came into my house and heart.

"You see, I knew about my husband's relationship with Madeline long before she conceived his child. Out of love, I chose to ignore his infidelity and concentrate instead on maintaining harmony in my home. When Edward told me that Madeline had given birth to his child and would be unable to care for it properly due to her circumstances, I immediately offered to take the baby and raise it as my own. I wanted a child most desperately. The fact that this infant was my husband's only made him more precious to me.

"Yet, I worried that someone would find out that Stephen was not my son. We filed all the appropriate adoption papers with the courts and had the records sealed, but I still lived in constant fear. As time went on, our best friends learned the truth but said nothing.

"Your questions and the disclosures that resulted from them have released me from a dreadful torture. I am sure that the information took Stephen by surprise. However, I would rather that he learn the truth now than to have it thrust at him in malice.

"Don't worry about anything, Honey. In time, people will forget their animosity toward you, especially when everyone sees the extent of my respect and admiration for my new daughter. I hope we will become good friends."

For a few moments, the room remained silent as if the two women sat frozen in their individual thoughts. Wiping the tears that had trickled down her cheeks, Honey replied softly, "Mrs. Turner, I cannot begin to tell you how much I appreciate your support and affection. I had no idea that in righting a wrong done to Jacqueline I would uncover so many levels of intrigue in my hometown. I only knew that I could not stand by and allow my friend to suffer. Even if I had never discovered that she was my half-sister, I had to do what I could for her. I apologize for any discomfort my efforts on her behalf have caused you."

Throwing her arms wide open, Christina Turner warmly embraced the young woman who would spend the rest of her life with Stephen. A sense of relief washed over her as their tears mingled. She knew that her son would be safe with this woman who loved him as much as she did. Stephen would have a helpmate in this brave girl during times of need. Her strength would help him when his own failed. Honey Tate would make a perfect wife and partner for her son.

"Aren't you two hungry yet? We're starving!" Stephen proclaimed as he entered the library after knocking lightly.

"What could you possibly have to say that would take so long?" Edward Turner huffed in mock despair. "You've monopolized that poor girl. I haven't even had a chance to speak with her. I am to be her father-in-law, you know."

Turning to face the men, Honey and Christina smiled as they wiped away the last of their tears. "Oh, Edward, stop growling," Christina ordered. "We have the rest of our lives to share with this wonderful girl."

Linking Honey's arm through his, Edward Turner replied, "Yes, but unless I steal her away from you, I'll never get a chance. I'm starving. Let's eat. You can tell me all about yourself then."

Smiling from ear to ear, Honey allowed her new father to lead her away as Stephen and his mother followed. The warmth and affection of her new family's home and hearts enfolded her. Their reception of her made her feel comfortable, content, and ready to face any odds.

Fifteen

The week sped by with Honey spending all of her days in preparation for the wedding and her evenings with Stephen. She supervised the placement of the furniture, rugs, and paintings in each room of the newly restored house. She had selected every vase and figurine with special care with concern that they would add to the atmosphere of the rooms that would become their home. Every painting had a purpose and a function above that of being pleasurable art. It had to help pull together the color in the fabric of the sofa and chairs with that of the rugs and walls. She had selected wallpaper with bold, rich designs, textures, and colors.

The rugs were not only of the best wool and silk Honey's money could buy, they were perfectly matched to the function of each particular room. In the living room, she instructed the men to unroll a rug with a light airy feel to its pastel floral background of sturdy, closely woven fibers. The library rug contained deep burgundy and navy swirls. The bedrooms welcomed silk rugs in subdued shades of green, rose, and blue.

Most of the drapes were made of raw silk that shimmered in the dazzling sunlight. In her bedroom, however, Honey added gossamer under curtains that fluttered in the breeze. Every room in the house was finally ready for the Friday wedding.

Tuesday, after a particularly trying afternoon, Honey sat on the front porch in the chairs Stephen had placed there for them. She had grown exasperated from trying to explain her vision for the south wall to the workmen who could not seem to understand her desire for a trellis covered in wisteria. Giving up, she had retreated to the comfort and solitude of the porch. As it had been in her childhood, this was her favorite spot in the entire house. From here she could see the Mississippi through the trees as it meandered past the house on its lazy course. She could smell the sweet aroma of freshly turned earth as the men prepared the fields for the late planting. Everything at Longmeadow House was as it had been during the prosperous days of her father.

As the sun began to set, Honey watched as a car sped up the rutted drive. Stephen had arrived to take her back to Jacqueline's for the evening. She had warned him against traveling at such great speed, but as usual he was in a hurry to see her. When the workmen finished with the last exterior touches to the house, they would begin work on the driveway. They had promised that everything would be in perfect order for the wedding on Friday. Considering the army of men that swarmed over every corner of her house, she could believe that they would complete the work on schedule.

Waving her hand, Honey ran across the lawn to intercept him. As he recklessly stood up in the speeding car with his tie and hair blowing in the wind, one of the wheels slipped into a deep rut, causing him to lose control of the car. As she watched, Stephen's expression changed from happiness to one of surprise and then of fear as he flew into the air and the car flipped onto its side. Honey watched as dust covered him from view and the sound of crunching metal and the groaning engine filled the air.

Unable to move, Honey stood transfixed at the edge of the lawn. The wheels of the overturned car spun in the dusty sunlight. With her hand at her throat, Honey once again ran toward the road. This time she did not wave with excitement but pushed forward through the thick, hot air that smelled of gasoline and burning rubber. Reaching the road, she stood for a moment and looked at Stephen's bloodied body as he lay face down in the dust.

Recovering quickly from the shock, Honey ran back to the house for help. She knew that she could do nothing for Stephen without the aid of the workmen. Shouting as she ran with her sandals beating out an urgent rhythm, Honey called, "Help me please. Stephen has had an accident. He's bleeding terribly. Come quickly!"

Immediately the men dropped their hammers and paintbrushes. As they followed her down the sloping lawn to the road, Josiah Mason, the foreman, stopped at his truck for a first aid kit and his cell phone.

The sight was even worse than Josiah Mason had imagined as man and car lay in a mass of torn, bleeding flesh and crumpled metal. To make matters more dangerous, gasoline flowed in a steady stream from the car.

Handing Honey the phone with instructions to call for a fire truck and ambulance, Josiah Mason quickly moved forward. Using a discarded door from one of the outbuildings as a back brace, he gingerly turned Stephen's lifeless body onto it. Checking his pulse, Josiah Mason instructed, "Tell them to hurry. His pulse is weak and he's lost a lot of blood."

"The phone is dead!" Honey shouted as she stared at the useless piece of modern technology in her hand.

"The sun must have sapped the charge, and I don't have an adapter," Josiah Mason confessed unhappily.

"Oh, no! That's the only phone we have!" Honey lamented as she ignored the blood on the ground at her feet and rushed forward to help Stephen. From the way he was lying, Honey could tell he had broken his right leg in the fall. From the amount of blood that caked his black hair, she worried that he might have broken his skull as well.

"Dr. Shaw lives up the road. Please send someone to get him and phone the ambulance. I'm so worried. We must do something," Honey cried as she held Stephen's hand in hers. His breathing was shallow but steady.

Calling over his shoulder as he raced to his truck, Frank Smith, one of Josiah Mason's men, replied, "He's not at home. I saw him at the barber shop next to Peterson's Hardware a few minutes ago when I went for some extra nails. I'll drive up to Scot's Hardware and use the phone to call an ambulance."

The time seemed to drag while Josiah Mason monitored Stephen's vital signs and Honey cried softly as she held his hand. They all listened for the ambulance that did not want to appear. The silence and strain were almost more than Honey could bear.

"Maybe I should go for Dr. Armstrong, Miss Tate. His house is further away, but, with luck, he'll be there," Josiah Mason said as he ran toward his car at the end of the driveway. Carefully easing his car around the ruts and the wreck of Stephen's car, Josiah soon vanished down the main road.

"Luke, would you fetch some water, please? I'll stay with Stephen in case he wakes up," Honey asked the painter standing in the sunshine as she sank to the ground beside him. He looked so ashen and lifeless. The concerned painter hurried into the house and to the kitchen.

Taking Stephen's hand in hers, Honey prayed as tears streamed down her face that the ambulance would arrive shortly. Stephen's breathing was so shallow that she feared he might die before anyone could help him. She had never seen so much blood on anyone, not even in New York where she had witnessed a shooting involving two street gangs. If only the doctor would hurry, she might be able to stop worrying.

The silence in the yard was deafening as Honey shielded Stephen's face from the hot sun with her hands. Periodically, she would stop fanning the flies away from the blood that caked in his hair and turn her head toward the main road to listen. Nothing but the sound of birds reached her ears.

With each passing moment, she repeated the litany that had become as familiar to her as breathing itself. With lips that felt cracked and dry, Honey whispered her prayers continuously. She would not stop although her throat ached and her head pounded as wildly as her heart.

Suddenly in the distance, Honey could hear the sound of cars slowly making the trip up the long driveway and the wail of a distant ambulance. Someone was coming up the rutted road! Afraid to release Stephen's hand for fear he would slip away from her, Honey strained to peer beyond the trees to catch a glimpse of the drivers. Listening carefully, she heard two voices. One she recognized as belonging to Josiah Mason, the other was a stranger to her. Behind them, she could make out the incessant cry of the siren.

"This way, doctor, he's right here," Josiah Mason's voice filled the hot summer afternoon.

"I came as quickly as I could, Miss Tate. Mr. Mason said that Stephen had suffered a bad accident. Step aside for a while so I can examine him," Dr. Armstrong ordered as he rolled up his sleeves and began to take Stephen's pulse. "It looks as if the ambulance arrived with me."

Unable to move under her own power, Honey allowed Josiah Mason to lift her gently before he returned to the doctor's side. As a trained EMT, he would be of far greater assistance than she would until the emergency personnel finished unloading their supplies. She hated to leave Stephen's side. She feared that he would awaken and she would not be there to comfort him.

Sinking into the fender of a nearby truck, Honey allowed the tears to flow once more. Stephen lay lifeless on the dry dusty road, and she could do nothing to help him. If only she could do something to turn back the clock and make him whole again.

Covering her face with her trembling hands, she sobbed for the life she feared they would not share. If Stephen did not recover, Honey did not know how she would be able to

face life without him. Since meeting him, Stephen had become the center of her happiness. They had talked of loving
each other forever and never parting. Quickly, she brushed
aside the thought that their forever might have arrived today.
Now, Honey prayed she would not be left alone without the
man who made her heart sing. Her tortured mind dared to
dream that one day she and Stephen would sit on the porch
as they had planned and watch their children play on the lush,
green lawn.

As Honey whispered one childhood prayer after the
other, the emergency personnel started working on the still-
unconscious Stephen. Dr. Armstrong stepped aside to allow
them access to the patient as Honey watched anxiously. She
listened closely as the men conferred and made plans to trans-
port Stephen to the hospital miles away.

As they loaded Stephen and the stretcher onto the ambulance, Honey asked, "Oh, let me go, too. I don't want to
leave him alone."

Seeing the strain on her tear-streaked face, the driver nodded and waved her into the back of the vehicle. Honey hardly
heard the wail of the siren or felt the bumping along the road
as she held Stephen's hand. The instruments clicked with his
breathing and constantly measured his vital signs.

"How is he?" Honey asked through trembling lips.

"He's stable for now, Miss Tate," the paramedic responded,
checking the instruments once again. "We'll have to wait until
the doctors assess his condition and clean away all that blood
before we'll know just how badly Mr. Turner is hurt. The leg
is broken for sure. I could tell that when I splinted it. I'm
concerned that he might have suffered a concussion."

The traffic appeared to move more slowly than usual as
Honey gazed lovingly at Stephen. Occasionally his eyelids
would flutter, causing hope to rise in her heart that he might
open his eyes. She watched and waited impatiently but nothing happened.

As the ambulance pulled up to the hospital door, Honey

looked wistfully at all the people milling on the sidewalk. They had no idea that Stephen lay lifeless in the ambulance. They did not know that she could barely breathe for worrying. They could not guess that not only Stephen's life lay in the balance but hers as well.

Honey joined the other families and patients in the waiting room as the paramedics rolled Stephen into the emergency room examining area, followed closely by Dr. Armstrong. She wanted to follow but knew she would only be in the way. She told herself she would have to wait patiently for the news of his condition.

Unable to sit, Honey paced the floor. She was filled with a strange nervous energy that would not allow her mind to settle on any one thought or her body to rest in the chair. Every time she tried to sit, she popped up from the chair as if stuck by a pin. Every thought that came into focus quickly blurred and flitted away. With her mind and body out of control, all she could do was pace the long room from one end to the other with her eyes straining for the sound of the doctor's return that did not come.

When Honey thought she would go mad with worry, Dr. Armstrong stepped into the doorway and beckoned to her. Immediately, she ran toward him. Anxiously, she studied his face for any sign that Stephen would be all right. Finding none, her heart stopped beating and her hopes vanished as she listened to the doctor's sobering message.

Placing his hands firmly on her shoulders, Dr. Armstrong explained slowly and kindly, "Mr. Turner has suffered not only a broken leg but a massive trauma to the brain. He has lost considerable blood and is in a very weakened state. The next forty-eight hours will tell. You have to prepare yourself, Miss Tate. If Stephen does not show signs of recovering within the next forty-eight hours, well, the possibility that he could leave us grows greater with each passing minute.

"The doctors here have done all they can for him at this point. They have set his leg and cleaned his head wound.

There is nothing more anyone can do now except pray and wait. I am sorry to be the one to give you such dreadful news. This should be a joyous time for you. I'll return later today after I see my other patients. If you need me, phone my pager. I will notify Mr. Tate's parents and Miss Du Prix of his accident. You shouldn't be alone at a time like this."

As Dr. Armstrong finished speaking, the sound of the ambulance's loud siren pierced the air as new patients arrived on stretchers. The excitement barely registered on Honey's dulled senses as she eased into the nearest seat and whispered, "Thank you, doctor."

Again Honey waited in the rapidly filling room. She was too tired to pace and sat with her head resting in her hands. She tried to control the tears that streamed silently down her checks, but she could not. Finally, she gave in to the grief that squeezed her heart.

After an eternity, the emergency room physician appeared. Calling her name, he walked toward Honey with Stephen's chart still in his hands. Laying a reassuring hand on her shoulder, the doctor said, "I'm sorry that I can't give you any words of encouragement, but we'll have to wait and see. Let's hope that time is on our side. You can go in to see him now."

Honey could only nod as she watched the doctor stride toward the next cubicle and another patient. The weight of his message and the futility he felt hung heavily on his stooped shoulders. Despite his large caseload, the young physician felt for every patient and family.

Entering the screened-off area, Honey found a nurse standing beside the bed adjusting the flow of fluids into Stephen's body. She recognized the woman as Patty Cross, a regular at Saint Philippe's store during sale events. Now that the doctor and Patty had cleaned the blood away from Stephen's pale face, he looked almost peaceful in his sleep. They had pulled the sheet up to his chin and folded his hands over his chest. Honey could almost imagine that he would awaken at any moment and speak to her. Had it not been for the constant beeping of the monitor and the tubes of precious fluids, she would have believed it possible that he was merely sleeping. However, they offered unpleasant reminders that Stephen was critically ill and possibly close to death.

Taking her place beside his bed and cradling his cool hand in hers, Honey turned her attention to Patty's composed face. Smiling bravely, she said, "Thank you for helping the doctor take care of Stephen. I know what you might think of me and I'm grateful that you didn't allow that to stand in your way of helping us."

"Think nothing of it, Miss Tate. I'm not one for judging a person based on rumor. You did a very brave and noble thing standing up for your sister like that against the opinions of small-minded people. Don't worry too much. I've seen much sicker patients than Mr. Turner pull through just fine. He'll be okay in no time. You might have to postpone your wedding for a while though. Now, if you'll excuse me, I'll leave you with him. If you need anything, press the button," Patty replied as she quickly left the room.

As Honey sat warming Stephen's hands in hers, she thought about the plans they had made and the dreams they had shared for a life together. She could not abandon the hope that they might still enjoy the life they had planned. She would not allow herself to think that her happiness had ended.

All the years that Honey had lived in New York with her mother, she had dreamed of returning to New Orleans and to the happiness of her childhood home. She had longed to run barefoot through the meadows and grass, gather wildflowers, fish off the little pier, and pick berries in the woods. Although she had gained fame from modeling, Honey longed for the quiet of living at home with her husband and children far away from the flashing lightbulbs. Every dream had been filled with the warm glow of sunshine, the smell of fresh air and growing crops, and the sweet song of the river as it passed the house.

Honey had always known that in New Orleans she would find the man who would perfectly complement and complete her soul. She had listened as the sweet-talking men of New York had offered her diamonds and furs if she would marry them. Some of them had actually been wealthy beyond her wildest dreams and quite capable of keeping their promises and making her life easy. At times, she had been tempted to abandon the runway for the financial rewards of marriage to one of them. However, they had never exactly matched her picture of the ideal man. Their voices had been too crisp, their accents too harsh, and their manner too direct for her taste. She did not want to become a trophy wife who would have to place her college degree and modeling reputation on the shelf to collect dust.

Honey had dreamed of finding a man whose voice rumbled like the Mississippi and resonated like the deep cypress forests. She had envisioned a man whose face would light up when he saw her and whose eyes would cling to her every move with deference. She longed for a partner whose desire was to sit and rock on the porch with her while they watched their children play on the lawn.

When she met Stephen, Honey knew she had found the man for whom she had been waiting. Their first dance together at Saint Philippe's masked party had shown her that they fit together perfectly. Their first stroll in the moonlight reassured her that Stephen's gaze would hold wonder and excitement and reverence as he studied her simple movements. The first time they sat on the porch and he spoke of his dream of watching their children, Honey knew that she cherished a man whose soul wanted the same peace and tranquility that hers did. Now, studying his peaceful face, Honey wondered if their dreams would ever come true. She prayed with all her might that they would.

As the afternoon shadows turned to twilight, Honey did not notice the nurse's return or the darkness invading the room until she heard the sound of someone speaking in hushed tones at the nurses' station. Leaving Stephen's bedside for only a minute, she looked out to see who had arrived to break the silence that had until then been punctuated only by the sounds of the clicking machines. Seeing Stephen's parents, Honey waved and motioned for them to join her. To Honey's delight, Jacqueline stood beside them as they listened attentively to the latest report on Stephen's condition.

Before Honey could reach the hospital room door, Christina and Edward Turner entered. Christina's eyes were red-rimmed from crying, and Edward's face was lined with worry. Both of them hugged her tightly and moved quickly to their son's side. Jacqueline followed closely behind them with her beautiful face contorted with worry. She immediately pulled Honey into her arms.

"We came as soon as we heard. Dr. Armstrong told us that we might not know anything for a few days," Christina explained as she turned her eyes from her son to the saddened face of the woman who loved him as much as she did.

"I'm so happy that you're finally here," Honey replied as she eased slowly toward the door. Although she wanted to give the stricken parents time alone with their son, she really did not want to leave.

"Thank you, my dear," Edward Turner said with a brave smile. He knew from the expression on Honey's tired face that the love she felt for his son was genuine.

"Have you eaten anything this evening?" Jacqueline asked, studying Honey's eyes, which were reluctant to leave Stephen as he lay motionless in the bed.

"No, I haven't left his side. I'm really not hungry," Honey responded as she allowed Jacqueline to guide her into the hall and toward the elevators that would take them to the hospital's cafeteria.

"You need to keep up your strength," Jacqueline advised as she gently pulled Honey away. "Stephen's care is in your hands. His parents are too old and fragile to be of much help. Let's go downstairs now and find you something to eat."

The ground-floor cafeteria was almost empty as Honey and Jacqueline entered. The evening shift had only just begun. They had their pick of tables as they studied the food machines with their luminous fronts.

"While you tend to Stephen, I'll take care of you. I know that unless I'm here, you'll forget to eat and get very little sleep. As it is, you'll probably sit up in that chair all night. You'll fall sick yourself from worry and neglect of your own needs. This salad actually looks pretty good," Jacqueline declared as she helped the distracted Honey unwrap the cover from the plastic bowl.

Taking her fork and knife in hand, Honey picked at the meal. The turkey was tender and sweet, the greens were crispy, and the tomatoes were juicy. For concession food, Honey would have found the salad was surprisingly good if she had noticed it. But that night, she could not stop thinking about Stephen long enough to enjoy the meal.

Pushing the barely touched plate aside, Honey said, "I guess I'm just not very hungry right now. I think I'll go back upstairs. I need to see if Stephen is all right."

Jacqueline smiled slightly in response, unable to find the words to comfort Honey and show that she understood. Honey had so much on her shoulders and had to carry the load by herself. No one could make it lighter for her.

As the elevator door opened on the first floor, Dr. Armstrong nodded and entered. His face was lined with care for his patient. He smiled gently at Honey and said, "The night will probably seem incredibly long to you. I would tell you to go home, but I know that you wouldn't listen. I'll return tomorrow around noon. I see you're not alone. You need company at a time like this."

"My sister Jacqueline and Stephen's parents are here. I should say, our sister Jacqueline. I will not be alone, I assure you, doctor," Honey replied as she entered the elevator and smiled weakly. Her legs felt very tired after the long afternoon of worry.

"Good. I'm glad to hear that. You need as much care as he does right now, maybe more. There's nothing we can do for Stephen except wait. We certainly don't want you worrying yourself sick at a time like this," Dr. Armstrong responded as he opened the door to Stephen's room. The bouquets of flowers could do nothing to cover the smell of alcohol and sickness.

Studying the faces of the Turners, Dr. Armstrong could tell that Stephen's parents had assessed the severity of his injury and were trying to prepare themselves for the worst. Their eyes said that they wanted him to tell them that their son would recover, but that they knew he could not make any promises.

As the concerned parents and Honey left the bedroom, Dr. Armstrong examined Stephen for signs of recovery. From his quick assessment, he could see that his patient had made little if any progress. Studying the on-duty physician's notes, he agreed that they would simply have to wait and see.

Sixteen

Long after Stephen's stricken parents had retired to their bedroom, Honey maintained her vigil in his room. Dr. Armstrong and the attending physician had assured her that nothing would happen to change his condition that night, but she did not want to leave him alone in case he woke up. After everyone had left, Honey settled into the stiff, uncomfortable chair beside the bed. Closing her eyes, she rested with her head on his hand.

The silent night gave Honey ample time to think about her new life. Overnight she had gone from being an only child of deceased parents to having a sister. She had changed from living in a lonely hotel suite to the renovated house of her youth. She had lived the relatively uncomplicated life of a model one moment, only to find herself the center of a far-reaching scandal the next.

Leaning back in her chair, Honey realized that much had changed around her in ways she could never have predicted. When she first returned to New Orleans, her only desire had been to earn a living, reestablish ties to her hometown, and rebuild her family home. Along the way, she fell in love, met wonderful people, found that unjustified prejudices governed the actions of many of the town's wealthiest citizens, and discovered a sister whose identity she had not known. Watching the patterns play on the wall, Honey mused that she had accomplished quite a bit in the short time since she had left New York.

Sitting back and watching Stephen sleep, Honey had a feeling deep in her soul that everything would work out all right. She had not done so much and come so far to stop short of having everything she wanted. She knew that Stephen would soon open his eyes and that their life would begin as it had been predestined. She had faced the death of her parents and survived. She had endured the censure of her hometown and proven herself capable of withstanding the criticism. She would be able to will Stephen to return to health. Nothing was impossible.

Resting her head on Stephen's hand again, Honey allowed her eyes to close and refreshing sleep to settle over her. She did not hear the door open as the nurse entered to check Stephen's vital signs.

Slowly the first day of waiting for Stephen to regain consciousness lengthened into the second and then stretched into the third. Everyone's nerves were drawn taut with watching for signs of recovery. Dr. Armstrong came each morning before he began his office hours and every evening after seeing his last patient. They could tell from the slump of his shoulders after he left Stephen's side that he had seen little if any progress, but they knew that Stephen would soon awaken from his injury and join them.

Early every morning Jacqueline cut flowers from her gardens and brought them to the hospital. She filled the many vases to overflowing with daisies and forget-me-nots and feathery ferns for contrast. She wanted Stephen to be surrounded with beauty when he woke up.

Every morning Honey shaved and washed Stephen's face and gently fluffed his pillow. She helped the nurses change his bed. She would spell his mother as they took turns sitting beside him as they read books that they would not remember later.

After a quick breakfast in the cafeteria, Honey would return to Stephen's room and read from the mysteries he loved so dearly until her throat grew tired and her voice cracked. Each time she stopped, she would adjust his covers and carefully spoon water between his lips. Then, sipping from the glass she kept on the table beside her chair, she would begin again. When her eyes ached and blurred and she could no longer see the words, she would wind up the music box her father had given her for her eighth birthday. Jacqueline had brought it to her so that she could have a bit of joy in her tiring day. Leaning back in her chair, she would listen to the sweet strains of "Love Story" as they twinkled on the gaily-painted floral instrument.

In the evening, Honey would leave the hospital room so that Stephen's many visitors could pay their respects. She would wander the halls or stroll outside. The air always smelled fresh after a day inside.

When night came and the guests had left, Honey, Jacqueline, and Stephen's mother shared the vigil at his bedside. Sometimes Honey crocheted or did counted cross-stitch until her eyes burned. She had already completed their intertwined initials on several sets of pillowcases and a sampler. Every time she fingered the satin-stitch letters, Honey thought about the long life she hoped she and Stephen would have together.

However, Dr. Armstrong no longer held the same hope. The forty-eight hours had passed and Stephen had not awakened. He was quite concerned that the young man had passed the point at which he could recover.

As morning dawned on what would have been her wedding day, Honey rose to stretch her tired body. She had napped with her head on Stephen's hand so that she would feel even the slightest movement. It was a pleasant morning for summer, barely sixty-five degrees. Opening the blinds to the fresh light of a bright new day, she massaged her shoulders and adjusted the fit of her clothing.

Honey wondered if she and Stephen would ever walk the lawns of Longmeadow again. She loved the old house almost as much as she loved Stephen. The house had drawn her back to New Orleans and introduced her to Stephen. The memory of the happiness she had enjoyed with her parents echoed through the halls and called to her heart. A pleasant thought resided round every corner and behind each tree. Honey knew that the elegant cypress on the south lawn would shade her children as they played under its boughs, just as it had protected her from the burning afternoon sun. And Honey feared that she would live there alone.

"Oh, Stephen," Honey whispered to the quiet room, "if you would only wake up to see this glorious morning."

Slowly she turned toward the bed. Stephen looked so peaceful and handsome as he slept despite the large purple bruise on the right side of his face and the ticking of the machines that logged his every breath and heartbeat. She could almost see him striding toward her as they met beside the minister at the altar.

Returning her gaze to the window and the Mississippi beyond, Honey sighed deeply. From the hospital room, she had a perfect view of the city and the paddleboats on the river. She was terribly tired, but she could not allow herself to rest until Stephen recovered. "Oh me!" she breathed as she rubbed the sleep from her eyes one more time.

"Good morning," a soft, fuzzy voice whispered from behind her.

Turning quickly, Honey looked at the door thinking that Stephen's father had entered and had not wanted to startle her. Seeing the door still closed and no one standing there, she lowered her eyes to the bed. To her surprise, Stephen smiled weakly and repeated through parched lips, "Good morning."

"Stephen!" Honey cried as she rushed to his side and took his outstretched hand in hers. Unable to control the tears, she buried her face in his shoulder as his arms weakly enfolded her.

"Don't cry, Honey. I'm all right now. Just a little bump

on the head, that's all," Stephen whispered as he lightly stroked the top of her head.

"Stephen, you don't understand," Honey explained as she wiped the tears from her cheeks and folded her hands in a prayer of thankfulness. "You've been unconscious for three whole days. You had us scared to death. Your parents and Jacqueline have been staying here with me so that we could take care of you. The nurses and Dr. Armstrong have been monitoring you almost nonstop. You had us so worried."

"Three days? You mean I've missed our wedding?" Stephen asked with disbelief in his weak voice.

With a merry little laugh, Honey replied, "No, darling, I've postponed it until after your leg heals. You have a pretty bad break. That's one way to leave a girl waiting at the altar."

"All of this happened because I stood up in the car to wave to you. I don't remember anything after that," Stephen mused. "How's my car?"

With a slight shrug, Honey replied as she lightly kissed his forehead and practically floated toward the door, "Let's just say that it could use a major overhaul. Don't worry about that now, Stephen. You need to focus all your energy on getting well. If you're feeling all right, I'll run and get the nurse, and your parents. Your mother has been beside herself with worry."

Stephen did not answer. He only smiled as her kiss warmed his tired body. The memory of the accident had begun to return. He could hear the crunching of metal and feel himself flying through the air. Closing his eyes again, Stephen willed the memories to be silent and his head to cease its throbbing.

"Well, I see you've returned to us," the day nurse commented cheerfully as she entered on the last of Honey's words. "I'll stay with him while you get his parents. Then I'll call the doctor to give him the news."

"Thank you, Miss Jones. I'll return in a few minutes," Honey bubbled with renewed energy. She had completely forgotten her stiffness and fatigue.

Rushing to the waiting area, Honey found Stephen's parents

reading in silence as the rays of the early morning sun filled the room. They seemed to have aged during the three days they had waited for their son to regain consciousness.

Speaking softly so as not to frighten them, Honey said, "Mr. and Mrs. Turner, Stephen is awake! The nurse has sent for the doctor. You can go in to see him if you'd like."

Fresh tears of relief and happiness sprang from Christina's eyes as she quickly hugged Honey before dashing toward Stephen's room. As Edward lightly kissed her on the cheek and joined his wife, she could hear Christina's quick steps rushing down the hall toward Stephen's room. Her voice drifted back to Honey as she cried, "Oh, Stephen, you're back! My son is back!"

Practically running toward the elevator, Honey impatiently pushed the button and waited until the door opened. Rushing toward the cafeteria, she searched for Jacqueline in the sea of faces ordering their morning coffee and bagels. Easing between the people, she called out her sister's name.

Looking up as Honey approached, Jacqueline asked, "Has something happened to Stephen?"

"He's awake! He opened his eyes just now and started talking just as Dr. Armstrong said he would," Honey announced to her sister's worried face, which immediately changed with the good news. "His parents are upstairs with him now."

"Wonderful! I'm not hungry anymore. Let's go," Jacqueline said as she quickly stepped out of line and followed Honey from the cafeteria.

In a few minutes, the two sisters returned to Stephen's room. Honey quickly walked to his side. His mother stood holding his hand and gazing into his battered face. Although he looked as if he had suffered numerous injuries at the hands of an unidentified assailant, Honey was relieved to have him with her again regardless of his appearance. Jacqueline happily brushed away her tears as she gently kissed Stephen on the forehead.

Hearing Dr. Armstrong's voice in the hallway, Honey intercepted him before he could reach the room. She wanted to be the first to greet him. Bubbling happily as she made the announcement, she commented, "You said it would take a few days for him to return to normal and it did . . . almost. I'm so grateful for all your time and effort. It's so wonderful having him back with me."

As he studied her haggard face, the kindly physician said, "Now that our patient is on the road to recovery, maybe you'll get some rest before you become sick yourself. But remember, Honey, Stephen has a long way to go before he's totally well. That leg of his will require at least six weeks of rest, and he'll probably have fierce headaches for a while. You won't be able to walk down that aisle for a long time yet."

"Don't worry, Dr. Armstrong. I'll see to it that he takes it easy," Honey replied happily as she mentally planned the picnics and long evenings on the porch she would spend with Stephen.

After the torment of being poked and probed by the doctor, Stephen napped most of the day. However, by dinnertime he was hungry and ready for company. All of his family members took turns entertaining him as he asked about the events of the last few days during which he was unconscious. He listened attentively to the smallest detail about the new trellis and his father's discussion of court cases.

Honey allowed herself to go home and sleep in a bed that night rather than in the chair. As she lay under the canopy of her large, mahogany, four-poster bed, she thought that if Stephen had not been hurt in the car accident this would have been their wedding night. As it was, this was the first time she had slept in the house since she was a little girl and the first time she had occupied the master bedroom as its owner.

Despite her fatigue, Honey's heart pounded so loudly at the excitement of being at home and at Stephen's recovery that she could hardly fall asleep. She lay for hours listening to the ticking of the grandfather clock in the hall, the familiar creaking of the floors, and the distant sound of the frogs. Turning on her side to face the window, she watched the moon and stars play in the vast sky until her eyes closed for much-needed rest.

As the days passed, the bruises that disfigured Stephen's handsome face faded and the headaches stopped. Slowly, his appetite returned and with it his sense of humor. On the way home from the hospital, accompanied by Honey, Jacqueline, and his parents, Stephen insisted that they stop at his favorite Chinese restaurant for fried rice with shrimp. He had endured enough of hospital food.

Demanding to use the wheelchair and crutches Dr. Armstrong had provided him, he chased Honey and Jacqueline around the lawn until he was winded. Then he would sit on the front steps and watch the sun set red on the Mississippi. Honey could tell from the expression of total happiness on his face that he loved the house as much as she did.

Seeing their son returned to his old self, the Turners kissed Honey on the cheek and returned to the city. Although they enjoyed the tranquility of the house in the country, they wanted to rejoin their circle of friends and their accustomed social life.

Honey's relationship with Stephen grew stronger every day. She had not imagined they could share so much warmth and companionship and become so comfortable with each other in such a short period of time. As they revised their wedding plans, Honey marveled that their thoughts were in step regarding even the tiniest details of the day.

As soon as Honey felt comfortable leaving Stephen to his own devices, she drove into the city to confirm her wedding plans. Visiting all the same vendors, she spent the day in discussion over flowers, food, decorations, invitations, and music. With a little juggling of their calendars, they were able to accommodate her wedding.

Stopping at Saint Philippe's, Honey found the shop buzzing with activity and gossip as usual. Instead of positioning a live model in the window as he had while she worked for him, he now displayed his creations on the usual female preformed figures posed in lifeless stances. Despite the change, his outfits looked breathtaking.

The women stopped their conversations and parted the way as Honey walked toward the back of the shop. She could tell they were still overflowing with criticism for her behavior on Jacqueline's behalf, but she did not care. She had learned from watching at Stephen's bedside that the most important thing in her life was the love she shared with him and Jacqueline. Everything and everyone else did not matter.

Approaching his desk, Honey smiled and extended her hand as Saint Philippe rose to his feet to greet her. Looking radiant now that she could breath easily about Stephen's health, she said, "Saint Philippe, I hope the delay in my wedding hasn't inconvenienced you too much. Stephen's doing very well now. I was quite scared for a while. I won't bore you since I'm sure you heard all about it."

"Oh yes, we all did," Saint Philippe replied nervously. "Dr. Armstrong kept us informed about his progress. I understand that he's living in your house right now. Are you sure that's a good idea? I know I sound old-fashioned, but I worry about these things."

"I couldn't begin to think of asking him to move. Dr. Armstrong says that Stephen's leg needs six weeks to heal. Besides, we're not alone. Josiah Mason and his men are still working on the house. Jacqueline is with me every night and almost every day when she's not taking care of her garden here in town. She helps me do the grocery shopping. She's a much better cook than I am and really helps out, leaving me plenty of time to take care of Stephen. Stephen and I are hardly ever alone. Besides, we can't get into too much trouble with Stephen's leg held together by surgical pins," Honey responded in a loud, clear voice for all the listening ears in the shop to hear. She did not want anyone to have to strain to make out her words.

"Well, if you think it's all right. I still think he should stay in his parents' house. But that's only my humble opinion, not that you asked for it," Saint Philippe added as he turned his attention to his favorite topic of fashion. "At any rate, on a different subject, I have completed the alterations to your dress. I can have one of my men load it into your car now if you would like."

"That would be wonderful," Honey commented with a mischievous glint in her eyes. "Thank you, Saint Philippe. I'm glad that everything worked out so well during Stephen's illness. The only thing I've had to do is change the wedding date with the engraver. My car is out front. I'd appreciate the help. I'll see you at my wedding, I hope."

Honey watched Saint Philippe struggle with his desire to see her wearing his stunning dress in opposition to the fear of lost revenue he would experience from associating with her. She would not have to wait long to discover which one of his desires would surface as the winner.

With an almost helpless expression on his carefully powdered face, Saint Philippe answered in a lowered voice as he darted his eyes around the room at the listening customers, "Of course, I wouldn't miss it for anything. I'm looking forward to receiving your invitation."

"That's great, Saint Philippe," Honey replied as she eased toward the door. "I'll be counting on seeing you."

Sinking into the ornate desk chair, the tormented man dialed his delivery man on the intercom. As he gave instructions for the delivery of Honey's dress to her waiting car, Saint Philippe knew that he was hopelessly trapped in a no-win situation between his assorted temptations.

As Honey turned the station wagon toward the road that led out of town, she was relieved to leave the people who continued to treat her with contempt. She was so content with her life she did not care if they ever welcomed her into their circle again. She would not mind at all if they did not attend her wedding. Honey had all she needed with Stephen and Jacqueline.

The trio filled their waiting days listening to Jacqueline entertain them on the piano, strolling along the grounds with Stephen skillfully piloting his wheelchair, reading or watching television in the family room, and tending the thriving flowers. Occasionally, they would play cards. When he grew tired, Stephen napped in a hammock Josiah Mason rigged between two trees near the riverbank. If he wanted to eat, either Jacqueline or Honey would serve his favorite treats.

Jacqueline had grown strong on the fresh country air, too. The hurtful gossip of the city seemed far away as she spent time in the garden with Honey and divided her daylight hours between Honey's place and the city. As she had promised when she first met Honey, the gardens around Longmeadow were now almost as splendid as her own in the city.

Honey happily welcomed the hours spent with her new family. She had been alone for so many years that she savored every minute with Jacqueline and Stephen. She delighted in the fact that Jacqueline usually returned to the country house after a day in the city. She seemed to relish the conversation that gave new meaning to her formerly solitary life. Honey was always happy to see Jacqueline slow her car and make the turn into the driveway. Now that the pavement had been repaired, she did not worry about anyone else having an accident on the drive to the house.

The days lengthened into weeks as Stephen's recovery showed steady and almost remarkable progress under her loving care. His leg mended so rapidly that Dr. Armstrong pronounced it healed at four weeks rather than the customary six. However, he cautioned Stephen that if he wanted to dance at his own wedding, he should still tread gingerly for a while. Although the break had healed, the pin holes would still need time.

As Stephen limped around the grounds with the help of a cane his father had lent him, he was very careful to treat his newly healed leg with respect. He had waited a long time to make Honey his bride and to taste the sweetness of her kisses. He did not intend to do anything that would prevent him from enjoying the favors of his beautiful wife to the fullest.

Watching her fluff the pillows under his foot or pick flowers in the meadow, Stephen was filled with an overpowering respect for the wonder of the woman who never seemed to tire of doing for him. She always seemed to anticipate his every desire or need. She made sure he was comfortable before she tended to her own needs.

Although the news of Honey's split with Saint Philippe had reached New York, she refused to leave him for even the most lucrative modeling jobs. When she would not go to the Big Apple, it came to her. Trucks of lighting equipment and cars full of photographers joined the ducks on the lawn.

Stephen watched proudly as Honey pranced and turned before the snapping cameras. She tilted her head and laughed happily as the fabric of the skirts twirled around her slim figure. She climbed onto rocks and sat in the boughs of trees in the latest in sports clothing. And Honey stood ankle deep in the little creek that trickled through the backyard while she modeled a revealing swimsuit.

The grace and beauty with which Honey moved her hands when sewing, posing, or massaging his tired shoulders made him want to trap them and cover them with kisses. The gentle sway of her hips drove Stephen mad with desire as he watched her ease soundlessly across the room. The soft soprano of her voice sent ripples of pleasure coursing down his spine as she whispered little nothings in his ear while they sat on the porch swing. The way Honey turned her head to the side when listening to a distant sound and smiled when she recognized it made him want to pull her into his arms and never let her go.

Although Honey remained determined that they would not sleep together until their wedding night, Stephen constantly wished that she would back down. He would just have to wait.

Seventeen

Everything was ready on that Friday afternoon as the inhabitants of the house waited to see if any of the three hundred invited guests would arrive for the wedding and barbecue to follow. Honey realized that her relationship with Jacqueline and her exposure of Edward Turner's long-hidden secret might jeopardize the success of her special day and turn it into a private affair. She was so happy, though, that she did not care if no one from the community shared the day with her. Surrounded by her sister and her fiancé, Honey could think of nothing that would make her happier. She did not need the approval and good wishes of the people of New Orleans to make her life complete.

The invitations had again been mailed, the flowers from the florist had been mixed with the ones that grew in abundance in her gardens and that of Jacqueline's home in town, and the banisters and balconies had been draped with white bunting and bunches of baby's breath and pinks. White sheeting led from the house to create a flower-lined aisle down which she would walk toward the canopy that would shade the altar as she and Stephen exchanged their vows.

As the aroma of ribs, chicken, and beef roasting on the barbecue wafted through the open windows on the unseasonably cool day, Honey stretched languidly in her soft bed. She had slept late that morning after staying up past her usual bedtime the previous night reading. She had been too excited

about the wedding to sleep after Stephen kissed her good
night at her bedroom door. She had convinced Stephen that,
although it was old-fashioned, they should wait until their
wedding night to unite their bodies in the passion that burned
within them. She wanted everything about their marriage to
be special.

Now, throwing off the light covers, Honey slipped into a
green and white silk robe covered in soft yellow flowers and
walked to the kitchen where brunch and Jacqueline awaited
her. Honey doubted she would do much more than pick at
the feast she and Jacqueline would share, but she knew she
had to try to eat something.

Honey had thought of all the little details that would make
the day spectacular from start to finish. She had purchased
bags of rice and enclosed its pearly grains in little silk
pouches. Each guest would receive one at the appropriate time
along with a slice of wedding cake to take home. Although
she had not seen Stephen since the previous night, she would
prepare for him a special breakfast of crepes with strawberry
sauce and scrambled eggs with corn. He was still recuperating
from his accident and needed his strength. Besides, he would
need all of his energy for that night.

After her meal, Honey found little to distract her as she
and Jacqueline walked into the yard and inspected the gardens
one last time before going to their rooms to prepare. The
china, crystal, and silver waited in the tent in spotless stacks.
The food was in its final stages of preparation and being
supervised by the caterer's expert eye. The wine had been
chilling for a week and only needed uncorking. There was
nothing left for them to do except sit and wait.

Alone in the room that she would soon share with her
husband, Honey sank into the rose-scented water of her bub-
ble bath. The warmth quickly penetrated her body and quieted
her nerves. She slowly rubbed the suds over her skin and
then poured a handful of her favorite shampoo into her hair.
Rising to turn on the shower, Honey allowed the water to

flow over her hair until the suds vanished. Quickly wrapping a towel around her head, she eased her shoulders under the surface of the water again as she rested her head against the high back of the tub. The soothing motion of the whirlpool almost lulled her to sleep.

Honey listened to the chirpring of the birds in the cypress trees and the buzzing of the bees in the wisteria vines. Closing her eyes, she allowed herself to be lulled by the sounds until she did not feel the passing of time or the chilling of the water. She knew that, when they had children, she would not have the time to enjoy the luxury of a long soak in the huge bathroom.

"Honey, are you decent?" Jacqueline called from the hall as she slowly opened the bedroom door and stepped toward the bathroom.

"I'm covered with bubbles. You may come in," Honey replied without moving. The water felt too comforting. She could not even lift her arms.

"Why Honey Tate, you're going to be late for your own wedding if you don't get a move on. The minister has already arrived and is chatting with Christina and Edward Turner on the porch, which, I must say, does look terrific with all those pots of flowers and greenery," Jacqueline scolded lightly as she sat on the chaise lounge.

"You're not dressed either," Honey observed through a slit in her eyelid. She could not bear the idea of opening her eyes to the sunlight that shone in mad abundance through the large picture window. With her eyes closed, she could hear for miles and miles. She loved the feeling of total freedom. On quiet afternoons, she sometimes wondered how it would feel to be a bird and soar above the trees, houses, and troubles of the world. Sighing deeply, she snuggled into the bubbles again and tried to block out the sound of voices in the yard and cars coming up the road.

"I'm more dressed than you are, Honey. I simply have to step into my dress. You haven't even begun to do your hair.

You really must hurry. Your guests have begun to arrive," Jacqueline urged as she unfolded the huge bath towel that lay on the floor next to the tub.

"All right, I'll get out. Just give me another minute. I haven't heard that many cars yet. Who did you say has arrived?" Honey asked as stretched one last time and rubbed in the scent of the bubbles.

"So far only the minister, the Turners, and Saint Philippe who, by the way, is having an absolute chicken to see you in his dress," Jacqueline replied. "But don't you fret, the others will be along soon. I've told you that nothing will keep our so-called friends from attending this wedding. They love nothing in this life better than gossip, and your wedding should give them plenty of material for that.

"Besides, Mrs. Turner said that people have been talking all week about what they would wear when they attended your wedding. It's not likely that they will pass up the opportunity to show off their Sunday best. Every time I drove past Saint Philippe's shop, it was packed with women. I don't think I've ever seen such activity. Enough talk. You've stalled long enough. It's time you got out of that tub." Jacqueline turned her face away and held up the towel for Honey.

"All right, you win. I'll get out. The water's getting cold anyway. Don't leave. I'll need you to help me into my gown," Honey conceded as she wrapped the towel around her trim body.

"I swear I've never seen anyone take so long to get dressed on her own wedding day," Jacqueline complained as she straightened the massive skirt on the wedding gown which lay across the bed.

"How many other weddings have you attended?" Honey asked mischievously from the bathroom.

"None, but that's beside the point," Jacqueline called over her shoulder as she lifted the veil to admire the delicate seed pearls that covered it.

Chuckling, Honey toweled off and slipped into her undergarments. The batiste fabric of the camisole and tap pants felt cool against her skin. She eased her feet into her white satin slippers before taking a seat in front of her mirror.

Tossing the wet towel into the bathroom, Honey shook out her damp hair. Bending forward, she carefully brushed and blew it dry. Shaking it into place, she watched as the curls slowly framed her face. Carefully, she gathered the front and sides and pulled them into a mass of curls on the top of her head. She secured them from underneath with a white satin ribbon that would blend with the ones on the cap that held her veil.

Critically studying her face, Honey discovered that the hours of walking and gardening in the fresh air had given her skin a healthy, rosy glow. She would need neither blush nor powder to augment her natural beauty. A light application of mascara, eyeliner, and shadow was all the makeup she needed.

As the sound of gravel crunching under the tires of arriving cars floated up to her open window, Jacqueline said as she unbuttoned the pearl buttons down the back of the gown so that Honey could step inside, "I'll help you pull up the dress. It certainly is a beautiful day. It's wonderfully cool for this time of year . . . and not a cloud in the sky. The cars are arriving in great numbers now."

Looking at her reflection in the mirror as Jacqueline positioned the little cap that held the veil, Honey saw a vision in white satin. She had modeled the dress in Saint Philippe's shop, but she had not taken the time to reflect on the way she looked in it. Even yesterday when she sat for her photography session, she had not thought about her image. Sitting for the photos was so similar to her usual line of work that she did not consider herself as other than a model. Now, looking at herself in the mirror in the privacy of her bedroom, Honey realized that she had become the image of the bride that she had once tried to portray.

"Oh, my! You look so lovely!" Jacqueline declared as she stepped back to admire her sister.

"Thank you, Jacqueline. If I haven't already told you, let me say it before the festivities begin. I couldn't have wished for a better sister than you have been to me. You've helped me immeasurably during Stephen's illness. Your presence has given me incredible joy. My only regret is that we didn't spend our childhood together. We never would have been lonely with each other for company," Honey said as tears of gratitude and love welled in her clear green eyes.

Embracing her sister, Jacqueline mingled her tears with Honey's. In a strained voice, she replied, "I wouldn't be here at all if it weren't for you. You're the only one who has ever believed in me enough to fight for me. Even if we hadn't discovered that we're related by blood, our hearts were united when we first met. I'm so happy that you're truly my sister."

Smiling at her sister and giving her a light shove toward the door, Honey said, "Well, we'd better hurry. We have to be downstairs soon and you're the one who isn't dressed."

"I'll only take a minute!" Jacqueline replied with a happy grin.

As Jacqueline left to change into the blue creation that Saint Philippe had fashioned for her, Honey sighed contentedly. She knew her sister would look stunning in the dress with the snug waist that accentuated her trim figure, and the color brought out the richness of her brunette complexion.

A gentle knocking sounded at the door as Saint Philippe entered and gushed, "Everyone is waiting for you, Honey. Oh my, I don't think I've ever seen you looking more elegant. If I do say so myself, and I will since you're not paying any attention to me, that gown is divine. Surely the most fabulous wedding attire I've ever created. The Paris and New York houses will be on the phone with me as soon as they see the drawings and photographs. I'll have to hire more seamstresses in order to keep up with the demand for my designs. You've simply made me the toast of the South!"

Laughing, Honey lightly kissed his powdered cheeks as she replied teasingly, "You were already the premier designer in this part of the country. That was one of the reasons why I came to work for you. Now, you are the best in the country."

Blushing, the beaming gentleman waved her away and responded with feigned modesty as Jacqueline returned, "Flattery will get you everything! You'll turn my head with all those well-deserved compliments. Now, Honey, I didn't come all the way up those stairs in these uncomfortable shoes to bestow or receive compliments. The minister sent me up here to tell you that it's time for you to make your walk down the aisle."

"Oh, gracious, I guess it is. Jacqueline, will you accompany me, please, for our grand entrance?" Honey asked playfully as she linked her arm through her sister's. Standing together, the sisters made a striking pair.

"It would certainly be my pleasure, sister dear," Jacqueline replied as they walked into the hall. Their dresses whispered softly as they navigated the wide stairs with Saint Philippe carrying the train to Honey's gown.

Stopping at the front door, Jacqueline gasped and asked, "Honey, who have you asked to give you away?"

"Oh, no! I forgot all about that!" Honey moaned as she stood facing the long walk past the rows of chairs in which sat the assembled guests. With all the planning, she had forgotten this one necessary item. "After Stephen was injured, I put everything out of my mind. It's a shame that Daddy isn't here to see his two daughters together at last. We don't have any close male relatives that I could have asked. Besides, I can give myself away. I don't have to ask a man to do it."

"Maybe so, Honey, but not at my sister's wedding," Jacqueline responded softly to keep her voice from drifting into the lawn and to the guests. "This is the most special day of your life. I want everything to be perfect for you."

Suddenly Honey's green eyes widened as she turned toward Saint Philippe, who had been so preoccupied with removing the minute specks of lint from his jacket that he had not heard their whispered discussion. Stepping toward him where he stood on the other side of the foyer, Honey asked sweetly, "Saint Philippe, as you know, I have no one to give me away. Would you do me the favor as my oldest male friend in New Orleans?"

Saint Philippe was totally taken aback. Sputtering he replied, "Honey, I would be most honored, but I'm not appropriately dressed. Although new, this suit is simply not sufficiently elegant for escorting you down the aisle."

"Oh, Saint Philippe, you're the most elegantly dressed man here, and you know it. No one else has your sense of style or your eye for fabric and design. The other men come to you to learn the latest in fashion because you're the trend-setter among them. All the men here are wearing styles that you designed. Please, Saint Philippe, I have no one else to ask or else I wouldn't put you on the spot like this. You and Stephen are the only men in my life."

"Well, I'd hate to let you down at a time like this, and you certainly can't walk down the aisle without someone to give you away," Saint Philippe commented as he linked Honey's arm through his. "I don't care how modern women have become. That simply isn't done. All right, I'll do it and with a great deal of pleasure."

Seeing them finally in place at the door, the wedding consultant handed Honey and Jacqueline their bouquets of baby's breath, carnations, and roses and quickly fashioned a boutonniere for Saint Philippe's jacket. Then she signaled to the string ensemble inside the large canopy to begin the music. With the fragrance of barbecue making the guests' mouths water and hinting at the feast to follow, everything was finally ready.

As the first strains reached Jacqueline on the bottom step, she turned and smiled at Honey before beginning her walk. Again, seeing her dear friend and sister standing at the top of the porch stairs, Jacqueline was struck by the radiantly happy face. With the afternoon sunlight shining on Honey's face and hair, she looked like a goddess from antiquity wearing a regal crown.

Standing behind the last row of chairs, Jacqueline knew that this would be an important moment in the spotlight for her, too. Although she was not the bride, she was on display nonetheless as the daughter of Madeline du Prix and Morgan Tate. Everyone would comment on her attire almost as critically as on Honey's gown. Straightening her shoulders and holding her head high, Jacqueline glided past the critical eyes of Creole New Orleans.

For someone who had until recently sought only anonymity and the quiet companionship of her flowers, Jacqueline showed herself to be very strong and resilient despite the whispers that greeted her as she walked down the white runner. With great dignity, she proceeded toward her waiting brother, turned slightly, and cast her gaze toward the back, from which Honey would soon make her entrance.

Watching Jacqueline take her place to the left of the altar, Honey touched Saint Philippe on the arm and said, "It's our turn, Saint Philippe."

Saint Philippe gushed as he squeezed her hand affectionately and said, "Before we go, I'd like to tell you, Honey, that you are not only the most beautiful woman I've had the good fortune to know and dress, but you're also one of the bravest. What you did for Jacqueline, although I didn't approve at the time, was remarkable. I'm very proud to be the man who escorts you on your wedding day. I probably should impart a few words of fatherly advice, but I can't think of anything that would direct your steps. Therefore, I'll simply wish you much health and happiness."

Smiling sweetly, Honey replied, "Thank you, Saint Philippe. Although we haven't always seen eye to eye, I've always known that you were silently standing behind me."

All heads turned from Jacqueline and the altar at the front of the tent to Honey as she and Saint Philippe entered. She could tell from the expressions on their faces that many of the guests had been engaged in gossip about her sister. Now that their gaze was focused on her, Honey knew they would soon be dissecting her with the same or perhaps even greater vigor. Walking with her shoulders back and her head held high, Honey did not care what they said or how they said it. This was her day and she was going to enjoy it.

Honey was surprised to see that Jacqueline's prediction about the people of New Orleans had come true. Guests filled almost all of the three hundred seats on the lawn. Yet, as she walked past the critical eyes on the arm of a beaming Saint Philippe, she did not really see any of them. The grass in front of the porch could have been empty for all the notice she took of its inhabitants.

Even the barely hushed whispers of the critical did not faze her as Honey looked directly ahead at the incredibly handsome man waiting for her beside the white-draped altar. Stephen's usually windblown hair had been freshly brushed into submission. He beamed at his stunning bride as he leaned lightly on the gold-handled cane. His tailcoat and trousers fit him perfectly. Even his tie, usually crooked, was straight and neatly tied.

Casting a quick glance to Stephen's right, Honey saw that Edward Turner cut a dashing figure as he stood beside his son as his best man. Tears glistened in the elderly gentleman's eyes as he watched the happiness of his son and his bride. He smiled warmly at Honey as she took her place next to Stephen.

Saint Philippe played his part beautifully as he stood between and slightly behind Honey and Stephen. When the priest asked the ancient question, Saint Philippe spoke up clearly and replied "I do." The guests snickered at the strength of his response that clearly overwhelmed the voice of the cleric. Grandly, he linked Honey's hand through Stephen's arm before taking a seat reserved for him on the first row of chairs. He wept silently and dabbed at the tears that threatened to disturb the carefully applied powder that concealed the age-revealing spots on his cheeks.

Christina was also moved to tears by the sight of her grown son taking a wife. She had longed for the day that Stephen would find someone to love and care for him as much as she did for her husband, despite his infidelity with Madeline. Now that Honey had unintentionally exposed the truth of his birth, Christina was even more relieved that her beloved son had found a woman who loved him enough to look past his parentage to see the wonderful person that her son had become. If they would only give her grandchildren, Christina would consider herself the luckiest woman in New Orleans.

Amidst the songs of happy birds and the deep rumble of the river, the guests watched the joining of more than the lives of two people and two families as the bride and groom repeated the ancient vows. At that instant, Stephen's birth to a courtesan mother was legitimized by the love that Honey offered him. The warm embrace of Stephen's family negated the hostility that New Orleans Creole society felt toward Honey for exposing their dirty linen. As Honey's sister and maid of honor, Jacqueline's public appearance with her family ended the long years of scandal and solitude that had saddened her life and caused her to take refuge in her garden. The guests themselves in attending the wedding out of either curiosity or a genuine desire to share the special day, added their own tacit acceptance of the families, the individuals, and the circumstances that brought them all together.

As the priest delivered his final blessing, the musicians struck the notes that signaled the beginning of a new life and the restoration of a tradition of elegant parties and merry barbecues at Longmeadow. Their wedding reception marked the first party given by a Tate at the house since her father's death. Turning toward the applauding guests and their smiling faces, Honey and Stephen beamed their happiness. Passing before New Orleans society and receiving its recognition, they recessed past the smiling faces with Jacqueline and Saint

Philippe and Edward and Christina following close behind them.

Honey bubbled with happiness as she stood beside her husband and received the greetings of their guests on the flower-filled patio. As they walked toward her, she watched as they exchanged pleasantries with each person in the receiving line. They were cordial to Jacqueline and did not dare snub her. Even those who only a few weeks ago would not have welcomed her in their homes behaved with the utmost civility. Now, the Tates, the Turners, and the Du Prixs were one big happy family.

Mingling among her guests, Honey invited all of them to eat heartily of the barbecue feast that awaited them. She thanked them for their kind words regarding her efforts to restore Longmeadow to its former grandeur as she encouraged them to stroll the grounds and tour the rooms. To each one, she repeated the information that Jacqueline had been responsible for the thriving gardens they enjoyed that afternoon.

As music and laughter once again filled the rolling lawn and gardens of Longmeadow, Honey stood beside Stephen as they surveyed the scene that unfolded before them. From the porch, they watched as their guests mingled, chatted, ate, and drank in carefree merriment. Everyone put all thoughts of unpleasantness from their minds as they relished the delicious food and perfect weather on the glorious afternoon.

When the barbecue ended and the dancing began, Honey allowed Stephen to lead her to the south lawn, where a specially constructed dance floor lighted by swaying lanterns and torches awaited them. The orchestra played a stately waltz as the couple glided around the smooth, polished boards. Under the soft dusk sky, they held each other close while the music carried them in its hypnotic spell.

The nearness of Stephen and the aroma of his spicy cologne made Honey's skin tingle with anticipation of the evening that soon would be theirs. Unable to take her eyes from his, she felt her cheeks grow warm under his penetrating gaze.

Her small hand felt as if it were on fire in his warm embrace. She could feel the pressure of his fingers through the many layers of clothing as he pulled her even closer. Knowing that he shared the same thoughts, she blushed even deeper. When the dance finally ended, everyone clapped and cooed as Stephen kissed his bride on her upturned, trembling lips.

As they switched partners, Honey found herself constantly looking at Stephen while her new father-in-law guided her around the floor. Although a once skillful dancer, age had dulled his agility and made him a more plodding partner. He did not swoop with the turns but mostly eased into them. She was relieved when Saint Philippe cut in and Mr. Turner began to dance with Jacqueline.

Saint Philippe could not contain himself as they danced. He chatted merrily about the success of the day saying, "I've never in all my life seen a more beautiful wedding. It's not only because you're wearing the most stunning dress ever created, although that certainly added to the celebration. The weather is superior, the flowers are spectacular, and the food was exquisite. I'm sure this will be the wedding that sets the standards for all the others for the rest of the year."

Laughing at his infectious merriment, Honey replied, "And do not forget that the bride was given in marriage by the most famous designer in the South."

"Honey, I could never forget that!" Saint Philippe retorted happily as he launched into a series of perfectly executed turns despite his sore feet in their too-small shoes.

Jacqueline also seemed to be having a wonderful time as she danced with Edward Turner under the watchful gaze of Creole New Orleans. She smiled proudly as he steered her around the floor and did not mind that his style was not as elaborate as that of younger men who waited anxiously to become her partner. She was so happy to be in the company of people that nothing could spoil the evening.

Honey smiled as she watched her sister change partners and dance with one of Stephen's first cousins on his mother's side. Robert Beauford from Savannah, Georgia, was quickly becoming infatuated with Jacqueline's shy ways, charming personality, and skillful dancing. His face wore an expression of immediate devotion. When she was not in his arms, he hugged the sidelines and waited for a chance to dance with her again. He returned to her side as often as possible considering that Jacqueline had become the center of much attention. Watching Jacqueline's face, Honey could tell that her sister had fallen under his spell also and looked for him in the crowd whenever she changed partners. Honey would not be at all surprised if Robert became a frequent visitor to New Orleans and Longmeadow house.

As the candles began to sputter on the tables and the little lights in the bushes tried to outsparkle the stars, the ensemble started playing a tango. Everyone grabbed partners and joined in the sensuous dance. Now that the sun had set and the air had cooled even more, they were ready to participate in the more intricate and energetic steps.

Honey and Stephen smiled expectantly as they twirled and slithered through the sultry movements that made their hearts pound. Her heart throbbed to the music as Stephen pressed her against him for yet another dip. Her fingertips lingered on the back of his neck long enough to send sparks down his spine before flying away in yet another turn. They were oblivious to the dancers around them as the sky grew dark and the stars came out to play.

When the last glass of champagne had been drunk and the last slice of cake eaten, Honey and Stephen waved good night to their guests and watched as they climbed into their cars for the drive back into town. From the porch, they watched the long procession of vehicles wind its way down the drive and through the trees. The party had been a great success. Finally the night belonged to them.

Joining the newly married couple, Jacqueline announced, "I should be getting back to my poor garden in town. I've neglected it shamefully these last few weeks. Now that the wedding is over, I'd like to spend some time in my own home. Besides, you two need some privacy. Good night, my sister and brother."

Honey and Stephen did not try to stop her as Honey hugged Jacqueline tightly. "Thank you, Jacqueline," Honey said softly, "for all your help during Stephen's recovery and in preparation for our wedding. I truly am blessed with a wonderful sister."

Smiling at both of them. Jacqueline said choking back tears, "No, I'm the fortunate one."

As Stephen helped Jacqueline load her bags into the car, Honey waved from the porch. They called their good-byes as the car joined the others on the road back to town. Waving to the vanishing guests with their arms around each other, Honey and Stephen sighed contentedly that the long-awaited day had finally ended.

Alone at last on the porch, Honey and Stephen kissed in the moonlight. With the fragrance of magnolias perfuming the air, they clung to each other and tasted the passion they had kept under control for so long. As their hands took on a new boldness, their lips relished the sweetness of their kisses. Unable to resist any longer, they linked hands and entered the house.

Honey blushed heavily as they mounted the stairs to the bedrooms. Glancing at her new husband as he opened the bedroom door, Honey hoped she would neither fall short of his expectations nor be disappointed herself. They had waited to begin their sexual relationship after marriage, something seldom done anymore. Now, she hoped the reality would match the expectation. Feeling her hand tremble in his, Stephen knew that containing himself and his desire for her would be no easy task.

The familiar bedroom looked large and foreign as Honey and her husband entered. Someone had already turned back the bed, removed the spread, and drawn the drapes that Honey always kept open to the night air on cool nights. Her white silk nightgown lay discreetly across the foot of the bed.

"I'll help you undress," Stephen whispered in a voice already tense with the thrill of anticipation.

Unable to speak, Honey closed her eyes as Stephen's fingers skillfully loosened the tiny pearl buttons on the cuffs and down the back of her dress. As he slid the fabric from her shoulders and his hot hands brushed her cool flesh, she shuddered as if a cold breeze had blown through the room. His breath came in short puffs as he slipped the camisole and tap pants from her body and dropped them onto the pile of satin on the floor.

Turning her toward him, Stephen lightly kissed first Honey's forehead, then her eyes, followed by her nose, and then her lips as his hungry fingers caressed the softness of her skin. "I love you, Honey," he whispered as his mouth traveled down her neck to her bare shoulder.

"Oh, Stephen, I love you, too," Honey cried as the new thrills ran down her spine, making her tingle all over.

Stephen's hands tangled in her hair and pulled off the ribbon that kept the curls carefully in place. As her hair cascaded over her shoulders, he buried his nose in its rose-scented sweetness. Pulling her head back, he teased the corners of her mouth until she groaned softly. Then, he pressed his lips firmly to hers and enjoyed her freely given kisses.

Honey's hands grew bold as waves of pleasure swept over her body. Tentatively at first and then with increasing assurance, she massaged his shoulders and neck and teasingly ran her fingers down the front of his shirt. As his breathing quickened, she slipped her probing hands inside and caressed his hair-covered chest.

Stepping back slightly, Stephen finished unbuttoning his shirt and threw it on the floor beside her dress. Then he stepped out of his trousers and dropped them onto the growing pile. Quickly he bent and picked up Honey in his strong arms.

Gasping, Honey cried, "Stephen, your leg! You'll hurt your leg again."

With his face buried in the sweetness of her neck, he replied, "No, I won't and if I do, I won't feel the pain."

Depositing her on their bed, Stephen pulled Honey into his arms and buried his face in her womanliness. Honey sighed as she held him close and ran her fingers over his strong back.

Without releasing her, Stephen pulled off his underwear and slipped naked into the bed beside her. Studying the body that now belonged to him, he marveled at the shapeliness of her hips and thighs and the curves of her calfs and ankles. He traced burning kisses up her body to her lips as his hands explored the delicate regions between her legs, making her writhe and moan with desire.

With passion as her guide, Honey ran her hands timidly at first and then with growing boldness over his body. She teased his nipples until he moaned and then followed the hair on his muscular chest to the spot where it blended with that of his pubic region. He gasped as her fingers tangled in the furry patch.

As she allowed her hand to wander even further down the length of his body, she exclaimed, "Why Stephen, you devil you!"

With a chuckle, he rolled over and took possession of his bride's eager body. They would not need any of Patrice Auguste's famous love potions to sustain them as the nightingales sang in the trees and the fragrance of night-blooming flowers drifted through the open window.

Coming in May from Arabesque Books . . .

Arabesque Romances by FRANCIS RAY

__BREAK EVERY RULE   0-7860-0544-0 $4.99US/$6.50CAN
Dominique Falcon's next man must be richer, higher up the social ladder, and better looking than she is . . . which Trent Masters is definitely not. He doesn't fit into her world of privilege . . . but his passion is too hot to ignore.

__FOREVER YOURS   0-7860-0025-2 $4.99US/$6.50CAN
Victoria Chandler needs a husband to keep her business secure. She arranges to marry ranch owner Kane Taggert. The marriage will only last one year . . . but he has other plans. He'll cast a spell to make her his forever.

__HEART OF THE FALCON   0-7860-0483-5 $4.99US/$6.50CAN
A passionate night with Daniel Falcon leaves Madelyn Taggert heartbroken. She never thought the family friend would walk away without regrets—and he never expected to need her for a lifetime.

__ONLY HERS   0-7860-0255-7 $4.99US/$6.50CAN
R.N. Shannon Johnson recently inherited a parcel of Texas land. There, she meets Matt Taggert who makes her prove she's got the nerve to work a ranch. She, on the other hand, soon challenges him to dare to love again.

__SILKEN BETRAYAL   0-7860-0426-6 $4.99US/$6.50CAN
Lauren Bennett's only intent was to keep her son Joshua from powerful in-laws—until Jordan Hamilton. He sought her because of a vendetta against her father-in-law. When he develops feelings for Lauren and Joshua, he must choose between revenge and love.

__UNDENIABLE   0-7860-0125-9 $4.99US/$6.50CAN
Texas heiress Rachel Malone defied her powerful father and eloped with Logan Williams. But a trumped-up assault charge set the whole town against him and he fled. Years later, he's back for revenge . . . and Rachel.

__UNTIL THERE WAS YOU   1-58314-028-X $4.99US/$6.50CAN
When Catherine Stewart and Luke Grayson find themselves unwitting roommates in a secluded mountain cabin, an attraction is ignited that takes them both by surprise . . . can they risk giving their love completely?
